SUBURBAN

HELL

W9-BWB-033

SUBURBAN HELL

a novel

MAUREEN KILMER

G. P. PUTNAM'S SONS
NEW YORK

OCT 2 4 2022

PUTNAM
— EST. 1838 —

G. P. Putnam's Sons
Publishers Since 1838
An imprint of Penguin Random House LLC
penguinrandomhouse.com

Copyright © 2022 by Maureen Kilmer-Lipinski
Penguin Random House supports copyright. Copyright fuels creativity, encourages
diverse voices, promotes free speech, and creates a vibrant culture. Thank you for
buying an authorized edition of this book and for complying with copyright laws by
not reproducing, scanning, or distributing any part of it in any form without
permission. You are supporting writers and allowing Penguin Random House to
continue to publish books for every reader.

ISBN 9780593422373 (trade paperback)
ISBN 9780593422380 (ebook)

Printed in the United States of America
1 3 5 7 9 10 8 6 4 2

Title page art: Hand with glass © tetti.rd / Shutterstock
Book design by Alison Cnockaert

This is a work of fiction. Names, characters, places, and incidents either
are the product of the author's imagination or are used fictitiously, and any
resemblance to actual persons, living or dead, businesses, companies,
events, or locales is entirely coincidental.

OCT 2 4 2022

For Ryan, Paige, and Jake

SUBURBAN HELL

CHAPTER 1

NONE OF THIS would have happened if it weren't for the She Shed. We thought it would be a place to have our ladies' nights in peace—away from the children waking up at midnight, away from the husbands giving a cursory wave before heading upstairs to watch sports in the dark, away from the dirty dishes piled in the sink. All we wanted was a place to call our own. To have *something* that belonged to us. What we got was our lives and homes ripped into bloody shreds.

It was the She Shed that started it all, a blissfully ignorant idea that transformed our cheery suburban enclave into something demonic.

The suburbs were hell . . . literally.

———

IT ALL BEGAN in June, when we gathered at Liz Kowalski's house for our monthly movie night. Well, we called it "movie night" but it was really just an excuse to get together on a semiregular basis. Something to look forward to during the monotony.

My next-door neighbor, Jess, and I arrived at Liz's house around the corner at the same time, each of us taking a different route on Maple Leaf Drive.

"Yo, Amy, I did wind sprints out of my house tonight. Shit, I need a night out more than anything." Jess wore white workout shorts and a tight tank top and held a bottle of tequila above her head as she walked up the pathway to Liz's house. Her blond hair flowed freely down her back, and in the dark, her six-foot frame stretched a long shadow in the automatic lights on either side of Liz's door. Jess's husband, Del, worked for a liquor distributor and always had high-end bottles of alcohol on hand, which made her very popular at parties.

"You do know this is a wine night, not spring break in Cancún, right?" I said as I eyed her bottle of tequila while hitching my sauvignon blanc into my armpit. I had found it on sale in an endcap at Target. I grabbed it out of impulse as I sped through, trying to buy the ingredients for dinner and new water shoes for my two kids before someone had a meltdown.

Jess frowned as we reached Liz's door. "It's George Clooney's tequila, not Jose Cuervo. And Del told me that tequila has less sugar than any other alcohol."

"Yes, I obviously attend these nights to watch my weight," I said as she pushed open Liz's door.

"Well, I have CrossFit at eight tomorrow morning, and I can't be hungover. Hey, do you want to join? It's Bring-a-Friend Day."

"Sorry, Jess. I always appreciate the invite, but my answer is still going to be no. Always," I said as I followed her inside the house.

I never understood why Jess would willingly work out in a build-ing without air-conditioning, doing exercises that mirrored the worst days of gym class. Most of the other moms in Winchester took barre classes, running around town after their workouts in high-waisted Lululemon leggings and tank tops with built-in bras while drinking kombucha.

Jess opened her mouth to espouse the wonders of CrossFit just before Liz rushed forward, arms outstretched.

"There you guys are!" She looked down at our shoes, and we quickly added them to the pile next to the front door. Liz's en-tire first floor had white carpeting, impressive since she had two energetic boys: Carson, who was seven, and Luke—their oops baby—who had just turned two.

Liz placed our bottles on the kitchen island, next to a collec-tion of air plants in a raffia basket that she had gotten on sale at HomeGoods. The island was covered in an almost embarrassing amount of food for four people. If nothing else, no one would ever go hungry at her house, although I knew she overprepared out of anxiety rather than hospitality. Once, she'd run out of toilet paper during a party and nearly had a meltdown.

Jess poured herself a tequila on the rocks as she scrolled through her phone for a playlist. She made a new one each month for our get-togethers, titled "Suburban Lady Jams," and filled it with whatever new songs had just been released.

Liz turned to me, her brunette topknot making her seem taller than her five feet. "I have wine open already." She pointed to her fridge, and I opened the white door and saw a box of pink wine on the shelf, spigot waiting.

I could already feel the pounding headache from the liquefied candy inside the box, but I didn't want to turn her down. Liz was a sensitive soul who'd worked as a pediatric nurse before she had kids, and her feelings would be hurt if I declined. I gritted my teeth as I stuck a goblet large enough to double as a vase under the spigot and watched as bright pink liquid sloshed into it. I smiled at her over the glass before I took a sip. The sugar immediately went into every groove of my teeth, straight to the nerves, like chewing on aluminum foil.

"Yum," I said as I forced a smile, and Liz beamed. I could see Jess smirk in my peripheral vision as she pulled a lemon out of her bag, halved it with one of the sharp kitchen knives from the block on the countertop, and squeezed it into her drink. We might both regret our decisions come the next morning, but me definitely more than her.

Liz gave me a motherly pat on the arm. "Guess what, ladies? Construction on the She Shed starts tomorrow." She clasped her hands together in prayer form.

My eyes widened. It had started as a joke a few months ago, that we should have a clubhouse. We sketched it out on the back of a field trip form. It had a wet bar, a wine fridge, a flat-screen television mounted on the wall, pink velvet couches, fiddle-leaf fig plants ("I think those are supposed to be kept in the house," I said, to which my friends waved their hands around. "The plant will be kept alive by witnessing our friendship," Jess responded.), jute rugs, fuzzy blankets, and himmeli on the wall. Basically, a living Instagram post that we would enjoy without any hint of irony.

The next week, Liz texted all of us: Ladies, the She Shed blue-prints are safely in my care.

Before Jess or I could react to the news, we heard a thud and a bloodcurdling scream from upstairs. Liz gave an exasperated sigh, waiting a moment to see if her husband, Tim, would leave his home office to intervene. Through the door, we could hear his elevated lawyer-speak. When he didn't so much as peek his head out, she threw her hands up and ran up the stairs to investigate.

I felt the wine/gasoline course through my veins and exhaled loudly. It felt like the longest day of my life. My son, Jack, had had his last day of first grade. He ran out of Winchester Elementary, screaming, wearing a handmade Dr. Seuss hat covered in marker, to where his five-year-old sister, Emily, and I stood. We waited outside Door 1, politely chatting with the other moms, lamenting that I couldn't have volunteered more during the year due to my busy schedule job hunting for a social worker position.

I still hadn't found one.

After school, it had been ice cream, a playdate that left my couch covered in marker, another pizza dinner, and more ice cream to celebrate the last day of school. All the while waiting for my monthly movie night with my neighbor friends. It sometimes felt like these nights were my only true escape, among people who understood and accepted me.

Liz appeared back down the stairs, wearing old gray sweatpants instead of light-colored jeans.

"Sorry, ladies. Luke wanted another drink of water. It's his latest trick for stalling bedtime. Of course he spilled it all over me," she said. "Bedtime is just so hard."

I glanced at the clock. Nine fifteen p.m. "Where's Melissa? Is she still coming?"

We turned as we saw a flash of light, Melissa's giant Infiniti SUV pulling into the driveway.

"On cue," Jess said as she took another swig from her glass of tequila. "Only Melissa would drive two blocks instead of walking."

All four of us lived in the Whispering Farms subdivision, a suburban enclave thirty minutes outside of Chicago. Well, thirty minutes with no traffic. With traffic, it took over an hour, making the city seem much further away than it was, an inverse mirage. I wasn't sure whether the city or our suburb of Winchester was the palm tree with water. Whispering Farms was our bubble, so close to the city, yet at times it felt like another dimension. The further we got away from the city, the more suburban stereotypes became like actual real life.

The front door squeaked open, its metal hinges rusty, and Melissa walked through the door. She still wore her work clothes, a smart black suit with four-inch heels and dangly earrings. Her curls drooped, and her lipstick was smeared. In her hand, she held a six-pack of Spotted Cow beer. It was only sold in Wisconsin; she and her husband stocked up on it twice a year after a state border crossing and guarded it furiously.

"Sorry, but I had a work call run late. Y'all, I finally just said my kitchen was on fire." Her voice still held the faintest hint of a lilting twang. She actually grew up in southern Ohio, but when people asked about her accent she usually said, "The South," even though her voice was more country than belle. People usually pictured Savannah or Charleston, as opposed to the truth: Chillicothe, Ohio.

Melissa's heels click-clacked through the foyer before she stopped and kicked them off. She padded toward us and set the six-pack down on the counter.

"Ah, you brought your contraband smuggled across state lines. Spotted Cow: favorite beer of FIBs," Jess said with a laugh. Jess was raised in Wisconsin and never failed to remind us of our FIB status (Wisconsin lingo for "Fucking Illinois Bastard"), despite living in enemy territory.

Melissa responded with a smile and a head shake as she opened a beer bottle. It was a running joke between them. "*Fancy* Illinois Bastard," she said as she clinked her drink with Jess's.

"Damn straight you are," Jess said.

"Oh, you need more wine, Amy," Liz said, and, before I could stop her, filled my wineglass to the brim from the box in the fridge. I looked longingly at the beer in Melissa's hand before Liz handed the wine to me and lifted her own glass. "Cheers. Thanks for coming over. I live for these nights with you all."

We had started the movie/wine (well, tequila, beer, wine, whatever) nights the previous fall, when we were all forced to attend our school's curriculum night. All of us had kids in first grade, and we huddled in a corner, trying to avoid the PTA moms with clipboards, signing up volunteers for class parties. Melissa had whispered that she needed a drink, and we all nodded furiously. Three hours later, we were in her gleaming kitchen, next to her Viking range, drinking too much and laughing too loud. On the way out, before I stepped onto her expansive front porch, I turned and said, "We should make this a monthly tradition."

We had found each other, at first banded together by the fact that we all seemed to be on the edges of wanting to be in suburbia. We wore the costume of suburban moms, yet it only covered us on the outside like a camouflage, just enough to hide the parts that didn't belong. Then, after we got to know each other, we were bound by true friendship and love for one another. And a lot of laughter.

"C'mon, everyone. Let's go pick out a movie to watch." Liz gestured for us to follow her down to her basement, to the leather sectional where Jess had spilled a rare whiskey at the Super Bowl party as I shamelessly inhaled queso dip and pigs in a blanket.

"Amy, hon, it's your turn to pick," Liz said in an encouraging, motherly tone.

We rotated who chose the movie, usually landing on a mid-to-late nineties or early-2000s classic. Last time, we'd watched *10 Things I Hate About You*, cheering for Heath Ledger as he serenaded Julia Stiles on the field.

I flipped through the romantic comedy movie selections, noting we had watched nearly all of them. Rather than a rewatch, I had a thought. "What about something different, like a scary movie?" I laughed when I saw their faces. "C'mon, everyone. I was a serious horror movie fan as a teenager. *Halloween*, *Nightmare on Elm Street*, the Jason movies, all of it." I held up my hand as I ticked away a few more. "I'd much rather watch a fictional horror than a realistic tearjerker where someone's husband dies. Real life is much more traumatic than anything on-screen."

There was a pregnant pause in the room as everyone remained silent. They knew I didn't want to talk about my sister that night—or any night, for that matter.

Melissa cleared her throat. "My childhood was enough of a horror movie, and it turned me into a wimp." Except, she was the furthest thing from a wimp: she was a senior vice president at a large banking corporation run mostly by old white men who'd asked her to fetch coffee and to fudge expense reports during her first week there. Her husband, Tony, stayed home with their kids and swapped sous vide recipes with all the neighbors. This was less than approved by her conservative parents, who were high-ranking members of a wealthy megachurch that held Sunday services with a laser light show and fog machines, like a Jesus nightclub.

"I'm all in," Jess said as she plopped down, tequila cradled in her elbow like a newborn. "You guys know there's very little I will say no to."

"Jess, trust us. We know. Did you ever hang those bedroom blinds?" Melissa said.

I settled down on the couch, pulling an embroidered blanket over my lap. "I'm the one who lives next door to her and has front-row seats to the nightly show. What are you guys complaining about?" I smiled at Jess.

"You're welcome," Jess said as she tipped her glass to me with a laugh.

"No complaints here," I replied. "Del's a lucky guy."

"If you choose a horror movie, I'm leaving," Melissa said as she began to rise from the couch, her black suit bunching.

I gestured for her to sit down, and we tried to find something else, but no one could agree on a movie. Instead, we chatted about how glad we were not to deal with homework since it was the summer, what we would do with our kids for the next three months, how none of us had gotten our kids into that fancy vacation Bible school camp that all the other moms mysteriously did, and how our neighbor Greg Spadlowski's new hair plugs gave us Nic Cage vibes.

Then Liz said, "Let's go outside and christen the She Shed location!"

We refilled our drinks and followed Liz outside. I eyed her tiki bar on the deck, covered in straw and colorful parrots. It was a source of pride for her, so much so that we'd had to gently talk her out of hosting a Jimmy Buffett–themed party for Tim's stuffy law firm partners last summer.

"But who doesn't love 'Margaritaville'?" she had said, confused. "His concerts at Alpine Valley are so much fun."

"I know, but probably not the most appropriate theme for a group of corporate suits. My office's last party was themed 'Bourbon and Bites,'" Melissa had replied.

We followed her to the edge of the fence, where an area of grass had been cleared out. Liz reached into her pocket and pulled out four small, woven circles. "These are for each of you. I saw an ad on Instagram and had to buy them." She passed out the circles, black bracelets of woven string, with a small charm in the middle, engraved with *Stronger with You*. I did a slight internal eye roll at the corniness, but I knew it was genuine.

"Liz, you're the best," I said as she passed them out.

After we put the bracelets on, Liz lifted her glass in the air. "To our friendship, and having a place to call our own. I love you girls."

"To those who wish us well, and the rest can go to hell," Jess added, her volume rising with every word, before we clinked our glasses together and then poured a little of our drinks into the dirt.

As the liquid absorbed into the ground, a strong, chilling breeze whipped through the yard and tinkled the wind chimes across the street. We paused and looked at each other, glasses still held in the air.

"Well, that was weird," I said.

"I think that was a good sign," Liz said with a laugh.

I can definitively say, now, that it was not.

———

ON MY WALK home later that night, I was careful not to trip on any cracks in our uneven sidewalk. I tightened my sweatshirt around my waist in the cool night air. It was technically summer, although Chicagoland didn't really warm up until July. Then we would have two glorious months of warmth before the Midwest weather reared her head and we'd have to dig out the snow boots and pants and buy more gloves because one always mysteriously disappeared, banished to the Island of the Unmatched Winter Paraphernalia.

I took a deep breath and looked around as I inched along. The Whispering Farms subdivision was built in the 1960s, as a planned community. The houses in the neighborhood were one of four styles: colonial, Dutch Colonial, ranch, and split-level. A few houses had been torn down and replaced by custom-built homes—one of which Melissa lived in. We lived in a decidedly non-updated Dutch Colonial version with a powder-blue furnace that I think saw the Kennedy assassination.

I walked up to my front door, *Foster Family* neatly stenciled on the mailbox, and slowly pushed it open. I tiptoed past Mark, who had fallen asleep on the couch. I winced as the steps creaked and glanced at the clock next to my bed: midnight. The kids would be awake in a few hours, early risers since they were born. The next day would be filled with the splash pad, more snacks, staving off requests to bring the Playskool inflatable bounce house (my nemesis) outside, dragging out the sprinkler, more snacks.

And I was going to feel like hell.

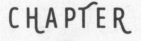

CHAPTER

"M OM, CAN I have the iPad now? Jack has had it since he woke up. He's been up forever, and I haven't had a turn yet." I slowly opened an eye, startled when I realized I was nose to nose with my daughter, Emily. I blinked a couple of times, my eyelashes crusty from the mascara that I had been too tired to remove before I fell asleep.

My head pounding, I hoisted myself up and brushed my hair out of my face. Every part of my body was sore, and I winced in pain as I reached for my glasses. The bracelet from Liz was still on my wrist, and I painstakingly slipped it off.

"You look weird," Emily said as she scrunched up her face.

"Tell your brother five more minutes, and then you can have a turn." My voice was hoarse and brittle, and I reached over and took a long gulp of water from the glass on my nightstand as Emily scampered out of the room, screaming that it was her turn.

Jack screeched downstairs, and I assumed that Emily had

wrenched the iPad out of his hands. We had debated whether we should get two—one for each kid—but I'd waved off the notion like a rookie, assuming they could share. And besides, they weren't supposed to be on tablets all day anyway and wouldn't need to have their own. Like I said, rookie mistake.

Mark walked into the bedroom as I swung my legs over the side of the bed, cursing Liz's boxed wine. Anxiety began to fill my bones as I thought of the long day ahead with the kids. I knew I should have come home sooner, had water instead of wine.

"What time did you get in last night, Amy? You look . . . tired." He strode over to me, dressed for work. He worked downtown in technology sales for Genitech, a media conglomerate. Unfortunately, Genitech also owned a major cell phone provider, and thus any time a family member or friend had poor service, they had to let him know, as though he personally oversaw the maintenance of the cell towers.

"After midnight. And thanks, I feel . . . *tired*." I stood up and took in a long, deep breath.

Mark leaned forward and gave me a kiss on the cheek. "I put two ibuprofen next to you, and made a pot of coffee."

"My kingdom for coffee," I said as I turned and downed the painkillers. I was filled with gratitude for his small, nonjudgmental gesture. I doubted Liz was getting the same treatment from Tim. "Thanks. I need all the help I can get."

"Rosé?" he said with a laugh, his blue eyes crinkling at the corners. He leaned forward and studied my face.

"Boxed-wine gasoline," I said as I rubbed my forehead. At thirty-seven years old, the hangovers came much swifter than they had a decade before, when all I had to do was drink a glass of water before bed. Now, anything more than two drinks, and I felt it the next day. Not to mention the consequences if one of those drinks contained the sugar equivalent of a liter of Mountain Dew.

He shook his head, chuckling. "Well, that would explain it." He picked up his phone from the dresser and glanced at it. "I have to head out. I have a meeting with my sales team in an hour." He leaned forward and was about to kiss me on the mouth but thought better of it, and his lips brushed my dry cheek.

"Thanks again. You're the best," I said.

"You know it." He winked at me and then turned to leave our bedroom. "A cold shower might help."

I saluted him as he disappeared into the hallway, wholly unprepared to start the summer.

TWO HOURS LATER, my headache was mostly gone, thanks to copious amounts of caffeine. I sat outside on the front porch, watching as Emily and Jack ran back and forth in the sprinkler. From around the corner, I could hear the rev of a backhoe as it dug into Liz's yard, prepping the corner of it for the She Shed. I imagined her hangover wasn't helped by the noise, either.

I smiled as I thought of our ladies' night, of allowing ourselves to be people, even if it was for a fleeting moment. It felt like so much of my time was devoted to everyone else. When I did get an evening of respite, it buoyed my spirits for days. It also helped that my three friends were some of the best people I had ever met.

I held a sweating can of LaCroix in my hand as I scrolled through my phone to find a recipe for dinner, determined not to make pizza or pasta again. In my peripheral vision, I saw Melissa walking across my yard. She was an impossible figure to miss, her glossy dark hair cascading down her back, as she strode closer with a confidence I had always envied. She had her shit together.

"Amy, what is that ridiculous noise? How can you sit out here?" Melissa appeared on my sidewalk, wearing black workout pants and a white tank top. Her kids, seven-year-old Rachel and six-year-old twins Ethan and Owen, trailed behind her. They all broke into a run when they saw the sprinkler, standing over it in their clothes.

"Kids, I told you not to get wet or dirty, and I meant it." Her eyes flashed with annoyance before she shook her head in defeat. She could silence a conference room full of men with one gaze, but she struggled to keep her brood in line. As we all did.

"I can't hear anything, let alone my children, so it's a trade-off," I said as she strode across the lawn, carefully avoiding the oscillating sprinkler. "Why aren't you in the office?"

She sat down on the wicker chair next to me. "I asked to work from home today after I woke up at four a.m. with a terrible headache. I will feel like myself by noon."

I shook my head. Only Melissa would time her hangovers like a scheduled conference call.

I wordlessly slid another LaCroix that I had brought out over to her, and she cracked it open with a satisfying click. We watched as an Amazon delivery truck slowed down the street, and we waved to Michael, the driver, whom I saw almost more than I saw Mark. It stopped in front of the Hacker house across the street.

"I just got an e-vite for Heather Hacker's kitchen remodel reveal party." Melissa leaned back and closed her eyes as she sighed. "I already declined. She always asks me when I'm going to stop working and stay home, like my career is a hobby. Or if Tony is really fine with staying at home with the kids, like I'm emasculating him."

"Well, at least she didn't call you a dirty hippie, like she did to Jess." Last year, at the school midsummer carnival, Heather stood behind the lollipop-pull table and "whispered" about Jess to one of her cronies. Of course, it didn't help that the crony in question was Del's ex-wife, Sharon, who was more than gleeful about a chance to gossip about her ex's girlfriend. Thankfully, only Melissa and I heard it, as Jess was waiting in line for an ice-cream sandwich. My chest still burned with rage when I thought about it, but I didn't tell Jess because the dynamics of a divorce could be tricky and I didn't want to put her in the middle.

"Did you get an invitation?" Melissa asked.

I snorted. "Nope. Sorry, I guess I'm not worthy of being in on the reveal." Heather Hacker was PTA royalty extraordinaire. She had grown up in the area and knew everyone. Her sister had been the president of the PTA before her and had passed the title down. It was like living among a sorority that I had no desire to join but that ran everything around me. On brand, she also was on the HOA board and somehow managed to fit all of those arbitrary rules into her immediate consciousness. Apparently, mailboxes have standards, and ours was not up to snuff.

A month ago, she'd tried to sell me herbal supplements that she was peddling. She looked me up and down at school pickup and told me HerbaFit would help me "lose the baby weight" even though Emily was five.

"What exactly is a kitchen remodel reveal party anyway?" I asked.

Melissa leaned back and closed her eyes again. "Heather had her kitchen redone and wants to show everyone. The invitation called it an 'unveiling.'"

"So it's like a gender reveal party, but for appliances? I wonder if the stove will shoot pink and blue confetti at everyone."

I wasn't surprised that only Melissa had received an invite. Heather generally dismissed our group but was strangely drawn to Melissa, likely because she had the best clothes and the biggest house. Money talked with Heather, which is why she was unbothered by the fact that her husband unironically wore brightly colored Crocs. His extensive family money gave him carte blanche to dress like a circus clown. As if that weren't enough, he also had a "Salt Life" decal on his BMW.

Melissa smirked in reply, her eyes still closed.

I tucked my feet up on the chair and wrapped my arms around my shins. "Such a fun night last night, and sounds—literally—like we will have a clubhouse soon." I cocked my head, remembering. "Although, that moment when we toasted, we all had that weird feeling. Hopefully it wasn't a sign of bad karma or something." I laughed.

She opened one eye. "Don't be ridiculous. The wind blew. We'd all had a few drinks by then, so I don't exactly trust our recall or reactions."

"True. I can always count on you to be the sensible one," I said.

"Occam's razor. My life motto. Well, adult-life motto," she said. Melissa's parents had told her that things that go bump in the night were real, that Satan was lurking around every corner, waiting to influence someone. That life should be lived with a healthy dose of fear of all things unseen. After she left Ohio and her parents' church and had actual life experiences that didn't involve spying on the neighbors to see if they were pagans, her worldview changed: the simplest, most rational explanation is usually the correct one.

I looked across the yard to Emily, who was ripping grass out of the front yard that we had meticulously resodded twice over two years, due to clay soil. Heather's HOA made sure to let us know that our yard needed "maintenance." I didn't want the kids to destroy what had taken so long to grow, but the backyard had a red ant nest that I still needed to clear out.

"Can you use your stern vice president voice and make that stop?" I said.

"No. That's only for—" Melissa started to say before she was cut off by a high-pitched screech. The kids in the yard stopped and put their hands over their ears as I winced. Then all the construction noise from around the corner halted.

"The hell was that?" I said, looking around.

Melissa shook her head, her forehead still due to the Botox she got religiously every four months. Then a loud boom made us all duck. I gripped the sides of my blue porch chair, my heart racing. It sounded like an explosion.

"Stay here with the kids," I said to Melissa as I leapt off my porch and ran to Liz's house. I banged on the front door. "Everything okay? What happened? We heard a noise."

When no one came to the door, I ran around the side of her

house and yanked the fence's gate open. A backhoe was paused in the corner of the yard, where Liz stood with a construction foreman, her arms crossed over her waist.

"What happ—" I stopped as a horrible smell filled my nose, a cross between raw sewage and moldy leftovers. I covered my face with my hand. "What is that?" Bucky, a mix between a German shepherd and a pit bull, began barking viciously inside.

"I—I'm not sure," Liz said, her voice small. She turned to me, and I saw that her eyes were ringed in red and her cheeks had a grayish tone, with small flecks of skin flaking off. Her greasy hair was pulled back into a knot at the nape of her neck.

"Whoa. Not feeling great today?"

She shook her head slightly but didn't answer, instead looking at the leathery construction foreman.

He shrugged. "We'll find out. Maybe a sewage line. We will stay on top of it." Then he walked over to his crew, who was peering down into the hole that they had dug, apparently halfway to a porta potty.

She turned to me. "I can't remember the last time I felt this bad. How are you feeling? Do you want me to make some coffee?" Of course, Liz would put her own malaise aside to see if she could help me.

I gave her a sympathetic look. "No, but thanks. Just take care of yourself for a change. Can I get you anything?"

She shook her head and trudged back into her house, her feet shuffling as she mumbled something about dinner in the Crock-Pot. I followed her, walking through her back door. My eyes widened when I saw her kitchen. The island was still covered in the trays of food from last night, and there were half-filled glasses of wine and tequila on the countertops.

"We made such a mess. I'm so sorry—let me help you clean." Liz had insisted that she could handle the cleanup after we left, nearly pushing us out the door. It was no secret that she actually liked cleaning her house after we were over. Maybe it was because it was one of the few times she was alone, a thought that was almost too sad to ponder.

I reached for a wineglass, still filled with candy-pink wine, as Liz leaned back against a kitchen wall and closed her eyes. "No, thank you."

I dumped the wine into the sink and turned on the faucet. She lifted her head as she heard the water.

"No. I said *no, thank you*."

I stopped, glass still in hand. Liz had never raised her voice to me. I had never heard her raise her voice to anyone, save for maybe once when Luke smeared Vaseline all over the bathroom walls.

Liz's eyes flashed in anger, something else I had never seen.

"Oh, sure. Sorry. I was just trying to help since you aren't feeling so hot," I said.

Liz didn't reply, her eyes narrowing. I quickly put the glass down into the sink and turned to face her.

"I'll get out of your way," I said quickly as I sidestepped toward the back door.

I walked back to my front porch, bewildered by Liz's behavior. Melissa had her palm pressed to her nose, the terrible smell in the air so thick it nearly had texture. The kids, of course, seemed unbothered, arguing and wrestling in the sprinkler.

"Did you find out what that smell is? I've never experienced anything quite so . . . ripe," she said as she gagged a little.

"I think Liz is sick or something. She looks awful, like she has the flu," I said. "And she's not in the best of moods."

"I wouldn't be in the best mood either if my backyard smelled like a garbage dump," Melissa said. She stood. "Sorry, I can't deal with it. I have to keep working anyway, since my hangover is almost gone." She checked her watch and gave a quick nod. Right on cue, almost noon. She waved her kids over and steered them down the street toward her house.

I tried to breathe through my mouth as I sat outside, knowing the kids would complain and argue even more inside, but the smell seemed to permeate everything. It filled my mouth and burned my lungs. It was like being surrounded by damp earth, with something dead inside.

And that's when I realized what the smell reminded me of.

Last year, Mark and I had bought a deep freezer for the garage. We had plans to split a cow with Liz and Tim, although that never really happened because the farm we were going to buy it from went bankrupt due to the wife's involvement in a Nigerian-prince email scam. So it sat in our garage, unused, for a month before we noticed a smell. We thought maybe a mouse had died in the garage, so we swept it out, set traps, but never found anything, and the smell persisted.

Finally, we opened the deep freezer and discovered the source.

It was horrifying. A thick cloud smelling of rotting flesh nearly knocked us over as soon as the lid was opened. I gagged and had to run away, taking deep breaths as I sprinted across the lawn. Mark did throw up, into an old painter's bucket in our garage.

It was a decomposing raccoon, covered in maggots and flies, with black sludge all around it, at the bottom of the freezer. We had no idea how it got inside or how long it had been there, but that was the epicenter of the stench: rotting, decaying flesh and maggots.

And as I sat on my front porch, the putrid cloud emanating from Liz's backyard, that's exactly what I was smelling.

CHAPTER 3

ROCKY DANCED IN front of me, a stutter step followed by a 360-degree turn, three times. I stared at him, waiting for Mark to offer to take him for a walk after dinner. I had made fettuccine Alfredo and garlic bread, which Jack announced was disgusting, and Emily drew a line in the proverbial sand and said that she would only eat the garlic bread. I always found it exasperating that I was the least picky person in the house, so I was relegated to making meals that were kid-friendly, and they still wouldn't eat them.

Emily and Jack were in the basement, engaging in what sounded like a dangerous battle with the lightsabers my parents had erroneously bought them for Christmas, and Mark was bent over his phone, staring at work emails.

He glanced up. "I have to go to Miami at the end of next week." He frowned. "Sorry."

I nodded mutely. Mark had been traveling more and more for work and was usually gone for at least a couple of days every month.

At first, I had panicked, but after a while, I barely reacted. It was usually last minute, so I quickly learned to shuffle things around as needed, whether it was dance carpool or a girls' night out. More than once, we'd had to reschedule our neighborhood ladies' night to accommodate his schedule when I couldn't find a babysitter.

I looked down at Rocky. "Give me fifteen minutes, then we'll go out, I promise." Of course, the only word he understood was "out," so he started hopping up and down. He was three years old, a pug mix that we had found at a rescue the year before. The kids had begged for a puppy, but I didn't want to wake up in the middle of the night, so we settled on an adult dog. From the moment I saw his little squished face behind the kennel door, I was in love. He had some breathing problems, so he snored, but I didn't mind. His snoring lulled me to sleep each night like he was a living white-noise machine.

Of course, getting a rescue in Winchester was not a popular choice. Almost everyone else in our neighborhood had some kind of doodle mix—because they don't shed!—like a peer-pressure puppy. I took pride in my small act of suburban rebellion.

I walked upstairs, into my bedroom, to the small desk next to my bed. Our bedroom wasn't really big enough for both a night-stand and a desk, so I had taken the nightstand out and shoved the desk next to my bed. On the corner sat a glass of water and ChapStick. I opened my laptop with a click and waited for my email to load.

No new messages, save for a few online retailers to whom I had relinquished my email for a "20 percent off first purchase" coupon, and then never bought anything.

I sighed and my shoulders slumped forward. A month ago, I

had applied for two different social work jobs at nearby hospitals, but it had been radio silence since I hit Send.

In my former, childless days, I'd been a social worker at St. Mary's Hospital in the city. I'd fallen in love with social work when I was in college, leaping at the chance to actually make someone's life better. At helping in a way that was tangible, real, goal-oriented. After college, I completed my master's in social work and was hired nearly instantly at St. Vincent's. I worked with all kinds of people, assisting with geriatric patients all the way to parents whose children were in the NICU. I organized home health care, medical equipment rentals, transportation to doctor appointments. I made sure patients knew their rights and comforted families when their loved ones received a devastating diagnosis like cancer or Alzheimer's.

It was often emotionally difficult work, and there were many nights I drove back to the apartment I shared with Mark and cried to him about what I had seen and had to do. But I never felt like I wasn't making a difference.

And I loved it.

Except it wasn't exactly conducive to having children, or really, a life at all. The patients I worked with required so much attention—well-deserved attention—that their needs superseded mine. When I got pregnant with Jack, I had visions of Making It Work, of proving that I could have it all. I could not. I couldn't keep up with the demands of a job that required me to put my work first and a newborn with more than a few fussy moments. After a year of stretching myself so thin that I was nearly transparent, I took a leave of absence. I reasoned that I could go back to work when Jack was a little older.

The leave of absence turned more permanent once we had Emily, and we left the city behind for the suburbs. When we did, I still deluded myself into believing I was just one more milestone, one more year, away from going back to work.

Now that the kids were older, I'd decided to dip my toe back into the social work world and begun applying for jobs. Six months later, I was still applying.

I needed more, something else to tether me to the person who I was, rather than the person I was expected to be. And yet, here I was.

The cursor blinked accusingly at me, shaming me for not finding a way to do what I used to love.

You. Failure.

Did you really think you could have it all?

My fingers hesitated over the keyboard, anxiety and inertia plaguing me once again, whispering that my social work days were behind me, that I was trying to force something that didn't exist, like desperately squeezing a ketchup bottle for drops and feeling only air come out.

I shook my head, closed my laptop, and stood up. Something would come along; I was due for a stroke of luck.

But for now, I was out of ideas.

ROCKY AND I started down the darkened street, the only lights the few gas lamps left over from the sixties. We had one in our yard when we moved in but noticed a faint gas smell in the air periodically from the driveway. We had the gas company come out, and they told us it was leaking and had to be shut off. After that we had a nonfunctional gaslight at the end of our driveway, but when I heard the cost to remove it, I decided it could stay even though it felt a little like having a broken-down car on cinder blocks sitting there. At least the HOA hadn't yelled at us about that . . . yet.

A few blocks over, I could hear a group of neighbors on someone's front porch, having drinks. Whispering Farms was the kind of subdivision where you'd find porch beers in the summer and hot toddies around a firepit in the winter. It was socially engineered to keep people in the bubble, for it had everything you could want.

Rocky and I walked in the direction of Jess's house first, preparing to round the block toward Liz's. I had grabbed a bottle of Pedialyte from my fridge before I left and planned to leave it on her doorstep to help with her hangover or flu or whatever it was. The smell from her backyard lingered in the air, like clothes that had been left in the washer for too long. A rotting, old, cloying smell that made it hard to inhale.

"Looks like we picked the wrong night to walk down Maple Leaf Drive," I said to Rocky, who wagged his tail. We moved past Jess's house; she was strolling around her first floor without a bra on. Again. She grew up on what was essentially a hippie commune made up of former groupies of the singer Wavy Gravy in the north woods of Wisconsin. Some habits were apparently hard to break.

As we got closer to Liz's house, I saw that Tim had set their W flag on the front porch. He put it outside whenever the Chicago Cubs won a baseball game, but it was to remind the neighbors that he had season tickets more than to remind them he had team pride.

The smell intensified, and Rocky started whining and pulling at the leash, wanting to go home. Finally, he stopped on the sidewalk and sat, refusing to move, his eyes shifting back toward our house.

"Really? It's not that bad. Let me just drop this off for Liz." But even as I said the words, the smell filled my nose, swirling into my mouth, and I gagged, bending down toward the sidewalk. "Never mind." I started to turn around to head the other way, back toward my house, when a flash of light from Liz's made me turn back.

It was a quick blaze of light coming from her bedroom window, and it happened so fast, I thought it might be lightning. I looked up at the sky and saw a spray of stars above me. Not lightning. I watched the house, waiting to see if another flash would come, and saw a dark figure move across the bedroom window. It was too big to be Liz or Tim, and it was angular, like it had sharp edges. From her house, I heard Bucky begin to bark, before he stopped with a yelp.

"What's going on in there?" I lifted my foot to take a step toward the house, to make sure everything was okay, but Rocky whined and refused to move, an immobile statue. I thought about tying him to the street sign on the corner to go over and check on Liz, but he started shaking in fear. So I pulled out my phone and texted her instead.

I waited for a moment, the night air seeming to pause, and my pulse quickened as I stared at her house, hoping for a sign of my friend.

Rocky started frantically pulling at his leash, snarling in the effort. I bent down to soothe him, and he maneuvered away, desperately trying to go home.

"Okay, you win." I gave one final glance toward Liz's house, which was dark again. Darker than I had ever seen it. "The exterior lights must be out," I muttered as I let Rocky steer me.

Liz didn't respond until Rocky and I were inside the front door and I was unclipping his leash.

I didn't see anything was the text back.

I shook my head as I put my phone in my back pocket. Maybe I had imagined it. Maybe a car had pulled into a driveway down the street. A thousand things were possible. I didn't want to press the issue and become one of the paranoid moms I saw on the Winchester Moms Facebook group, regularly posting about neighbors who didn't clean up after their dogs, teenagers speeding down the street, or people who had cut them off in traffic. It was the worst kind of policing and one that didn't do any good, just started fights on social media.

Years ago, I would have never imagined that I would live in a town that became embroiled in such petty drama so often. Mark and I had vowed we weren't going to become those suburbanites who talked about mowing their lawn and tree-trimming services. No, we were much better than that—we were city people. Who took our kids to fancy restaurants and walked everywhere. Who shared one car that we barely drove and always knew where to get the best Indian takeout.

I was deeply aware of how uncool and boring the suburbs were. And yet I would soon come to find that our suburb was anything but mundane.

CHAPTER 4

THE MOMENT WHEN the kitchen was finally clean after dinner and the dishwasher began to hum was always one of the best parts of my day. All that was left was bedtime. Although bedtime was usually an arduous epilogue that involved copious bribery and threats.

The dishwasher whirring behind him, Mark looked at me, Clorox wipe in hand, and sighed, his shoulders sagging.

"Done. Finally," he said as he opened the garbage and tossed the wipe inside. He held an arm out, and I slid next to him in a side hug. He squeezed my shoulders, and I briefly closed my eyes. It had been another long day with the kids. Jack had fallen four times, and I had run out of Band-Aids, so I had to borrow some from Jess, who only had cupcake bandages, which was apparently a tragedy worthy of the national news.

"Want some pie? I hid the last two slices in the back of the fridge," Mark said, and I nodded mutely into his chest. He turned and riffled around in the fridge, pulling out the leftover key lime pie. He extracted two pieces from the tin and presented one to me.

We sat down at the clean kitchen island, the kids in the other room playing hide-and-go-seek, and clinked our forks together.

"What day is it?" I said, and glanced at the calendar.

"Only Tuesday," he said with a grimace. He had gotten home late from the office and eaten dinner with us still in his suit and tie. He had been promoted from a manager to a sales director a few months prior, and while at first I was thrilled at the prospect of more financial breathing room, it also meant longer hours at the office. By the time he came home at night and dinner was finished, both of us were usually so exhausted we fell asleep on the couch right after the kids' bedtime.

"Thanks for making the tacos tonight," he said.

"I'm glad you liked them. One day, I shall make something everyone in this house eats." The kids had picked at their tortillas and essentially only eaten the shredded cheese, dipping each sliver into the mountain of sour cream they had each loaded onto their plate.

"We can only dream," Mark said. His phone buzzed from across the room, and he glanced at it but remained in his seat. It buzzed again, and I could see the messages stacking on top of one another on the screen. But instead of getting up and replying, he looked at me. "Why don't we watch a movie tonight? Your choice."

I lifted my eyebrows in surprise. "My choice? Really?"

He smiled. "Sure. Just not anything airing on Bravo."

I rolled my eyes. "Well, that eliminates about ninety-nine-point-nine percent of everything I watch. It really puts your own life into perspective when you're watching a grown woman flip a table and call someone a 'prostitution whore.'" I lifted my glass in salute to the mindless television that had seen me through many long nights as I nursed our kids. "True-crime documentary, then?"

"Now you're speaking my language." He stood up and grabbed our plates. "Let me slip into something more comfortable"—he wiggled his eyebrows at me—"and then let's do it."

"I hope by 'do it,' you mean watch the documentary." I stood up and went into the family room, settled down on the couch with a blanket, and queued up the television.

I scrolled through a few crime documentaries until I stopped on one titled *She Never Came Home*, about a mom who disappeared during a camping trip to Yosemite with her husband and children. The husband claimed she had just vanished, like a ghost in the night.

Murder mystery shows were one of the first things that Mark and I bonded over when we met. We were both in grad school at Northwestern, me for my MSW and him for his MBA. We were at a bar near campus aptly named Hole in the Wall, on a Monday night during my second year. I bumped into him on the way to the bathroom, spilling vodka cranberry all down the front of his shirt. I was horrifically embarrassed and profusely apologized, especially after seeing how attractive he was, but he laughed and shrugged it off without a hint of mockery. That was my first indication that he might be more than just a guy in a bar.

He insisted on buying me another drink, even though I had been at fault, and we talked at a scratched wood bar table.

"My Friday nights are usually spent watching *Dateline*, so this is a nice change," he said as we split a pitcher of beer.

My eyes widened. "Really? That's my favorite show. Don't laugh, but I have an intellectual crush on Keith Morrison."

He leaned forward, and my heart beat faster in my chest. His fingers brushed mine as he whispered, "Me too."

We only made it through another fifteen minutes before we went back to my apartment.

Two kids, a mortgage, and many car payments later, Mark appeared in the doorway and laughed when he saw the title of the movie I had queued. "*She Never Came Home*. Should I be worried?" He settled down next to me, wrapping an arm around my shoulders as I shared the blanket with him.

"You know it's the husband. It's *always* the husband," I said as I poked him in the ribs. "So make sure you really cover your tracks if you murder me, otherwise you'll end up in jail and the kids will have to live with your parents."

He narrowed his eyes and cocked his head to the side. "Well, I could at least get rid of your phone records. Mike in IT is pretty sweet on me."

I nodded. "Now you're thinking."

"I can flirt with the best of them," he said. "Cue it up, and let's see how long it takes for the husband's alibi to fall apart."

——

I WOKE UP the next morning feeling deeply unsettled. It wasn't from the documentary, where the husband, shockingly, did kill his wife and buried her in the woods behind their house. Mark and I had collapsed into bed together, too tired to do anything but kiss, and I had fallen fast asleep.

And then the dreams came. Of someone breaking into our

house, chasing Mark with a knife, before turning it on me. Of my children being pulled into a deep, dark, never-ending hole as I tried desperately to claw away the moist dirt that fell on top of them, swallowing them whole as I screamed.

At the end of the dream, I saw who had murdered us. It was a woman with no eyes or nose and long dark hair. The last thing I remembered before I woke up was her smile. Her mouth stretched up toward her ears, revealing rotting teeth.

She whispered, "I'm back."

My body buzzing with the lingering fear and panic from the dream, I glanced outside and saw that it was mostly still dark out, sunrise only starting over the horizon. I tapped at my phone: five forty-five a.m.

"Mom?" I heard Jack call from his room.

I padded down the hallway, trying to shake off the unease of my nightmare. "What do you need, buddy?" I said as he popped out of bed.

"I'm hungry. I need breakfast," he said. "The sun is awake, and I am, too."

"Give me a second," I said. I went back to the bedroom, grabbed my glasses from the nightstand, and wound my hair into a topknot. I looked over at Mark and Rocky. They were both snoring lightly, oblivious. If only I'd had a restful night of sleep like they had.

———

JACK SETTLED IN happily with some microwaved pancakes, and I held a hot cup of coffee as I sat at the kitchen island, watching the backyard slowly illuminate. In the far corner of the yard, I saw a movement of brown and white fur.

"Look! A bunny." Jack's head swiveled around as we watched the rabbit hop around the backyard.

"Good job. Keep going," I whispered as I saw the rabbit begin to munch on the weed patches I needed to pull out. "Too bad you guys don't eat red ants."

The rabbit then hopped over to the center of the yard and stopped.

"What's it doing, Mommy?" Jack said when it didn't move after a few seconds.

I looked at him and smiled, watching the rabbit hop away out of the corner of my eye. "I think there's a nest out there. The mama rabbit comes to feed the babies in the early morning and right before it gets dark out."

I stopped as my throat began to close, thinking of the rabbits my younger sister, June, used to keep when we were growing up. She had two that lived in a hutch outside, and they were her prized pets. It was a time of innocence, of summers spent drinking from the hose and riding our bikes home only when the streetlights came on. The bunny reminded me of a time before the darkness overtook her.

I still couldn't believe it had been five years since she died.

Jack pulled me out of my thoughts. "Bunnies? I want to see!" He leapt off his chair.

We carefully walked outside, making sure to close the sliding glass door behind us so Rocky wouldn't nose his way out. Sure enough, where the bunny had sat was a disturbed patch of grass with loose soil and a few tufts of rabbit fur. I grabbed a nearby stick and gently lifted the grass and fur.

Inside were four tiny, gray, squirming baby rabbits, eyes still closed.

"They're so cute! Can they be our new pets? Please, please, please?" Jack said as he crouched down lower.

I smiled. "They're cute, but they belong outside, with their mom."

He sighed in disappointment, and I carefully replaced the grass and fur on top. "We can check on them each day, though, and say hi."

"What if Daddy cuts the grass and hurts them?" Jack said.

"Well, let's mark it off." I went into the garage and found an old easel tripod that Mark had brought home from work a few years ago.

I stuck the tripod on top of the nest, careful to splay the legs so they wouldn't scare off the mom. As I did, a feeling of darkness settled around my shoulders. It raised the hair on my arms, and for a moment, a shadow seemed to move across the nest, although the sun was on the opposite end of the sky.

A word popped into my brain, a whisper more than a thought: *Death.*

The panic and fear I felt in my dream came rushing back, my vision narrowing and my ears roaring with pumping blood. Goose bumps popped up on my arms as I remembered the way the woman's mouth had stretched open, her rotting teeth like decrepit piano keys.

I'm back.

The words whispered against my cheek, nudging my skin in a tender caress.

Startled, I stepped backward, and just as quickly as it had appeared, the feeling was gone. Another trick of my mind, perhaps. Or maybe the lack of sleep was finally kicking in. I shook my head and turned to Jack.

"See?" I said. "All good."

We went back inside, and I picked up my now-cool cup of coffee. Putting it in the microwave, I took a deep breath. My pulse was still racing from whatever had happened outside, but I told myself it was just anxiety, just my tired mind warping my thoughts.

Occam's razor, I thought. I took a few more deep breaths, trying to center my body. I was safe in my house. Whatever I'd felt outside was in my head, created by a nightmare and the stress I felt over finding a job.

I reached for the fridge to grab more creamer. My hand paused as I noticed a flier on the front of the fridge that made me forget about my panic and fear: an invitation to the neighborhood block party. I had stuck it there when I found it in my mailbox, and then it promptly became part of the decor, like the spot on the rug in the family room.

HEY ALL YOU WONDERFUL NEIGHBORS!

IT'S TIME TO CELEBRATE THE START OF SUMMER.

PLEASE JOIN US ALL AT THE ANNUAL WHISPERING

FARMS BLOCK PARTY ON MAPLE LEAF, AT 4:00 P.M.

ON JUNE 23. BRING A SIDE DISH AND A DESSERT.

GRILLING MEAT WILL BE PROVIDED. CORNHOLE

AND BOCCE BALL TOURNAMENT TO BEGIN
AT 5:00 P.M. SHARP—RAIN OR SHINE!

It was tomorrow. Shit. That meant I had to go to the grocery store—again—and figure out what to make. I could always bring a tub of premade coleslaw and some grocery store cupcakes, but then I would be the only one bringing something not homemade. There would be casseroles, buckets of puppy chow, homemade cheese curds, and every kind of dip it was possible to make out of cream cheese and French onion soup mix. It was like the Super Bowl of the block, and I was never in contention to get the MVP ring.

I would have considered skipping it, but the epicenter of the party was two houses down, so there would be no way to hide.

I took a long gulp of my coffee before muttering, "Block party? Now, that's something to really be scared of."

CHAPTER 5

CROCK-POTS LINED THE folding tables, which were peppered with bowls of tortilla chips, pretzels, and unidentifiable dips, in the middle of the street outside our house. I walked out, a bowl of hot corn dip and bag of tortilla chips in one hand, a pan of caramel brownies in the other.

I pasted on a smile as I approached the group milling about in the street, which was blocked off by two sawhorses at each end. Next door, two bounce houses were inflated in Jess's yard, and across the street, at the Hacker house, preparations were under way for the cornhole and bocce ball tournaments. Andrew Hacker stood in his front yard, wearing his signature brightly colored Crocs. Heather was surrounded by her group of friends as she held court. She said something, and they all laughed, their dangly earrings swaying. I wondered what they were joking about, and whether it was again my friends and me. Further down, one of the neighbors was filling water balloons with a hose and still another was lighting sparklers for the kids.

I had watched the crowd gather from my bedroom window, trying to steel my nerves for a long afternoon. There would be so many neighbors, so many names and backstories to remember; the thought of it all exhausted me already. It always seemed like everyone else could recall the most minute details of each other's lives, whereas I just nodded and smiled and pretended to remember that Nancy Johnson had gone to Mackinac Island last month to renew her vows, or that Josie Spadlowski's son was accepted at Notre Dame and might walk onto the football team in the fall. "You know how much we love the movie *Rudy*," she would say.

I could barely remember the details of my own life, let alone anyone else's. At these neighborhood events, I often felt out of place and not quite complete, like a puzzle with a piece missing. Sure, someone could tell what the picture was supposed to be, but something wasn't quite right. I wasn't even sure I wanted to know what the missing piece was supposed to be.

As if all that pressure weren't enough, a heat wave had unexpectedly hit late that morning, and the heat index was nearly 100 degrees. It meant that everyone would stand around, remarking that the weather "really wouldn't be that bad, if it weren't for the humidity." As Midwesterners, we always seemed to get the short end of the meteorological stick, no matter the season.

I gave a nod to neighbors who lived two streets over—no idea what their name was—as I carefully nudged aside a Crock-Pot full of cocktail meatballs and placed my dip in between that and an enormous bowl of Josh Peterson's self-proclaimed "famous"

Buffalo chicken dip. I set my brownies on the opposite end of the table, in between two other identical pans of brownies.

Whatever. At least I tried.

I spotted Melissa holding a plastic cup of wine, on the edge of the group of neighbors. She sported a white sundress, wedges, and a bored look on her face. Her eyes lit up when she saw me, and she trotted over.

"This is terrible already. I know you hate these things as much as I do. I should have faked a work emergency and stayed home. No one would have questioned it, because they all get so uncomfortable whenever I talk about work." She sighed and peered at the food table. "What did you bring?"

I crooked a finger toward my bowl. "Corn dip."

"Looks good." She grabbed a chip and tried to scoop up a sample, but it broke in her hand. She tried again, but the top layer of cheese had hardened into an impenetrable fortress. "Oh."

I lifted my palms. "I guess I should have heated it up more. That'll show me for trying to bring something I've never made before." I glanced around at the table. "So, what did you bring?"

She nodded toward a dish at the end of the table and then took a long sip of her wine. "Tony made a charcuterie board. He carved the serrano ham himself from a pig leg he had imported from Italy." She pushed her sunglasses up, splaying her highlighted hair.

A trained chef, Tony had gone to culinary school and worked as a sous chef for a few years before he met Melissa. They met when she had dinner at Michelin-starred Alinea with some work colleagues, and their tab was high enough to be invited to tour the kitchen. After the introduction, she invited him to tour her bedroom.

Two years later, they were married. He bounced from restaurant to restaurant until they had kids, when they decided he would stay home and she would continue to work. Yet his passion for cooking never waned; he clearly missed having a creative endeavor. Something I understood all too well.

"Once again, you've earned your nickname of Fancypants. Next time I'm just putting my name on whatever you bring." I glanced around, spotted a sweating aluminum bucket of wine, and poured myself a glass of sauvignon blanc. As I took a sip, I surveyed the crowd. Most of the husbands were standing in a semicircle, gesturing toward the grills as though they were all part of an elite force of charred meat experts, except only Kevin Simpson was actually doing any work. He held the tongs in the air and clicked them together every ten seconds, like he was communicating in Morse code. As Mark approached the group, their faces perked up, no doubt ready to ask him about a discount on their cell phone bills. The older residents of the neighborhood sat on folding lawn chairs in the street, also in a semicircle. I spotted Jess inside her house, gathering things in the kitchen.

"Where's Liz?" I said. "Hopefully she's feeling better."

Melissa gave a shrug, her turquoise Kendra Scott earrings brushing against her cheeks. "Stalling, if she's smart."

I heard Emily screaming from across the street and saw that she had fallen down on the sidewalk and was holding her knee. I waited a moment to see if she would shake it off and get up, but when she didn't, I walked over. A steady stream of blood poured from her leg.

I crouched forward. "Oh, honey. What happened?"

"I tripped over my scooter." Tears ran down her dirt-streaked face as she stared at the cut. I put my hand over it to stop the bleeding, kneeling on the rough sidewalk awkwardly in my cutoff jean shorts. I glanced around, again looking for Liz. As a nurse, she usually was the first to arrive when any of our kids got hurt, but I didn't see her.

"Let's go home and get you a—" I stopped when I heard a rustling from the crowd. I turned and saw electricity run through the groups, like a lightning bolt moving horizontally, pinging each person.

I grabbed Emily's hand and placed it on her knee. "Put pressure on it for a second." I stood up, her blood streaking my palm, and craned my neck to see what the commotion was about.

The crowd was parting slightly, like royalty was entering a ballroom. The catalyst was a short woman, long hair cascading down her back in perfect beachy waves. She had on red lipstick and gold sparkly earrings that brushed her shoulders. She wore a short, strapless romper with white four-inch heels. Her skin was the color of honey, with patches of highlighter accentuating her shoulders and cheekbones.

It took me a moment to register who it was.

It was Liz. Hangover or flu apparently gone.

She surveyed the crowd coolly, her hair fluttering in the breeze behind her like Beyoncé with a wind machine. Her kids trailed her, with Tim bringing up the rear, his attention on his phone, nonplussed by his wife's transformation from someone who booked yearly Disney World vacations (complete with a social media picture of the MagicBands the day they arrived in the mail) and bought specialty s'mores sticks for the backyard firepit.

I caught Melissa's eye as she slowly turned toward me, mouth agape. I shook my head slightly and looked over to Jess, who had emerged from her house and was standing barefoot on her front porch, portable speaker in one hand, giant bottle of vodka in the other. She wasn't actively working against Heather's first assessment of her, something I respected. Jess was always herself, no matter what the situation.

She laughed. "Yes, Liz! Looking good, friend!" she shouted over the top of the crowd with guttural admiration.

Liz slowly craned her neck toward Jess, squinting in her direction as though trying to figure out who she was. Then her face broke into a smile, and she gave a quick wave to Jess before sauntering to the card table bar.

She picked up a pale pink bottle of rosé and wrinkled her nose at it before she put it back down on the table. I tipped my head to the side in confusion. That bottle was at least twice as good as the wine from her house the other night, and she was acting like it was poison.

As she lifted a bottle of Grey Goose vodka, I saw she had painted her nails bright red, a far cry from the Ballet Slippers she normally sported. Sexy Liz plucked a few ice cubes out of a sweating bucket, dropped them into a glass, and then filled it nearly to the top with vodka. I waited for her to add a mixer, but instead she whirled around, her hair streaming behind her, and began to walk toward Heather, who was now assigning teams for the cornhole tournament. I was too far away to hear what Liz said to her, but Heather's face changed from a smirk to surprise and then anger.

Heather's eyes narrowed into sharp slits as she slowly lifted her drink to her mouth, no doubt forming a plan to destroy Liz socially. Her minions had equally dark looks, as though Heather was the neck and they were collectively the head that had to follow. They all ran the school, and there were even more opportunities for them to exclude Liz now that they had a concrete example of why she didn't belong.

I bent down and gave Emily's leg another pat before I walked over to Liz, wiping the leftover blood on my shorts.

"Hey, that was quite an entrance," I said to Liz. "What did you say to Heather?" I glanced over, and she was still glaring in Liz's direction.

She lifted a meticulously drawn eyebrow and gave me a small smile. "I said to her what I have always wanted to say." Her words were stiff, formal, missing their usual warmth.

Melissa appeared next to us. "Liz, most of the husbands are staring at you right now," she said as she gestured toward the semicircle of men gripping sweating craft beer bottles, trying not to stare. "For that reason, I would advise avoiding Heather and her witches."

Liz didn't answer but took a sip of her vodka without a wince and nodded to the group of men. They quickly looked away. Busted.

"So what's up with you? Just woke up feeling edgy today?" I said as I waved a hand up and down her figure. "Performance art piece?"

She smiled again and took another sip, before her voice came out, deep and formal. "I am not sure what you are referring to. I have never felt more like myself."

Melissa and I exchanged a puzzled look as Jess walked up, still barefoot.

Jess clapped Liz on the back, hard. "Hell yes. Love this look. Shit, I'm so happy I was here to see"—she gestured up and down the length of Liz's body—"*this* happen." She wiped her sweaty brow with her forearm as she laughed.

Liz stared at her for a moment and then laughed along. A chill ran down my back at Liz's expression. It looked like she was *studying* Jess to figure out the appropriate response. Her teeth even seemed whiter.

She looked at each of us, pausing for a moment, examining our faces.

"Really, though, are you okay? You seem a bit . . . off," I said as I furrowed my brow.

"Of course," she said, and smiled again. This time, her smile was warm and her tone familiar, full of the Liz that we all knew and loved. "I just wanted to dress up a little today."

Melissa leaned in. "Nothing wrong with that. You look fantastic. Tim must have been thrilled."

We looked over at Tim, who was still buried in his phone, not looking up once, in contrast to the rest of the husbands.

"Yo, we can still see you guys, you know. Try harder," Jess called to them before they quickly looked away.

"When did you switch to vodka?" I asked Liz as I tapped her glass with my index finger. Her gaze was fixed in the direction of Emily, and I tapped her glass again to get her attention.

She finally turned toward me. "It was time for something new." She met my eyes, unwavering. "Like if you volunteered to help at school."

I lifted my brows in surprise. Liz usually wasn't one for off-handed sarcastic comments. "Good one. I just know if I downed that much straight vodka, I wouldn't be volunteering for anything, or walking straight," I said with a laugh.

"Oh, girl, not in those heels, you wouldn't." Jess pointed to Liz's.

Liz's eyes narrowed as she looked down at Jess's bare feet. "You should put on shoes. It's vile."

Jess shrank back and frowned, looking to Melissa and me for an explanation. For all of her bravado, Jess was a soft soul. I shook my head slightly in confusion and gave a tiny shrug.

Melissa cleared her throat and shifted, a deliberate movement to break the tension. Her gaze drifted over to a circle of our kids, leaning in and whispering conspiratorially. "Looks like the kids are planning something."

Liz's head turned slowly toward them, and a small smile appeared on her lips as Emily ran over from the group, her hair streaming behind her, her injury apparently forgotten.

"Mom, Mom, Mom, Mom," she repeated until I held my palm up.

"Take a deep breath, and then start over," I said.

"Mom," she said as she panted. "Can you show everyone the baby bunnies in our backyard?" She pointed to the group of kids behind us, staring, waiting. "They're so cute. Please, please, please . . ."

She continued her chorus of pleading until I nodded. "Sure."

Emily turned and screamed, "She said yes! C'mon, guys!"

"Now, everyone, remember, you can't get close to the babies or else the mom won't come back. I'm the only one who can lift up the grass from the nest, okay?" The group of kids nodded as they followed me. "And be really quiet, because we don't want to scare them. They're just babies, and I'm sure they would be nervous if they saw so many people standing around them."

I walked over the grass, the horde of kids following behind me like I was the Block Party Pied Piper, and picked up a long stick. Jack joined the group, whispering to his friends that they should be excited. I smiled, a warm feeling coming over me as I prepared to show them something special.

I gingerly approached the nest, tiptoeing across the grass as the children huddled around me. I moved the tripod and knelt down, then looked up at the kids crowding around and put a finger to my lips as they all tensed in anticipation.

The memory of the feeling I had when we first discovered the nest came flooding back, and my breath caught in my throat. I swallowed quickly, pushing it away, reminding myself it was nonsense. Just a bizarre moment, and nothing else.

I looked down at the nest, about to carefully use the stick to peel back the layers of grass, but paused. The covering wasn't patted down and placed over the nest as we had left it. Whereas before it had been almost indistinguishable from the rest of the lawn, the new arrangement made it clear that something was hiding.

I looked up at Emily. "Did you show your friends already?"

She shook her head furiously and knitted her brows together. "No, Mommy. I promise."

I looked down and lifted what was left of the covering, and the first thing I saw was red.

Blood. Mixed with fur.

Instead of baby bunnies huddled together, it was just bloodstains, fur, and scattered body parts. My eyes focused on a small severed bunny foot, the edges jagged, having been chewed off by something with very sharp teeth.

The children behind me started screaming in terror before they ran out of the yard, yelling for their parents. Bile rose in my throat, and I quickly dropped the stick and jogged out of the yard behind them. A wave of panic moved across the block party crowd as the parents saw their children come tearing out of my backyard, tears streaking their faces.

Mark jogged over and scooped up a hysterical Emily, bending down to hold her shaking frame. Jack slowly backed away, eyes wide.

"What in the world happened?" Mark hissed to me.

I shook my head, my heart racing. "The bunnies. Something got to them. There's . . . not much left."

The chorus of crying children and shouting parents seemed to billow around me as I bent down to Emily and rubbed her back. I scanned the yard for Jack, but he had already run down the street.

"I'm so sorry, honey. I'm so sorry that you had to see that," I whispered. I placed an arm around her, and Mark and held tight.

Emily buried her head in Mark's shoulder. "Who would do that?" she wailed.

"It's not a who, honey. It was some kind of animal. Maybe a coyote or something like that. It's awful, but it does happen. I'm so, so sorry," I whispered again.

"But why?" she wailed.

Out of the corner of my eye, I saw my friends doing the same thing with their kids—hugging them, picking them up, wiping tears from their faces with a palm, rocking them back and forth.

"It is nature, Em. It's really sad, but that's how some animals eat—by eating other animals," Mark said.

"But they were so small. They were just babies. Why couldn't their mother protect them?" she said, her breath coming in ragged gasps.

"I don't know," Mark finally said, pulling her close again.

I took a deep breath and looked around, my hand still on top of Emily's head. Most of the crowd was now dispersing, hysterical children in their arms. I heard whispers, promises of ice cream and special treats. Of toys bought from Amazon and trips to the neighborhood swimming pool. Of anything to calm their kids down.

Except for one.

Liz stood on the fringe of the crowd, her drink still in her hand. I didn't see Tim and the children, but I assumed they were also headed back toward their house. Yet she remained. Her head slowly turned toward me, until our eyes locked. Hers widened for a moment before she slowly lifted her drink to her mouth and took a long sip. She wiped the corner of her mouth, and as she brought her red fingernails up to her face, they didn't look like they were painted. From across the street, they looked bloody.

And then she smiled.

CHAPTER 6

"MOM, WHERE ARE my goggles?"

Jack stood in front of me, dripping wet, water pooling around his feet on the hot concrete. I sighed and fished into my pool bag, extracting the child equivalent of the Hope Diamond from the bag with two fingers. I wondered how many times, on average, per pool visit, I was asked to locate goggles. It had to be somewhere north of one billion.

"Thanks!" He snatched them from my hand and scampered off into the water to join the countless other children splashing around in the zero-entry pool. We had decided to spend the morning at the community pool, a decision I had immediately regretted when I saw the massive crowd waiting to gain entrance. In addition to the goggle requests, there would be pleas for ice cream; many, many applications of sunscreen (the spray kind, for which I would always get a few dirty looks as I applied it, because other children only wore sunscreen that was nontoxic, made from fairy dust and recycled water bottles); and lost swim towels.

My kids and the others in the neighborhood had recovered from the trauma of seeing the bunnies. Assisted, no doubt, by the ice-cream truck Heather flagged down after it happened. It seemed that Creamsicles and Choco Tacos could be a balm for any wound, physical or emotional. I, on the other hand, hadn't recovered. The combination of Liz's behavior and the possible foresight I'd had of the bunnies' being slaughtered had kept me up last night.

I leaned back in my lounger, eyes carefully trained on the group of kids at the water's edge.

"Havin' a fuckin' blast yet?" Jess mumbled as she dropped her bag down on the chaise next to me. I'd texted her, desperate to have someone for company who wouldn't ask for a Popsicle in the shape of a rocket ship.

Before I could answer, she plopped down next to me as her seven-year-old stepdaughter, Summer, scampered off to play. Jess didn't wear a cover-up—ever—and her red bikini barely covered her sensitive parts.

She scanned the pool, squinting across the crowd. "Yo, she's not here, right?"

"No. I would have warned you if I saw her."

Jess was referring to Del's ex-wife, Sharon. She lived a couple of miles from us, in a McMansion she'd bought after the divorce in a planned community that looked like a developer had bulldozed a cornfield and built as many cookie-cutter homes as the town would allow in one space. To say she wasn't the biggest fan of her ex's girlfriend would have been the world's largest understatement.

Whenever their paths crossed at a school event or holiday, Sharon took a few cheap shots at Jess. And of course she was friends with Heather.

Jess and Del had met four years ago, a year after his divorce, at the Country Thunder music festival in Twin Lakes, Wisconsin. She moved to Winchester to live with him a couple of years after that, forever scandalizing our town.

"Great. So, let's not shoot the shit and get right to it. What's going on with Liz? We need to discuss," she said as she leaned forward and put her forearms on her thighs, hands clasped in front of her.

I shook my head. "I have no idea, but it's really creeping me out. As much as I enjoyed watching her say whatever she said to Heather and the Mom Mafia, there's something obviously going on with her, and we need to ask her about it. She's arrogant; she's bitchy. It's like she's completely flipped her personality. Like she . . ." I trailed off.

"Dropped a bunch of acid," Jess finished as she lay back on her chair.

I rolled my eyes. "Yes, something like that. But, really. Do you think something's wrong at home? With Tim, maybe?"

"Probably," Jess said as she closed her eyes. "He's not exactly Husband of the Year or anything. I mean, the guy ignores Liz and the kids and only talks in weird lawyer corporate speak like 'touch base' and 'accountability.' And he only cares about money."

Liz and Tim were high school sweethearts and had been together for nearly twenty years. I imagined he had been softer and kinder at some point, since she'd fallen in love with him. If they had met in adulthood, I couldn't imagine that they would have chosen each other. While Liz was loving and motherly, Tim seemed to feel the only contribution he needed to provide was on his W-2.

"Well, I'm going to talk to her and see if she's okay. It's just too weird, with the clothing and general behavior," I said. I stopped before I allowed myself to tell Jess about all the other strange things that I had felt over the past week.

I looked up as Emily tenderly patted a younger girl wearing a swim diaper by the water's edge. She was sensitive, almost empathic. She had cried for what felt like hours the night that we had found the bunnies. The next morning, we'd held a small ceremony for them in the backyard and buried what was left of them in our flower bed. That afternoon, I saw her kneeling in front of the grave, telling them that they were safe now and not to worry. It broke my heart a little.

She had come inside and stood at the kitchen window, her eyes wide.

"Something bad happened to them, Mommy," she whispered. Her small body seemed to fold into itself, and she looked like a trembling baby bird. Her face was pale, her mouth pinched together in fear.

I knelt and wrapped my arms around her, but she didn't return the embrace. "It was just another animal, honey. It's just . . . nature."

She nudged my hair aside and whispered into my ear. "No. I saw it."

I leaned back in surprise. "You saw it? When? What happened?"

Her eyes were glassy with fear. "In my dream last night, I saw what happened to the babies. It was a scary old lady, with long teeth that dripped with blood. She went to the bunnies, and ate them, and spit out their bones."

I exhaled and shook my head. "No, it was probably just a coyote. Which is scary enough, I know. I'm so sorry that you had that terrible nightmare."

She shook her head in frustration, swiping her bangs from her eyes. "It was a lady. A really scary one."

I just pulled her to me again and gave her a tight hug. "It can't hurt you."

"I know." She wiggled out of my grasp, and I stood up. She started to leave the kitchen but stopped and turned to me. "But it can hurt you." And then she left.

I felt rooted to the kitchen floor, which was still dusted with crumbs left over from breakfast. A chill ran through me, and I wrapped my arms around my midsection.

I'm back.

I would have to talk to Mark later. Maybe he could explain what had happened to her in a way that was more concrete . . . and less creepy.

At the pool, Jess took a long swig of water from an aluminum water bottle as she watched Summer go down the slide over and over again. The sounds around us had reached a fever pitch from all the kids and parents yelling to *get out of the water, here's more sunscreen, find your flip-flops.*

"Is there some sort of rule that after you have kids, you can only wear a black bathing suit with a skirt?" she said as she looked into the crowd of women, all of them PTA members who always got the teachers their kids requested and had the principal on speed dial. I noticed they snuck disapproving glances at Jess from behind their sunglasses. Jess would forever be labeled as "the girlfriend" by them, and I could only imagine what Sharon told them about her. Plus, I was sure that they had all heard about whatever Liz said to Heather at the block party, and we were all guilty by association.

I looked down at my own black bathing suit, a high-waisted tankini. "Apparently." I didn't wear a swim skirt, as that was my line in the sand.

"Don't we all have stretch marks and veins and cellulite?" she said with a frown. "Shouldn't we all just say 'screw it' and wear whatever we want?"

I settled back with a laugh. "In theory, yes. But might I remind you that you don't have any of those things?" I glanced at her body, which was like looking into the past. She had never been pregnant—she harbored no desire to do so—and was nearly a decade younger than the rest of us at twenty-nine.

Meanwhile, the ill-advised heart tattoo on my hip that I got in college after a night of keg stands had stretched and contracted twice with my pregnancies and was now a sad shadow of its former design. "Only a deal with the devil would fix my body at this point."

Jess sat up quickly and jabbed her pointer finger in the air. "That's it! The devil." She lowered her finger as I narrowed my eyes. "She made a deal with the devil to escape the suburbs."

I nodded. "Oh yes. That is the only possible explanation." I rolled my eyes as I hitched up my bathing suit. "The eighties called and want their Satanic Panic back."

"I don't know what you're talking about," she said. "I wasn't even born in the eighties."

"Satanic Panic was when people in the eighties thought there were satanic cults everywhere, possessing people and abducting children for demonic rituals. Neighbors accused other neighbors of being devil worshippers and casting demonic curses."

She closed her eyes and smirked. "Cocaine. Everyone in the eighties was coked out."

I scanned the water until I located Emily and Jack and then sat back, closing my eyes for a minute. But I couldn't stop thinking about Liz, and a darkness settled onto my shoulders for a moment. I knew whatever was going on with her was something more serious than anything we were ready to admit.

CHAPTER 7

THE CURSOR ON my laptop blinked like an impatient child tapping his foot. *Do something. Something. Anything. A grocery list.* My fingers were poised over the keyboard, halted in midair, words stuck somewhere inside of me.

This was my allotted time to apply for jobs: the hour after lunchtime, when the kids were safely ensconced in the family room with a movie and a blanket. They had tired quickly at the pool, and I barely had time to have a full conversation with Jess before they started asking to leave. It took another ten minutes to gather all of our things, because of course Emily had left her goggles in the sand area and another kid had taken them. It took hostage-negotiator levels of conversation to get them back.

We arrived home, and I made them peanut butter and jelly sandwiches (incorrectly, apparently, due to the jelly/peanut butter ratio), flipped on a Disney movie, and then raced to my desk to work. Once I was there, though, *nothing*. It was like hitting a brick wall at top speed.

As much as I tried to focus on looking for social work jobs, my mind still lingered on Liz. I chewed my lip and looked outside, trying to crane my neck around the corner to her house, but all that was visible was the top of her chimney. I saw a thin plume of smoke wafting out from it and frowned. Strange to build a fire in the middle of the summer.

I leaned back and sighed. One more thing that was odd. Nothing exciting ever happened in our neighborhood, save for the time when Ginny Thomas's three-year old accidentally bit into a light-bulb last year and she had to call an ambulance. He wound up being fine, but the neighbors talked so dramatically you would have thought something actually serious had happened, like garbage day being moved.

I turned back to my laptop and rested my hands on the keyboard. But before I could type anything, Jack appeared.

"Mom, when can we go to Disney World?"

I heard the background noise of a commercial for the Magic Kingdom and sighed.

"Hmmm, not sure," I said. "Not sure" was always my answer for "nope." Never. Walking around a theme park when it was ninety-five degrees while spending approximately one million dollars was not high on my priority list. Christ, we could go to Hawaii for a month for the amount that I heard most families spent.

"Can I have a snack?" Jack said. "And I spilled my water."

I rubbed my forehead and gave my laptop a long look before I stood up, back into Mom Mode.

———

AFTER DINNER, I pulled my phone out of my back pocket. I'd texted Liz two hours before, asking if we could meet up. I wanted to talk to her in person about whatever it was that she was going through. No text back.

Since I hadn't heard from her, I texted Melissa and Jess.

> Have you guys heard from Liz? I want to check
> in with her.

Nope was Jess's response.
I had meetings all day and never looked at my phone, Melissa said.
Then, as if in collusion, they both responded:

> Go over there. See if she's on acid.

> Why don't you check in on her? I have to finish
> this performance review.

My marching orders given, I glanced again at Liz's house. The plume of smoke had stopped, and the house was still. A wave of anxiety built in my chest and spread across my body as I thought about what to say to my friend. Her behavior at the block party and at her house the day before was so out of character that I didn't know what to expect. I wanted to ask Jess and Melissa to come with me for solidarity, but I knew it was probably best if I went alone. Melissa wouldn't have patience if Liz was still acting bizarre, and Jess would brush it off and deflect. So that left me.

I almost decided not to go, to give it another day, but I knew it wasn't right to ignore the situation. She was my friend, and I needed to reach out. I had so many regrets when it came to my sister. There were so many times when I should have reached out and didn't; my guilt propelled me to ignore my anxiety and put on my shoes. Never again.

I told Mark I was walking around the corner and would be back in a bit. As I headed toward the door, Emily asked where I was going.

"Just around the corner for a moment, to Miss Liz's house," I said.

Her eyes widened and she shook her head. "Don't go."

I frowned. "I will be back in a few. Dad will put you to bed."

She shook her head more vigorously. "No. Don't."

I patted her on the shoulder. "I will be right back."

She opened her mouth but then closed it, her eyes wide. I started down the sidewalk, swallowing hard as my nerves began to rev up, telling myself to stop being ridiculous, that she was my friend and there was nothing to be anxious about. Yet as I ducked down under the large crab apple tree that George Simpson refused to prune, the neighborhood suddenly felt much darker, and colder, than ever.

Liz answered the door before I could even press the doorbell. My hand hung in the air, frozen, my pointer finger extended next to the W flag, as she gazed at me coolly.

"Yes?" she said.

I was momentarily speechless. She was wearing a black jump-suit with long earrings.

"Are you . . . going out?" I said.

"What makes you think that?" she said, her face stone. "I was tired of dressing like a slob every day." She slowly looked me up and down.

My mouth opened, but nothing came out.

"I—" I stopped when she bent over laughing, her hands on her thighs as she roared. I continued to stare, and she looked up at me, her hair hanging on either side of her face.

"You should see your expression," she said as she stood up. She exhaled, then brushed her hair back over her shoulders. She steadied. "Why are you here?"

"Oh, sorry. I just wanted to check on you. I was worried and—" I stopped as I saw Carson scamper into the other room behind her. She slowly turned and followed my gaze, before looking back at me expectantly.

"Is there somewhere where we could chat privately?" I said as I crossed my arms over my chest.

She frowned, but then cocked her head to the side and smiled. "Sure. The backyard."

I followed Liz to the outdoor couch near her Margaritaville tiki hut. She tucked her legs underneath her and stared at me. The horrible smell from the other night still lingered in the air, and I had to make a conscious choice not to put a hand to my nose.

"Sorry, I didn't mean to interrupt. I'm sure you're in the middle of the bedtime routines. I've just been worried about you and wanted to let you know that I'm here to talk if you need an ear," I said.

"I don't put them to bed anymore," she said with a shake of her head.

"The kids?"

She confirmed with a lift of one eyebrow. Liz had always put her kids to bed herself. She was often late to wine nights or dinners because she stayed home to do the task.

"Why not?" I finally asked when she didn't say anything else.

She ran her tongue around her lips and gave a slight shrug. "I didn't want to anymore. I told them to put themselves to bed. It's too boring."

"Oh," I said with a slight nod. "Well, it is. It's just always been something that's been important to you, which goes back to why I stopped by. You've been acting a little different lately, and I just wanted to check in."

She gave a small snort before she slowly looked over her shoulder, toward the back corner of the fence, where the She Shed construction had started. I couldn't see much in the darkness, other than the outline of the wood.

She turned back to me, and I saw Liz. The old Liz. The sweet friend who always remembered birthdays and checked in on the anniversary of my sister's death.

"I'm having a tough time," she said. Her eyes filled with tears, and I leaned forward and put my hand on her knee.

"What's going on? You don't have to tell me, but you can if you want to." I felt a tightening in my chest as I squeezed her knee. My anxiety about coming over disappeared, and shame and guilt entered. I had waited too long to reach out, to see if I could help. Liz would have been over to my house with a basket full of muffins and a fluffy blanket if she thought something was off with me.

She met my eyes, and I saw hers were full of fear before she buried her face in her hands.

"I don't know. I don't feel like myself anymore. It's like there's this other person inside of me." She sobbed quietly into her hands.

I stood up and knelt down in front of her, placing both of my hands on her legs. "We all have times like this. It's okay. I'm here." I put my arms around her shoulders and tried to hug her, but her body was stiff. "I'm so sorry you're feeling this way." I leaned back and released her, studying her face. I knew what it was like to feel scared, alone, unsure of what to do next. I wished there was something else I could say, but all I could offer was my presence and clumsy platitudes.

Tears streamed down her face as she looked at her hands, tightly clasped in her lap. She took a deep breath and exhaled loudly. Then her shoulders stiffened, and she slowly looked up.

I stood and took a quick step back at the change on her face. It was emotionless, her eyes black, all pupils.

She let the tears run down her face and drip into her lap, her mouth tight. Her eyes narrowed, suddenly dry, and her face turned to stone. She again glanced over her shoulder.

"Do you want to see something?" she said as she turned back to me.

"Um, sure. I guess." I didn't move for a second, not knowing whether she was messing with me. When I saw she wasn't, I followed her as she stood up.

I clutched my phone as we walked to the corner of the yard, toward where the She Shed would go. I tripped over an exposed tree root from the locust tree. Locust trees were notoriously unstable, awful trees. They had weak branches and grew like weeds. Last year, when a microburst came through the neighborhood, it took out two of them in our yard, one of the branches falling through our garage.

Liz stopped by the fence line. It was too dark to really see anything, and I stumbled my way to the edge of the grass. I could see my house from here, and Emily's light was still on, meaning that she had woken up and wanted someone to sleep in her bed.

"Oh! I should probably head home," I said as I pointed my phone in the direction of Emily's bedroom. "Seems like I have a kid awake."

"This will only take a second," Liz insisted. She motioned for me to come closer.

"Just for a minute." I slipped my phone into my back pocket before I took another step forward.

As I did, I saw what Liz pointed at. She had her forefinger aimed toward the ground, at the gaping hole in the earth. The smell hit me like a brick wall, making me stop and clutch a hand to my nose. My legs locked up, my body rigid as I tried not to inhale the unholy stench.

"Liz, I can't— What is that? It smells awful," I said as I took a quick step back, stumbling over the tree root again.

Her eyes widened and she hurried forward, grabbing my elbow. At first, I thought she was doing it to steady me, but then she tugged at my arm.

"Come on, just a few more steps." Her voice was insistent, her grip firm.

"What? No. Stop, please. You're hurting me." I could practically feel the bruise already beginning to form.

"One more step," she said again, gripping my arm so hard I thought it was going to pull out of the socket.

I tried to move away, to jerk my arm from her grasp and run back home, but I couldn't. She was too strong. Before I knew it, she'd shoved me, and I fell down, down toward the gaping black hole in the earth. I landed face-first in the dirt pit, about six feet below the grass. My head barely stuck out, and I grabbed for the grass around me, scrambling to try to lift myself out of the hole as I stood on my tiptoes.

Liz stood at the edge of the pit, a small smile on her face. She took a step back as I grabbed furiously for her.

"Is this a joke? What the fuck, Liz? Help! Give me a hand! I can't get out," I said as I clawed at the earth around me. My feet slipped on the moist dirt. I thrust my hand upward, my fingers waggling, reaching out for my friend.

But she only stepped back again. Her eyes met mine, like two black holes without any humanity behind them—without any *Liz* there. Then, her face changed further, melting into a rubbery mask of open, weeping, infected sores, red eyes, and a mouth full of black, rotting teeth.

"Sweet dreams," she whispered with a laugh. Then her face went back to normal before she turned and headed toward her house.

"No! Come back!"

She didn't stop, and I shouted some more, but my voice was hoarse and didn't carry very far. It dissipated in the wind like a puffy white dandelion seed. I clawed at the earth around me, but it fell into the pit, dropping at my feet. The stench was overwhelming, although I didn't have time to be bothered by it. Terror washed over my body and my breath quickened as I realized I was trapped.

At my feet, the dirt seemed to move. It was like the earth had opened up, and the more I tried to get any kind of leverage to hoist myself up, the more I sank down.

I screamed again. "Liz, get out here and help me! What the hell is wrong with you?" but my words were drowned out by the Kowalskis' air-conditioning unit turning on with a loud metal clanking noise.

I stopped and took a deep breath, my feet sinking a few more inches into the mud. I needed to calm down and figure out a solution. I always told my kids that for every problem there was a solution. I'd just never imagined that trying to climb out of a sewage pit in my friend's backyard was a problem that would need solving. I needed to use what I had.

My phone. I still had it in my back pocket.

I pulled it out and swiped at the screen with trembling fingers. Except the screen froze midswipe. I tried to turn it off and reboot it, but it kept searching for service. The terrible joke that I would have to complain to Mark about my cell service did not escape me.

Since the rectangle in my hand wouldn't give me a signal, I decided to use it as a tool. So much for the newest model with the upgraded camera. I spotted the errant locust tree root, sticking out of the mud near the hole. I reached and strained and finally hooked my phone around it. Now I had leverage.

Rain began to fall around me, sloshing into mud at the bottom of the pit. The water level quickly rose, and I realized if I stayed any longer, I could drown. Adrenaline coursed through my body as I pulled myself up, using my phone as leverage.

I felt my shoulder pulling out of its socket, a burning pain shooting up my arm as I strained to lift myself. I was never good at pull-ups in gym class, but now my life depended on it. Too bad I had never taken Jess up on her offer to try a CrossFit class.

I put my other hand around my wrist for stability as I slowly lifted my feet out of the mud. With my feet free, I pulled, ignoring the searing pain in my arm, until I got a foot against the edge of the mud pit. With my other hand, I clawed toward the top, hand-fuls of mud moving through my fingers like pudding. I stopped for a moment to take a breath, my chest feeling like it was going to explode.

As I did, I noticed a color change inside the pit. A green swirl was beginning to form at the bottom, like smoke gathering from a fire. And then the awful smell came back again.

My eyes widened in terror as the smoke swirled up toward me, encircling my leg. Inside, I felt the presence of something dark, something ancient. Something demonic.

I turned and pulled, pushing my feet against the mud with everything I had. My survival instincts kicked in, and I barely noticed when two of my fingernails broke off, lost to the earth.

The mist around my leg began to settle, and I felt a slight pull-ing sensation. It wanted me to come back down, to wash over me.

I had to get out immediately.

I grunted and screamed and finally, I was halfway out, my torso and face on the grass, my legs still in the darkness. I felt a tugging on my ankle, and I felt a different kind of pain, a burning sensation, before I swung it around out of the hole.

I was out, face-first on the lawn. Panting and sweating, I stopped for a moment to catch my breath and try to figure out what had just happened. Out of the corner of my eye, I saw the mist begin to swell up from the hole, plumes inching toward me.

I placed my palms on the earth and hoisted myself up, feeling another tear in my shoulder. My phone was still in my hand as I started to run, stumbling over more tree roots. I ran from Liz's backyard, down Maple Leaf Drive, straight for my house, covered in mud.

I threw myself at the front door, wrenching it open, leaving muddy handprints all over the front door. I shut the door behind me and closed my eyes briefly, trying to steady my pulse.

Mark heard the commotion and came running into the foyer. When he saw me—covered in mud, fingernails broken and bloody, trembling violently—his eyes widened.

"What in the world . . ."

I shook my head, still shaking, unable to articulate what had just happened. All I managed to say was: "Liz. She tried . . . I think she tried to kill me."

His arms dropped to his sides. "What? Liz? Tell me what's going on."

My teeth chattered as I held my stomach. "There's something wrong with her. There's something in her backyard. She threw me into a hole and tried to kill me."

He stared at me, no doubt assessing whether I had been drinking, and then stepped forward and pulled me to him. He didn't understand—he *couldn't* understand. He put a hand on the back of my head.

"I don't know what happened, but you're safe now," he said. "Just calm down and tell me what happened."

I shook my head. "No. None of us are safe." I bent down and pulled up my pant leg, where the white-hot pain still throbbed. I saw what looked like a burn mark, the imprint of a hand, the edges already beginning to blister.

"How did you get that?" Mark asked.

"I told you: Liz's backyard." I swallowed hard as I released my pant leg with shaking hands. "It was something in the pit—I don't know what it was."

He peered down at my leg. "It looks almost like an electrical burn. Was there a downed wire or something?" Before I could answer, he turned toward the kitchen. "Let me get something for it. It looks pretty bad."

I glanced at my reflection in the hallway mirror as I waited. Whatever I had thought was going on at Liz's house—nervous breakdown, drug problem, midlife crisis—would not have been able to char my skin. Not to mention what I saw happen to her face. I wiped sweat from my forehead as I remembered the mist rising. There was something dark, something evil, something *demonic*, in there. Whatever it was, it had a plan for me; I felt that in my core.

It was the same feeling I'd had over the past week—the panicked feeling that something wasn't right. And if it wasn't for that tree root and my phone, whatever was in that hole would have won.

The darkness already had Liz, and now it wanted me.

It wanted all of us.

Maybe the eighties really were back.

CHAPTER 8

THE NEXT MORNING, I lay in bed, afraid to look at my leg. Instead, I thought back to when we first moved to Whispering Farms.

After another sleepless night when Emily was three months old, when she had been up all night crying and our neighbors had started leaving notes under our door complaining about the noise, Mark had first brought up the topic of moving from the city to the suburbs.

After so many weeks of colic and lack of sleep, I agreed to go look at a few properties in Winchester. Mark had suggested it for the good public transit so he could take the train into work.

When we pulled up to Maple Leaf Drive, we saw groups of kids playing outside, and the driveway was lined with blooming lilacs, their scent filling the air as I walked to the front door. I felt my resolve soften like ice cream left out on a countertop. I looked down at the listing sheet and calculated that the mortgage would be less expensive than what we were paying in rent. What sealed the deal was the office on the first floor. I envisioned I'd soon go back to work, my laptop and paperwork strewn across a beautiful white desk.

The office was now our playroom.

And our long, lilac-lined driveway required the purchase of a snowblower the first winter we moved. We also discovered that in Whispering Farms, snowblowing was a sort of neighborly competition, the victor being the husband who woke up the earliest the morning after a snowfall to start on the sidewalks, earning bragging rights. Mark had never won.

I remember feeling as though a small part of me died when we packed up the last box and I watched the city skyline disappear from the rearview mirror of our rented U-Haul. I felt trapped in between two worlds, in a purgatory of my own making, one that involved leaf blowers and pressure washers.

As though the suburbs were my landscaped coffin, although I didn't know it yet.

———

"AMY, I ONLY have a few minutes before my next call. What is this big emergency?" Melissa said as she closed my backyard fence's gate behind her.

I shook my head in reply and adjusted my leg, which was propped up on the patio chair next to me. An ice pack covered my ankle, and I winced as it moved against my skin. I swore the wound had its own heartbeat.

Melissa stopped abruptly, hands on her hips, when she saw my face. She squinted down at me and pointed to my leg. "Wow. That looks terrible. What happened to you?"

I gestured for her to sit down and took a long sip of water as she settled in. The kids were playing inside, and I could see they were still on the couch through the sliding glass door. The night before, after I had regained the ability to speak, I had told Mark the whole story as I tried to drink a glass of wine in the kitchen, my hands shaking violently.

"I'm going to call Tim," he had said as he reached for his phone. "Liz is obviously having some kind of breakdown."

I snatched the phone out of his hand so quickly that I scratched his fingers. "No. I don't think he's even noticed—or even cares. It might make things worse. I think we should think through this first, come up with a plan, and then loop him in."

When he tried to reach for his phone, I held it away and added, "Please. Just let me talk to Jess and Melissa first, and then we can approach him." He folded his arms across his chest, leaning back in the chair at the kitchen island.

"Okay. So what do you want to do?" He craned his neck around and looked at my leg, wincing. "Should we go to urgent care?"

I gingerly lifted the bag of frozen peas off my leg and then quickly put it back on when I saw it was beginning to blister. "It's too late. I don't want to wake the kids. Let me see how it is in the morning before we do anything." Exhaustion overtook my body, and my spine felt like it had turned to dust. I slumped forward. "I just want to get some sleep."

Except, sleep never came. My leg throbbed and burned all night, and every time I closed my eyes, all I saw was Liz's black pupils, two dark holes in her head. I thought about texting her, asking her if she even remembered what had happened or if she'd had some kind of out-of-body experience, but I wanted to talk to our friends first.

When I woke up from my fitful dreams and gathered enough courage to see my leg, I saw that the wound had turned so purple it looked black, dotted with fresh scabs and angry red streaks.

And Mark had already left for work for the day. He'd left a note next to the bed, saying he didn't want to wake me and to call him later.

So I had limped around the house, telling the kids that I tripped on a crack in the driveway the previous night, while waiting for Melissa and Jess to get back to me. Emily had looked at me suspiciously when I told her the lie, even though I wore yoga pants so the injury was hidden. She had glanced down at my leg, at the exact spot where my skin was flayed. A chill ran through me.

Before I could begin to tell Melissa what had happened, the gate swung open again and Jess bounded through, wearing workout shorts and a close-fitting tank with a picture of a woman lifting a huge dumbbell over her head. Jess's blond hair was in two French braids down her back.

"What's going on?" she said. "Sharon is supposed to be over in a half hour to pick up Summer."

"It's Liz." I straightened up, wincing again. I had texted them an hour ago: Come over as soon as you can. I need to talk to you two. "She did something last night." I swallowed hard. "Something terrible to me."

Jess gave a laugh. "What, did she make you go to a Nickelback concert?" She snorted at her own joke but then stopped when she saw my face. "Oh, shit. You're not kidding."

"Does it look like she's kidding?" Melissa said as she gestured toward my elevated leg.

I nodded to the empty chairs, and they sat down on either side of me, stealing glances at my covered leg.

"This is going to sound wild, but Liz . . . I guess you could say, *attacked* me last night, but 'attacked' isn't the best word." Their eyes widened as they listened to my clumsy explanation of what had happened. Repeating it made the story sound even more ridiculous, like some fever dream. But I knew what had happened.

"And when I got home, this was on my leg, where I had felt the pain when I tried to escape the pit." I leaned forward and gingerly lifted up the leg of my wide black yoga pants, shimmying it up my calf.

"Are you being serious?" Melissa whispered as she leaned forward. "It looks like something bit you."

Jess didn't say anything as she slowly brought her hands up to her cheeks, mouth open.

There was a long, pregnant pause as I looked at them and they stared down at the oozing welt on my leg. I could hear the distant sounds of *Cocomelon* on Netflix inside and the hum of a lawn mower down the block. It was Wednesday, scheduled landscaping and mowing day for Seneca Drive. A leaf blower started up, the white noise of the Midwest.

For a while, no one spoke. We listened to the sounds of the neighborhood around us, to the kids beginning to mill about their front yards, to the neighbors exchanging muffled greetings. To dogs barking at each other and the Spadlowski teenager blasting nineties rap out of his bedroom window. To the distant hum of the

Kowalskis' air-conditioning unit turning on, the same noise I'd heard the night before the attack.

Melissa regained her voice first. "Why would she do something like that? Y'all, it doesn't make any sense." She slowly glanced over at the fence line toward Liz's house before she turned back.

"If I knew, I would tell you. That's why I wanted to ask you guys. In person, so you could see how bad it is." I rubbed my forehead and put my elbow on the patio table. "I know it sounds unhinged, but—but I think this is something bigger than us. Bigger than Winchester. Bigger than . . ." I trailed off, glancing at the empty hole where the rabbit's nest used to be.

Neither of my friends finished my sentence.

Jess sat back in her chair and ran her hand down the length of one of her braids, stopping at the end. "I can't believe Liz, of all people, would hurt you."

"She's obviously unstable," Melissa said as she looked at her phone. "Do you think she's on drugs?" She stole a quick glance my way before looking back down.

I shook my head slightly. I knew what that looked like, and this wasn't it.

"Maybe she's just trying out a new identity," Jess said.

I shook my head again. A new identity or personality change wouldn't have made her face melt into rubber or caused mist to rise from the pit. I had seen it, and an emotional problem or drugs, even, wouldn't have done that.

A wave of panic rose over my body, moving up from the ground to my head, down my legs, and circling my blistering wound as I thought of voicing my fears. But I had to.

"I think it's something supernatural. Dark." Melissa snapped open her mouth to protest, and I held up a hand. "When I was a social worker, patients at the end of their lives or after a traumatic incident would sometimes talk about ghosts or spirits. I never believed it, but it didn't matter because it's what *they* believed. I saw this with my own eyes, and I didn't imagine any of it. I know it sounds bonkers, but I'm afraid there's a supernatural explanation. I think—"

Melissa opened her mouth again, unable to hold back. "That's bullshit," Melissa said. "My parents used to talk all the time about how the devil was real and how Satan was always sending dark forces to mess with people, and I never believed it, because it wasn't true. My parents are liars, crooks, people who feed off other people's fears." She shook her head. "No, it's impossible. I think she's become unstable, maybe from that swamp gas in her backyard. There must be a rational explanation."

I lifted my eyebrows. "I hope you're right. Believe me, I know how all of this sounds."

Jess put her hands on her chair. "Who cares what the reason is? Ghosts? Spirits? It's semantics. How about 'weird shit'?"

I pressed my lips together, pulling back what I didn't want to say. I had seen demons and darkness, and they were nothing like my friend throwing me into a construction hole in her backyard. The demons I had seen were my parents' belongings disappearing one by one, being sold off to fund June's addiction. The middle-of-the-night phone calls, begging for money. The countless trips to rehab that always ended in heartbreak. An ending that no one wanted, one that I could never forgive myself for. One that in my darkest moments, I blamed myself for.

Melissa cleared her throat. "Really, though, my parents' church was into that stuff. They would get together and speak in tongues, and the pastor would cast out people's demons every Sunday, right after the light show where lasers would spell out 'Jesus' and everyone would cheer." I waited for her to laugh but then realized she was serious.

She continued. "It was deluded. Ridiculous." She rubbed her forehead and then stopped, probably remembering her aesthetician had said friction made her Botox wear off quicker. "Anyway, you know I barely speak to them now, and that's a large part of why." She crossed her arms over her chest. "Unfortunately, I have to see them in a few days when they stop through town on the way to a tent revival in Iowa."

I leaned forward. "Really? If they are into all of this hellfire stuff, maybe we should talk to them about Liz."

This time, she did laugh. "Absolutely not. And possibly the worst idea you've ever had. All they'll do is tell us to make a large donation to their church and maybe give us some fake holy water and a plastic crucifix made in China by five-year-old laborers."

"Well, the holy water and crucifixes can be plan B," Jess said. She picked up her phone and tapped away. "Plan A is a bit easier: I'm just going to text Liz." She held up the screen when she was done.

> Hey friend. How are you feeling? I talked to
> Amy and she said something happened at your
> house last night. Her leg is pretty messed up.
> What's up?

I startled and pointed at the screen as I saw three dots appear below the text—Liz typing a response. Jess held the phone out as we watched and waited. I don't think I exhaled at all. Then, they disappeared. Nothing. She wasn't going to respond.

I slumped my shoulders. "What now? Should you guys go over there?"

Melissa shook her head. "No, thanks. I don't want to get anywhere near her. Besides, I have that conference call soon, and I can't take it from the sewage pit."

I looked at Jess, who held her hands up. "Hard pass. I tried—I texted her. But maybe we can try and see what that sinkhole looks like now from a safe distance. Can you see it at all from upstairs?"

I nodded. "In my bathroom window, you can see a little bit. Not the pit itself, but most of the yard. Maybe she's outside or we can see what she's doing." *Hopefully not further plotting my demise.*

Jess and Melissa helped me hobble inside and steadied my arms as I hopped up the stairs one at a time. Before we walked into the bedroom, I said, "My bedroom is a total pigsty."

"Amy, that's not really what I'm worried about right now," Melissa said, but I noticed her eyes slid to the enormous pile of laundry on the floor, my unmade bed strewn with pajamas, and the five empty cans of LaCroix and two coffee cups on my desk.

"That's some good-looking underwear." Jess laughed as she pointed to the granny panties in my laundry pile.

"Sorry, I've been focused on not getting murdered by our friend and not my underwear collection," I retorted.

I led them into the master bathroom, equally disorganized with a hair dryer on the floor and towels in the corner. We crowded around the window, craning our necks past the giant oak tree to get a glimpse of Liz's house. It looked the same, nothing amiss. The sun shone on her back deck. I spotted Luke's water table, and a Wiffle bat in the corner. If it weren't for the oozing burn on my leg, I would have sworn that I'd imagined the entire thing.

"Maybe we should just give her space for now," Melissa said as she left the window and sat on my bed, pushing aside my crumpled pajama pants. "I don't want any part of this—whatever this is. I have too much going on right now to even try and add this to my plate."

"She's our friend, and might I remind you, I'm the one who bore the brunt of this," I said as I shook my head and hopped a little on my good leg. "We have to at least try and figure out what's going on."

"That's great, but I need all of my limbs for CrossFit, and your leg looks like it might fall off," Jess said.

"Stop," I said, and held up my palm as I leaned against the bathroom's doorjamb, injured leg bent behind me. "Enough. Let's all think this through and figure it out. We can't just abandon her."

Melissa sighed. "Fine. But I think we should keep a healthy distance in the meantime." She looked at her phone. "Time's up. I have to get home. My client waits for nothing, not even this."

Jess helped me down the stairs after Melissa left and paused at the front door before she opened it. "I'm game to help Liz out however I can, but we need to be careful. None of this is normal—not that Winchester ever is, but this feels wrong."

I nodded. "I know." I watched her jog across the front yard, a sinking feeling in my body. It wasn't just me who felt the darkness. And while I wanted to keep Liz at more than an arm's length away, I couldn't. I couldn't let someone else I loved slip away.

"I'm hungry," I heard Emily call from the other room.

"One second," I said. I hobbled over to her, and she stared at me.

"Does that still hurt? You should go to the hospital," she said. "Your leg is going to get worse. Yuck."

"I'm okay. Just a little cut." I kept my voice high and cheerful, too afraid to ask what she knew.

She stared back, something flickering behind her eyes that made my knees lock up. Then she turned and bounded into the kitchen. I steadied my breath before I followed her, pushing aside the idea that she was aware of far more than she should have been.

CHAPTER 9

WHOEVER SAID IT'S best to just rip off a Band-Aid clearly never had to yank a bandage off a blistering, infected wound caused by a supernatural force. I screamed so loudly at urgent care when the doctor peeled off the gauze pad that I heard a nurse drop something metal in the next curtained partition.

The doctor had jumped back, gloved hands in the air like she was working the overnight shift at a gas station and had no desire to be a hero that day.

"Okay, let's try that again, but maybe a little calmer this time," she said, narrowing her eyes at me over her blue face mask. "Just try and relax."

I gritted my teeth and nodded, wishing I had taken Mark up on his offer to come with me. After Jess and Melissa had left in the morning, I had tried to hobble around after the kids, telling myself it would be better by the evening. But the day came and went, and by the time Mark came home, I could barely move off the couch.

Every time I so much as twitched my leg, I would yelp like a neurotic, unsocialized Chihuahua. Mark took one look at me and told me I needed to go to urgent care, and he would call his parents to come over and watch the kids.

After thirty minutes of arguing that I did not want to call them—mostly because I couldn't figure out how to explain how I got the injury, but also because I didn't want to hear his mother's judgments on the state of the house and how the dish towels were no longer folded in the drawer as she had done it last, I finally agreed to go, but only if he dropped me off, and I would text him when I was done.

The receptionist gave me a pitying look as I hopped up to her desk to check in, no doubt wondering why I didn't have any family or friends to help me. "No babysitter and my mother-in-law judges my kids' unfolded underwear drawers," I whispered to her, and her look changed from pity to solidarity.

"My mother-in-law rearranges my bookcases when she comes over," she said as she slid a clipboard across the desk.

I explained to the intake nurse that I had fallen in my backyard, keeping it as vague as possible, but she looked at me in suspicion before she left. And then the doctor came in and asked if she could "take a quick look" by peeling back the gauze pad.

I almost kicked her.

I looked away as she removed the bandage, bile rising in my throat at the earthy smell of dried blood and charred skin. The fresh air felt like needles on the wound, and I clamped my mouth shut to avoid yelping.

"How did you say you got this again?" she asked. "It looks almost like a burn injury."

"I fell outside. In the backyard. By myself." Which, technically, wasn't a lie. I did fall outside, and it was in a backyard. And I was alone after Liz pushed me.

There was a pause during which I refused to look at her. My entire life, I've been a terrible liar, which most people would think is a good trait but did nothing to help me in high school when I was trying to go to a party but convince my parents I was seeing a movie. My tell was that I usually provided an excruciating amount of unnecessary detail, like I was having a conversation with myself, and I didn't want to end up describing the color of our gutter guards or how we had a skunk infestation last year.

"Well, at a minimum you're going to need a hefty dose of anti-biotics and follow-up care. If it doesn't get better, then you might need to consult with a plastic surgeon for the scar."

That made me look.

"A plastic surgeon?"

She nodded. "The scar isn't going to be pretty—it's pretty jag-ged around the edges. A plastic surgeon would be able to make it look cleaner after it heals. They might end up recommending a skin graft."

My stomach turned at the thought of removing skin from one area of my body to attach it to another, like a paring knife slicing off the peel of an apple. I made the mistake of glancing down at my leg, then looked away again. My entire ankle was red and swol-len, puffed out like it could be popped with a safety pin. The burn itself was black and purple, with bleeding scabs and fluid oozing. And it was all in the shape of a small hand, like a child's.

"Are you sure it was just a fall?" the doctor said.

I nodded quickly. "Oh yes. I'm so clumsy. Those darn locust

tree roots." And then I launched into my knowledge of locust trees and essentially the history of every tree growing in our neighborhood, like the crab apple trees that attracted bees and smelled terrible.

"Anyway," I blabbered as I watched her eyes get wider and wider, "I'll have to call that plastic surgeon. Maybe I can get a two-for-one special with a tummy tuck." I gave a high-pitched snort as she continued to stare. I had lobbed her a verbal football, and she let it hit the ground next to her without attempting to catch it.

An hour later, I was home. Mark and the kids had picked me up and then driven through Walgreens to get my prescriptions, which were handed to us in a giant grocery bag. There were antibiotics, painkillers, creams, clear sheeting, and more sterile bandages and flexible tape. And a giant ACE bandage to wrap around it.

Emily and Jack presented me with cards they had made while I was at urgent care. Jack's said, "I'm sorry your leg is gross," and Emily's was a picture of two stick figures holding hands. On the taller stick figure was an angry blob that she told me was my "owie."

Mark told the kids to head upstairs to bed and then sat down next to me on the couch, carefully avoiding my leg propped up on a cushion. He clasped his hands in front of him.

"I talked to Tim," he said quietly.

I lifted my eyebrows and sat forward. "You went over there? I asked you to keep it quiet for now."

He shook his head. "I'm worried. I thought he should know what's going on." He glanced at me, frowning. "It didn't really go anywhere. He didn't apologize and asked if you had paid attention to the tree roots in the backyard. 'Personal responsibility' was what he kept saying."

Anger flooded through my body, and the scab on my leg throbbed. "So he's worried we're going to sue?"

Mark nodded slowly and then lifted his palms. "Seemed like that. You were right. He was more concerned about their liability for the accident than the fact that Liz caused it."

"Or why she caused it. And it wasn't an accident," I added quickly. I adjusted the ice pack on my ankle and sat back. "I'm really worried about her, and all of us. What if this is just the beginning? What's next?" I swallowed hard, thinking of how many times I'd said that to Mark during the last two years of my sister's life. *What's next? What new low will she find next? Is her rock bottom infinite? What will make her stop?*

Of course I knew the answer to those questions now.

Mark had remained the positive, supportive relative, while I descended into anger and hurt. I stopped answering her phone calls and blocked her text messages. I would change the subject whenever my parents brought her up, unwilling to keep carving off pieces of my soul to help someone who had no desire to save herself.

"Give it time. Maybe it was just a bad night. See how she is going forward, and talk to her when the dust has settled," he said.

We heard a loud bang upstairs, followed by a wail from Jack. He shouted down that Emily had broken one of his *Star Wars* LEGO displays. Mark slapped his thighs and stood up, briefly placing a hand on my head before he went upstairs.

As Mark put the kids to bed, I looked over the cards again, smiling. Yet a stillness ran through me as I studied Emily's a second time. She had drawn our house in the background, a simple box with a triangle roof. In the upper right-hand corner was a black circle that I hadn't noticed before. She had filled it in with black, pressing the crayon so hard that I could see flakes of wax ground into the paper. An angry black hole.

In the location of Liz's house.

CHAPTER 10

DON'T TOUCH THAT!" I called across the enormous table of books at the library, begging Jack not to upend the collection of Transformers a local kid had loaned to the library for display. I had visions of having to scour eBay auctions in order to reimburse an eight-year-old.

Mark was in Miami, and my leg still wasn't up to snuff, and there were only so many activities to do outside in the heat, so we'd packed up and gone to the library. Emily made a beeline for the play area with the plastic kitchen and ice-cream cart, and Jack pulled books off the shelf and sat down in a kid chair while I settled into the couch, moving carefully.

Within seconds, I was sweating. The air-conditioning was on, but the mercury had already soared to ninety-five degrees, and freon could only do so much in the aging building. There was condensation on the inside of the door and windows. And I was wearing long gray yoga pants to cover up my bandage. It was too much effort to determine what version of the story I wanted to tell curious neighbors, and after my experience at urgent care, I didn't think anyone wanted to hear about our landscaping in minute detail.

I was glad for my foresight when I saw Heather Hacker walk through the library doors, flanked by her two kids. Remy and Ruby were six and eight years old, dressed in identical pink-and-green Lilly Pulitzer dresses. Heather wore a headband with the same matching pattern and a spotless white maxidress. She spotted me, and her face lit up. Normally, I would have quickly stood up and feigned being late for something, but I was stuck. Like a bear in a forest trap, but I couldn't chew off my own leg to escape.

"There you are, Amy! I haven't seen you in forever. How are things?" She plopped down next to me and clasped her manicured hands on her knee. She studied me, her head tilting to the side in concern as I saw her gaze move to my hairline, where I could feel beads of sweat appearing.

I had just seen her at the block party, but I didn't remind her of that. I had learned that no matter when you last saw another Winchester mom, you had to pretend like it had been eons. "Good. Just trying to get into a routine for the summer. You?" I said quickly as I moved my injured leg away from her.

"Same, same." She cocked her head to the other side, in what I'm sure she imagined was a contemplative pose, before she launched in. "I've been meaning to call you about something."

I lifted my eyebrows. Heather had never just called me about anything, something that I appreciated, honestly.

"I wanted to see if your friend Liz is okay. I ran into her on a walk yesterday, and she seemed very strange." Heather's eyes widened in fake concern. "And then, of course, there was her concerning behavior at the block party." She smiled and stopped, waiting for me to fill in the blanks. Like socially engineered Mad Libs.

I stared at her for a moment, unsure of how to answer, before I finally said, "I think she's doing okay."

The standoff continued as we held polite smiles, each of us waiting for the other to say something.

She broke first. "Well, that's good to hear." She rolled her eyes. "The only good news. I'm so incredibly stressed right now. We can't find anyone to chair the school's midsummer ice-cream social and carnival, and I'm just too busy to do it myself. If only we had more hands on deck." She slowly looked at me and smiled.

I was about to protest when she forged on. "Sharon was the previous chair, and she has a lot on her plate as a divorced mother. She did such a wonderful job in the past, and I know Summer enjoyed it last year. It's great how some parents are so involved, but others just skate by and enjoy the fruits of our labor. I'm sure Summer will be so disappointed, but she knows that her mom does everything else for her."

I thought of Jess and Del's house, and how nearly every time I went inside, it looked like they had been robbed. It looked that way because Jess was always setting up elaborate obstacle courses for Summer or using their dining room table as an art studio, with paint and markers scattered everywhere. Or the afternoon dance parties I saw through the window. When Summer was at their house, Jess shared her best self. Of course, that didn't mean anything to Heather. Her barometer was calibrated on a different level—one that meant Jess and the rest of us would never be worthy.

My lips curled down into a frown, and before I could stop myself, I said, "I'll do it. I'll organize the event."

She paused, hand frozen in midair above her headband, and I repeated the offer, feeling panic rise through my chest. I had only attended the event once, last year. There was a bounce house that Jack loved, a lollipop pull, a ring toss, an ice-cream truck, and concessions.

"I wasn't aware you had joined the PTA. Only *members* can organize events," Heather finally said.

I made a mental note to click on the emailed membership link to join when I got home. I smiled sweetly at her. "It will be a great event."

"I'm sure it will be. I will get you the information binder from last year. Well, I should be going. I don't know if you heard, but I had my kitchen redone recently, and I have a meeting with my designer to do a final walk-through. So stressful, am I right?"

I smiled thinly. "I can imagine. I did hear you talk about it recently. Congratulations." Of course I knew about it. It was all she'd talked about for nearly a year. It would be like if I asked whether she knew there had been a presidential election. You would have had to be living off the grid to miss it. I waited for her to get up, but I had miscalculated, and she leaned in, thinking it was an invitation.

"I couldn't believe how many options there are. Open versus closed shelving, smart fridges that connect to Wi-Fi, dual dishwashers, no-touch faucets, farm or traditional sinks." She sighed dramatically, slouching back in the chair as though the weight of so many decisions had exhausted her. "That's why I had to hire a designer. Who can make all those decisions on their own?"

I nodded slightly, thinking of the grand plan I'd had last

summer to paint our kitchen cabinets white. Our kitchen had been remodeled in the early aughts, during the time of dark wood cabinets, tan and cream granite, and nickel fixtures. When we bought the house, we remarked that it looked like a Mafia sit-down room. Of course, we moved in with plans to give it all a facelift that never materialized. So after a late night on Pinterest during which I almost decided to rewire a vase into a lamp, I decided to paint the cabinets on my own. I dragged the kids to Home Depot, bought hundreds of dollars' worth of supplies, and unloaded them in the garage. They were still sitting there, next to the leftover wood from when we had our fence replaced.

Heather stood up, her lament about home renovations complete. "Well, I should scoot. I will be sure to get you the binder on Wed—" She stopped abruptly. "Soon," she finished.

The kitchen reveal party that only Melissa had been invited to was on Wednesday. I smiled sweetly at her. "Good luck with the party." I wanted an invitation to the party like I wanted a hole in the head, but I wasn't going to let her slip-up go unnoticed.

She frowned and then turned to leave but stopped.

"Actually, I would love it if you came. Eight p.m. sharp. Light appetizers and drinks."

I shifted uncomfortably, trying to think of a plausible excuse. Mark would be home that night, and she would see his car in the driveway and know he was back. I couldn't even use the excuse that he had a work dinner thanks to his conspicuous Honda.

The path of least resistance it was.

"Thanks. I'd love to stop by." I regretted the words the second I spoke them, wanting to reel them back in with my mental fishing rod.

"Invite anyone you like. Just maybe not you-know-who."
Heather whirled around, her hair floating, and then left with her
robotic kids.

I sighed and glanced over at my kids, who were still happily
playing and quiet. Scanning the library, my gaze fell on the horror
section, and then on nonfiction.

I was in the perfect place to do some quiet research.

I glanced around as I sat down at one of the computers and
typed in a keyword search for demons, possessions, dark spirits.
As I waited for it to load, the air in the library seemed to grow
colder, and I rubbed the tops of my arms. I scanned the results
and found the section where the occult books were shelved.

The stacks housing the books seemed quieter and darker than
the rest of the library. They were in the corner furthest from the
kids' section, which I appreciated when I plucked a title off the
shelf and looked at the cover—a black lake, with a skeletal hand
reaching out of the water, pointed up toward the sky.

I swallowed hard and opened up the book.

Ten minutes later, I had a stack of books to check out next to
me, all about blood sacrifices and demonic possessions. One book
had a picture of a dark shape floating above a bed; underneath lay
an elderly woman covered in scratches. I shivered as I thought of
Carole, one of my last patients. She would scream all night, terrified of spirits attached to the ceiling. She would scratch at her
arms until she drew blood, calling for help. The doctors told her
family her delusions were due to her dementia, but now I wondered just what she had seen.

I scanned the back cover.

Demons, once they have been able to enter our mortal world, will become addicted to creating evil. Much like an addict who won't stop until they destroy themselves, dark spirits will cause havoc and pain until they consume everything they can.

That, I understood.

I put the book down quickly and rubbed my forehead.

I paused, realizing I couldn't hear any distant chatter from Jack and Emily. Pushing myself to a standing position on my good leg and hoisting the books under one arm, I used my other to steady my balance as I made my way out of the stacks. As I got closer to the children's area, I didn't see either of them.

I called their names, moving faster throughout the library, thinking they had wandered to another section. But nothing. My heart pounding, sweat beginning to trickle down my back, I huffed and puffed around the stacks on my injured leg. Dark thoughts began to run through my mind, almost to the beat of the pain coursing through my ankle.

Where are they?

I have them, a voice seemed to whisper from the cobwebs of my brain. *They are mine.*

"Emily! Jack!" I screeched across the quiet library, ignoring the head snaps in my direction. A librarian looked up from the children's desk, hand to her chest.

"We're over here, Mom," I heard Jack call from a distant corner.

I limped along toward his voice and found them, piles of books at their feet, snuggled into a beanbag chair. I put my hands on my thighs and exhaled.

"What's wrong?" Emily asked as she slowly closed her book.

I shook my head and brushed my hair out of my face. "Nothing. I was just—nervous. Time to go."

I saw Emily staring at the books in my arms, and I pressed them tightly to my chest, concealing the dark images on the covers. She frowned and walked toward the checkout desk.

"Oh, over here. Let's do self-checkout," I said. I didn't want any more strange glances from the librarians. A limping mother who has a screeching panic attack in the library and then checks out books with titles like *Blood and Dirt: Modern Demon Worship*—I would get Child Protective Services called on me before we even reached the front door. I needed to pull it together, or at least project the image of someone who wasn't slowly unraveling.

As we loaded into the car, I carefully set the books down on the passenger seat, silently praying that they held the key to bringing back my friend and protecting the rest of us.

CHAPTER 11

"YO, WHAT IN the fresh hell is that?" Jess hissed in my ear on Wednesday night as we stood huddled around Heather's gray-and-white farmhouse table in her dining room.

I swatted at her outstretched pointer finger. "Stop. You have to be discreet. If she sees you making fun of something, our kids will never be invited to any birthday parties again."

"Promise?" she said.

I glanced at the corner of the room, where she had pointed, and stifled a laugh. "It's a maternity photo shoot picture."

"Why would someone do . . . that?" she said.

The black-and-white picture was of Heather and her husband, his arms wrapped around her from behind. She wore a button-down shirt that was open to show her enormous stomach, and both of them had their eyes closed, as though they were locked in a lustful embrace. It looked like something out of a porn fetish website.

"Stop," I hissed.

She was undeterred. "Can you imagine what their sex life is like? I bet she keeps her shirt on."

I smirked. "That, or she's a lady in the streets but a freak in the sheets."

"God, I hope so," she said. "You know he keeps those Crocs on."

I shifted and smiled sweetly at Violet Peterson as she inched by us, her plate overloaded with her husband Josh's famous Buffalo chicken dip. Apparently, at the block party, Josh had told Mark it had just won an award. Mark said he didn't realize Buffalo Chicken Dip Olympics was an event. I did find it odd that she always ate most of it at neighborhood gatherings, like she was hoarding her family's appetizer talent. Although, she won, because it hadn't even occurred to me to bring anything that night.

I had slowly gotten ready for the evening, sighing deeply as I looked through my clothes, hoping to get a text that the party was canceled. I offered to stay home multiple times with Mark, but he shut it down immediately, urging me to go out and have fun, especially after I confirmed that Liz wasn't invited. So I threw on a maxidress that I had bought off Amazon last year that had faded from black to gray. It was long enough to cover my bandaged ankle, and this was the last group I wanted to watch me stammer out explanations.

"There's an agenda," Melissa said as she sidled up to us. In her hands, she held a piece of pink paper with Heather's initials embossed at the top. She wore white linen pants and a pink short-sleeved top.

I scanned the paper.

8:00 p.m.: Wine, cheese, and light appetizers
8:30 p.m.: Welcome toast by Mrs. Hacker
9:00 p.m.: Presentation in the formal living room
9:30 p.m.: Proceed to the kitchen for the reveal

"Are you shitting me? We have to wait around until almost ten for the actual reveal? This is a hostage crisis," Jess said. She reached forward and defiantly put a huge glop of artichoke dip on the Vera Wang grosgrain china appetizer plate. I only knew that was the pattern because Heather had lamented that it had gone out of production. "I should have made a playlist for tonight. All Cardi B and Nicki Minaj, just to scare everyone."

A drop of the dip landed on Jess's shirt, and she swiped at it with her finger and then wiped it off on her plate.

"I think this is more of a U2-and-Coldplay crowd," I said.

Jess didn't respond, still wiping. A shadow of dip still remained on her black RAGBRAI shirt. She'd participated in the bike race last year, biking across Iowa with her mother.

When she had met me on the sidewalk, I'd lifted my eyebrows and said, "A RAGBRAI shirt? You really put that on, looked in the mirror, and went, 'Yup. This is the one'?"

"I did."

"I think it's great, but I'm not sure Heather will approve," I said.

"Yeah, because that's what I care about," she responded. "Let's see her try and bike across an entire state."

Jess was inordinately proud of completing the race, despite the road rash she got when she fell off her bike after a tipsy participant T-boned her. She also had a blister on her inner thigh that got infected, something she dropped her shorts and showed me in my kitchen, bending over right as Mark walked in.

"Didn't realize the nudity started this early on your ladies' nights," he said with a laugh as he slowly backed out of the kitchen.

"It's five o'clock somewhere. Or whatever the naked version of that is," Jess called after him.

All in all, the RAGBRAI T-shirt was a better choice than the high school gym shirt she'd worn to the kids' spring recital at school.

Melissa popped a bacon-wrapped date in her mouth and looked down at the appetizer's description placard. "'*Sponsored by Elderberry Kitchen*'? Who solicits sponsorships for a party at their house?"

"Incoming," I muttered as I saw Sharon move through the crowd, a large white binder in her arms. She had on a black shift dress and pink heels, and her hair was pulled back at the nape of her neck. Her full face of makeup was laser-focused on Jess, a small smile on her pink lips.

"Ladies," she said. "So nice of you all to join us." She looked at Jess, her eyes lingering on the stain from the dip. "Isn't it nice to have an evening together and . . . dress up?"

Melissa made a noise, and Sharon frowned in her direction before turning to me. "I understand you've volunteered to chair the carnival. How generous of you." She held out the white binder. The front of it read, *We All Scream for Ice Cream*. "Here is all the information from last year. It's quite a lot of work. I hope you've started building your committee."

I swallowed hard. That thought hadn't occurred to me. "Yes." I gestured with my thumb to Jess and Melissa, who turned to me in unison, mouths open in silent protest.

Sharon laughed. "Well, good luck, then. What a unique event it will be. I will be looking forward to it."

Jess shrank back slightly, and Melissa stepped forward. "You should," she said.

Sharon gave Jess one more look before she turned, disappearing into the crowd of women around the ice sculpture.

"Sorry, guys. I should have asked for your help before I said that," I said as I clutched the binder to my chest. I looked to Jess, who shifted uncomfortably as she watched Sharon across the room. She hid it well, usually, but I knew Sharon made her feel unworthy. She only played the game for Summer's sake.

I gave her a sympathetic look, and she took a swig of her wine. "Sure. I'm game to help. I think my mom is still friends with some carnies from the commune."

Heather appeared in the doorway, hands clasped in front of her chest. She wore a long red jumpsuit with lace sleeves. "Ladies, thank you so much for coming. It means a great deal that you all took time out of your busy schedules to be here to support me." Her gaze briefly stopped on Jess, eyes flicking down to her now-stained T-shirt before she smiled again. "Now, if you will all grab your plates and follow me into the formal living room, we have a fantastic program for you."

Jess, Melissa, and I loitered around the food under the guise of filling our plates, especially when we saw a projector click on in the next room.

"It feels really weird to be together without Liz," I said as I watched the other women obediently file into the "formal living room."

"I know. She never responded to my text," Jess said with a frown.

"I'm really worried about her," I said. "Do you think we should reach out again?"

"I think—" Melissa quickly stopped as Heather appeared in the doorway. "You should go with the larger-sized air fryer," she finished smoothly. It wasn't hard to see how she was the youngest senior vice president at her company. Her ability to maintain her composure in the face of stress was something foreign to me, as evidenced by my blabbering about locust trees at urgent care.

"Hurry up, ladies. We paused everything so you could join us," Heather said with a smile, a murderous look in her eyes. In her arms was her doodle dog, a white-and-tan fluffy little thing wearing a pale blue collar.

Jess patted the dog—Astrid. I remembered when Heather had first gotten him, she'd paraded him around the neighborhood in a tartan leash and collar. We were in our front yard and did the obligatory gushing (me) and real excitement (the kids).

Jack held out a hand and asked, "What is it?"

Heather replied, "A Cavapoo, of course. Bred from a champion Cavalier King Charles spaniel and Best in Show toy poodle." She then leaned over to me. "Cost far too much and the waitlist was two years long, but the best puppies come to those who wait."

I nodded at her while I ignored the sounds of Rocky barking inside my house, no doubt having gotten into the garbage again and torn apart the tampons in the bathroom. It was his favorite activity.

In Heather's living room, I settled in next to Marianne Baker, one of the original residents of Whispering Farms, the founding families of the neighborhood. She had moved away before Mark and I moved in. She shifted aside on the pristine white couch draped with a blue kantha blanket made by underprivileged women in India.

"How are you, Amy?" she said. Her eyes shifted to my injured leg, as though her eyeballs could bore right through the polyester to the bandage, and then up to the thick white binder in my lap.

"I'm doing well. It's going to be a very busy summer, since I volunteered to chair the school carnival," I said.

She balanced a plate of blue-cheese-stuffed dates in her lap. "That's wonderful. I remember taking my kids to that event years ago. My son's favorite game was the cakewalk. Do they still have that?"

I nodded, remembering last year. The cakewalk was numbered squares placed in a circle. Children would walk from square to square as music played. When it stopped, a number was chosen out of a hat, and whoever stood on that number won. The prize was selecting a donated baked good from a table inside. I wondered if this year I could just buy a bunch of cupcakes from Costco.

"Baking cakes is something of a hobby of mine, so if you need some extra prizes for the game, I'd be happy to help," she said with a smile.

Relief and gratitude flooded in. "Yes, please. I would love that."

"Please, ladies, let's begin," Heather said from the front of the room. She turned and started up the presentation, complete with handheld remote and background music. It began with drone footage over her house, flying through the front door to the kitchen. I had to stuff a date into my mouth to keep from laughing.

———

"MY HOUSE. DRINKS," Melissa hissed in my ear as Jess and I walked out of Heather's house. "Right now."

We slowly walked toward Melissa's house, arms linked, sadness overtaking my shoulders as I glanced down the street to Liz's house. It looked quiet, no lights on except for one upstairs. She should have been there with us, listening to Heather's ridiculous presentation and taking home promotional materials from the remodeling company—no doubt part of a discount, like a very elaborate, very expensive pyramid scheme. There was a Liz-shaped hole in our group, and I noticed Melissa and Jess stealing glances at her house, too.

"I miss her," Jess said as she shook her head.

"I know. Should we go and see if she's home?" I asked as we slowed on the corner of Maple Leaf and Seneca Drives, as much as every fiber of my body told me not to go over there, not to get near her backyard.

Jess and I looked at Melissa, who crossed her arms over her chest. "We need to plan first. We can't just show up unannounced. She didn't like that even before the . . . before."

She was right. Liz was too anxious to ever feel comfortable with people stopping by unannounced, as she was always convinced her house wasn't clean enough. Never mind that my house consistently would be classified as a hazardous environment on a child welfare check.

"True. I did check out some books from the library the other day. On spiritual warfare and supernatural forces." I looked quickly to Melissa, whose face had hardened in anger. "Please. I know you don't believe me and think there's a different explanation, but humor me, okay?"

Melissa didn't answer and closed her eyes slowly, shaking her head.

"I'll run in and grab them," Jess said quickly.

"Amy, this is ridiculous," Melissa said as Jess ran through the front door and up to my bedroom, where I'd told her the library books were stacked.

"I know it sounds like that, but I know what I saw. Please," I said.

She tightened her arms around her chest as Jess came jogging out of the front door, books in her arms. Laughter followed her across the lawn to where we stood.

"I've never heard Mark say the F word so many times," she said.

I cocked my head to the side in confusion. "What? Why?"

"Your dog really likes tampons, huh?"

CHAPTER 12

"WHAT ELSE CAN I get you ladies?" Melissa's husband, Tony, stood in the kitchen and surveyed the scene. Within less than a minute after we'd walked in the door, he had assembled a charcuterie board, hummus, and a veggie tray.

He continued. "I have some homemade limoncello if you'd like?"

Jess laughed. "Did you just whip up a quick batch of that when your wife texted that we were coming over?"

Tony frowned. "No, but I did put coffee grounds in the French press with a stout if anyone would like an infused beer." He gestured to the stainless-steel French press filled with a dark amber liquid.

"Who could turn that down?" I said as I gingerly lowered myself onto the blue velvet overstuffed chesterfield.

Tony's face lit up as he went over, plucked a pint glass from the Guinness warehouse in Dublin, and poured a milky, frothy beer, as Melissa pulled out a bottle of white wine from the fridge and poured herself a hefty amount.

"That's a Maple Leaf pour right there," Jess called out as she tucked her legs under her. We called a double pour the Maple Leaf pour, for the street that Jess and I lived on, as opposed to the fancier Oakton Lane, where Melissa's and Heather's houses were. Liz was the one who coined the term, and I smoothed my hands over the library books in my lap, wondering how we had gotten here.

"Jess?" Melissa lifted the carafe in the air and gestured toward her.

"None for me, thanks. I have—" She stopped and rolled her eyes at us before continuing. "A workout in the morning. See? I didn't say it that time."

Melissa and I grumbled as Tony handed me the drink, and Jess settled in next to me. The couch shifted as she sat down, and I maneuvered my body so the dark liquid that sloshed out of my glass hit my black pants instead of the velvet fabric. We always joked that Melissa needed to put plastic coverings down when any of us came over since we had the fine motor functions of toddlers.

I noticed Tony was still standing in the kitchen, staring at me, waiting for me to try the drink. I took a cautious sip, and the bitter taste of the beer filled my mouth.

"Mmm," I murmured.

Tony beamed and then launched into a soliloquy about how he had secured the rare varietal of the Goose Island Bourbon County beer in January, standing outside the liquor store at 4:00 a.m. like a college student on a bender.

"I think I hear the twins," Melissa said with a wave of her hand. "Can you go check on them?"

He nodded and said over his shoulder before he left the room, "Have Mark text me next time and I can get some for him." He frowned. "You do have a French press, right?" He looked at Melissa and then continued upstairs when he saw her expression.

There was a pause as Jess opened her mouth, but she closed it when she saw Melissa's warning face. Without Liz's kind presence, her ability to smooth the edges in the group, the tension was much higher. No one really knows what a group is actually like until one piece is missing, one cog breaks off, and then the whole operation starts to veer slightly off track.

I cleared my throat. "So, here are the books that I found." I spread the collection across the gray reclaimed-wood farmhouse coffee table in front of us. There were five books, each with a more horrifying title than the last: *Demon Inside Her*, *The Possession*, *To Hell and Back*, *Dark Places*, and *True Stories of the Demonic Realm*.

Melissa shrank back from the books, hand poised in the air. "I don't know if I can do this." She closed her eyes and shook her head. "I thought I could, but this brings back a lot of memories."

I made a sympathetic sound. I couldn't imagine growing up in her family. Each week she would attend their megachurch, hear fire-and-brimstone rantings about going to hell, and then have brunch at Cracker Barrel, musing over the various possible demonic activities they had all witnessed in the past week. Neighbors accused other neighbors, and Melissa told me her parents once ran a family off the block for having tattoos and piercings, a definite sign of the devil. None had anything to do with God.

"Did you know they canceled Halloween? The head of the church said that it was Satan's holiday and shouldn't be celebrated. No costumes, no trick-or-treating. Nothing," she said with a head shake. "I'm sorry, Amy. Really. But I just don't believe in any of this."

"Let's humor her, Mel. I'm not saying it makes sense, but you guys know I've never turned down an adventure," Jess said as she flipped open one of the books. She turned it around and tapped one of the illustrations, that of a naked woman rising above a terrified man in the bed below. "Maybe this is why Tim isn't concerned."

I grunted and reached for a book, scanning the accounts of people changing their personalities, of unexplained noises in the night, of electrical problems that couldn't be explained by ComEd.

"It's hard to know what any of this is. I feel like half of these things could be attributed to nervous husbands or a midlife crisis. I mean, how often in history have women been accused of supernatural things when they were just being humans?" I said. "Look at Salem. Scary groupthink is a real thing, and I don't want to veer into that territory."

Melissa brushed her hair back from her shoulders. "First of all, we aren't setting Liz on fire. And besides, you were the one who checked these books out, Cotton Mather."

We heard footsteps and quickly closed the books, turning them over so the covers weren't visible. Tony appeared in the doorway.

"I just remembered that I have some excellent brie en croûte that I could heat up for you all if you want," he said as he hooked a thumb toward the kitchen. He took a step toward it before we said anything.

"Heather had so much food, we are all full," Melissa said quickly. They exchanged a long, silent conversation before he nodded and walked back upstairs again.

"That was strange," Jess said, her eyes shifting toward the stairs. "He seems obsessed with feeding us."

Melissa waved her hand. "Cooking is his only outlet, and he wants to share it. He also likes hanging out with you both. But, please, don't tell him about any of this. He would worry too much, and he already worries enough for five people."

I held up *Demon Inside Her*. "Sure about that? He might change his mind if he sees these illustrations."

Jess snorted. "Or he'll wonder how he can get one of the sex demons over here." She picked up the book and leafed through it. "I told Del about Liz's behavior, and he joked that she has probably been hanging out with Sharon."

"Did he take you seriously?" I said.

Jess shook her head. "Nope. He's too rational. Demons are too much of a stretch for him to just accept."

Melissa eyed the book. "He and I have that in common."

"Well, I appreciate you guys' humoring me, and I'm open to any other ideas that spring to mind." I lightly tossed the books toward them, dividing them up equally between the group. "But we have work to do, and a limited amount of time before Tony comes back and offers to make risotto, so let's get to it."

CHAPTER
13

THREE FIFTEEN A.M.

That was the time I woke up the morning after Heather's kitchen reveal party. I tried to will myself back to sleep, steering my thoughts from darkness to light. Grocery lists, recipes, lyrics to R.E.M.'s "It's the End of the World as We Know It (And I Feel Fine)," although that one was slightly less cheery. After about an hour, I gave up and checked my phone, which had two texts from Jess.

> I can't sleep.

> I need to drug myself with an Ambien. Do a
> wellness check if you don't hear from me by
> 10 am.

The images we'd seen earlier that night flooded my brain. Images of naked women being devoured by demons with claws and horns. Terrified children huddling in the corner as a dark shape overtook their room. Broken bones and bloody wounds.

The stuff of nightmares.

Mark was snoring gently, so I quietly tried to go to the bathroom, and as I put my uninjured foot down on the carpet, I felt the softest whisper of a touch against my ankle, like something was brushing against it from under the bed.

I yelped and retracted it, pulling my legs toward me. Mark didn't so much as roll over.

It's all in your head. You just read too many disturbing things last night and now your brain is overcompensating.

It was my worst fear as a child: that something lurked under my bed, waiting for me to put my feet down at night so it could grab at my legs. So much so that I made my parents remove the bed skirt around the perimeter so they could check every night before they tucked me in.

I knew it was likely some kind of brain trick, but there was no way I was getting out of bed.

I lay there for a couple more hours, trying to ignore my full bladder and contemplating whether I could finagle peeing into the glass next to my bed, until I saw the sun begin to peek through the roman shades in my bedroom and figured it was safe. The under-bed creature wouldn't dare come out during the day.

We had read in one of the library books that demons were most powerful during the nighttime, specifically at the 3:00 a.m. hour. It was apparently a perversion of the time when Jesus died, which was 3:00 p.m.

"So is that adjusted for time zones? Like, do demons say, 'Oh, it was three p.m. in Mesopotamia in 40 AD or whatever, which would be noon here'?" Jess said.

I shot her a look. "We have to take this seriously, or not at all."

"Oh, 'not at all' is an option? Because I'd like that for five hundred, Alex," she said.

Melissa put her hand over one of the books. "No, it's an actual belief in religious circles. Demonic energy is most powerful at three a.m. My parents used to tell my brother and me that if we woke up during that hour, we should hold the Bible on top of us to ward off any bad energy." Her eyes glazed over, and her mind went somewhere far away. "They believe it," she said again with a look of disgust.

"Del told me he made a lot of bad decisions in college around that time," Jess said as she pulled her hair into a knot on top of her head. She hadn't received her bachelor's, instead working on a cruise ship for a couple of years as a waitress after high school, so her college points of reference were limited to fraternity-heyday anecdotes from Del.

"Yeah, I'm sure it was the demons and not jungle juice," I said.

Still, I made sure to step far away from the underside of my bed when I stood up the next morning.

I didn't want to go downstairs, as one of the laws of parenting was that the kids would wake up the second I opened my bedroom door, so I shuffled over and sat down at my computer, slowly opening it. I scanned my email and opened the daily job-posting digest for social work positions.

I stopped when I came to the third one.

The posting read:

HOSPICE SOCIAL WORKER, MONARCH HOSPICE

> This position is responsible for providing social work and
> bereavement services in line with federal and state
> regulations. The individual will be responsible for
> providing emotional support and counseling to families
> and patients from intake through end-of-life. They will
> develop a Plan of Care and present it to the
> interdisciplinary team, as well as assess family factors to
> estimate capacity to cope with terminal illness and
> death. They will provide counseling to individuals and
> families as requested and needed. They will assist in the
> dying and grief process for all involved parties. Position
> is located in Winchester, Illinois.

My fingers hovered over the keyboard as I read through the posting several times, the pressure in my chest building. I had never worked specifically as a hospice social worker, although my experience in a hospital meant that I'd seen patients who didn't have much time left, and assisted them and their families. Most of them were terrified of the word "hospice," although it really just referred to a different style of nursing, one where the focus was on keeping the patient comfortable rather than trying to diagnose or treat the underlying illness. It was to provide respite, comfort, and emotional healing before they passed.

I remembered one family I assisted, before Jack was born and before my sister was in the last throes of her addiction. Mary Peterson was ninety-one years old, and most of her family lived in California. She was alone most days and seemed anxious to talk to someone, anyone. So I would sit with her and just listen to her talk about her life. She told me about her sisters, growing up on a farm in Indiana, and how she met her husband at a neighborhood dance.

A few days before she passed, when she was still lucid, she thanked me. She told me that because I had sat with her and listened to her stories, she felt that they would live on after she was gone. It was one of the most rewarding moments of my career.

Before I let any doubts diminish my hope, I sent a cover letter and my résumé via email. I read through the description one more time, thinking it could be the next right career move, before I shut my computer and sighed. I knew I should go downstairs and start prepping for breakfast, but the exhaustion from the past week began to creep behind my eyes. I crawled back into bed, throwing the comforter over my head, and fell fast asleep before I could think about what might be hiding under my bed.

———

BY THE TIME I woke up, Mark was already downstairs. I heard Jack and Emily laughing—not fighting, for once—and smelled the heavenly scent of coffee. I padded down, disoriented when I saw that it was after 9:00 a.m. I found the kids in the kitchen, happily digging into Froot Loops (a breakfast I normally relegated to the weekends, but I was willing to let it slide for those extra minutes of sleep), and a full pot of coffee on the counter.

Mark entered the kitchen, dressed for work with his phone in his hand.

"Did you get some sleep? You were tossing and turning all

night," he said as he poured coffee into a travel mug and then pulled out a mug and poured me some.

"I did. Thanks for getting up with the kids. Shouldn't you be on your way by now?" I said gratefully as I took a small sip.

"I moved some things around." He looked at me sympathetically, I'm sure thinking, *You don't look so good.*

"Thanks." I rubbed my forehead and took another sip of coffee.

"Any communication from Liz?" he said.

I shook my head. "Nothing." I gestured to the supernatural library books I'd stacked in a corner of the kitchen after I got home last night. "Although I convinced Jess and Melissa to do some research last night."

His eyebrows lifted in surprise. "Melissa went along with that?"

I waved my palm in the air. "Barely. Begrudgingly. And Jess never says no to anything."

He walked over and gave me a kiss on top of my head. "You need a break. Give it time. I'm sure Liz will snap out of it, and you all will be back to being friends."

I didn't say anything, instead closing my eyes and wishing with every part of my being that would be true.

Magical thinking, as it turned out.

———

I SENT THE kids outside after breakfast, still in their pajamas, to collect caterpillars. Well, I had suggested ladybugs until Emily reminded me that we had a lot of Asian ladybugs around our house, the kind that were yellow and bit. So I suggested they find caterpillars, even though we had seen them only once in the past three years.

I walked outside on the front porch, coffee cup in hand, and glanced around the neighborhood. All the other kids were beginning to break free from their houses, a collective roar of shrieks and shouts that formed one giant child swarm. I looked to my right, at Jess's house, just as she emerged onto her front porch. She saw me and jogged over, still wearing the tank top and pajama shorts that she'd slept in.

"Howdy, friend," she said. She stopped suddenly, midjog, in my front yard. "Oh, maybe I shouldn't say 'howdy.' Wasn't the name of the demon in *The Exorcist* Captain Howdy?"

I answered affirmatively by lifting my coffee cup in the air.

"Did you sleep at all last night?" I said as she bounded onto my porch. "I sure didn't."

"Same," she said as she tossed herself into a chair next to me. She looked down at her hands, picking at a hangnail before biting it off. When she looked up, her eyes were wide, filled with tears. "Amy, this is so screwed up."

I nodded and sat back, closing my eyes. "I know. I spend half of the time convincing myself that I made it all up—wondering if I'm the one who has the problem—and the other half of the time expecting the furniture to start moving around on its own."

"I saw her just now," Jess said quietly, tucking her legs to her chest. "Through the window."

"And . . . ?" I leaned forward, sneaking a glance toward Liz's house.

"She didn't see me, but she was going for a walk, and she looked the same. Normal. Like our friend. Like maybe we are just a bunch of paranoid housewives who are being assholes and turning on our friend for no reason," she said with a sigh. She looked down at her hands again. "You know, what if she's actually fine—happy, even—and finally just doesn't give a shit about anything and is doing what she wants? What if we are the ones who are actually in suburban hell?"

I didn't say anything but glanced across the street, where Caroline Endicott was deadheading her enormous hydrangea bushes. Jess's words reminded me of our conversation at the pool about the Satanic Panic in the eighties. From all accounts, the people involved truly believed in the accusations and were deluded enough to think the devil had entered their neighborhoods or preschools. We weren't doing the same, were we?

I turned to Jess and leaned forward, nudging her leg with my knee. "I know. I think—"

I was cut off by a screeching and thumping sound.

Thump. Thump.

"Mommy!" Jack yelled from the family room. I sprang out of my chair, heart racing.

I ran inside and slid across the wood floor in my socks, Rocky at my heels, barking. Jess jogged behind me. I stopped when I got to the threshold, Jess and Rocky running into my legs.

"What the—"

Jack stood on the coffee table of the family room, eyes stretched wide, pointing down at the ground.

Thump, something sounded again.

My first instinct was to reach for him to grab him off the table, so I outstretched my arms, and then looked down toward the floor. I saw the source of the terror was Darlene, our Roomba. I had named her that because when Mark had given her to me for Mother's Day, she had seemed so pleasant and agreeable. I would press Clean on the app, and she would do it without argument. Darlene was the name of one of the nurse managers at St. Vincent's, and she had been like a mother hen to all of us. So the Roomba became Darlene; it was the nicest tribute I could think of.

Yet Darlene was anything but pleasant in that moment. She was spinning around in a circle, churning up the throw rug and making a horrifying whirring sound. Then she reversed and sped straight toward the coffee table leg with a sickening thud, as though trying to break it.

"Darlene, what has gotten into you?" I kept my voice light and forced a laugh so Jack would calm down. I leaned down to press the Stop button, but it jerked away from my touch as I got closer.

"Okay. I see you've gained some AI, Dar." I laughed again and looked at Jess, who stood frozen in the doorway, eyes wide.

I stepped toward Darlene again, and it again maneuvered out of my grip. This time, it reversed as though it were a pinball and the plunger had been pulled back, and then quickly released toward me, shooting across the carpet at an unnatural speed before crashing hard into my ankle on my bad leg.

"Damn it!" I shouted as I bent down to gingerly touch my leg. It felt like my heartbeat was pouring out of my lower left side, and pain swarmed in front of my eyes as black spots appeared.

"Amy, move!" Jess shouted. I watched as the Roomba pulled back again, ready to ram into me once more. I was able to hop on my good leg out of the way, and Darlene crashed into the corner of the coffee table again, sending a large crack spidering up to where Jack stood.

I reached for him again and pulled him off the table, quickly passing him to Jess as we left the room. Darlene zipped after us, nipping at our heels, while Rocky brought up the rear, barking at it.

"Emily! Stay in the kitchen," I shouted through the doorway. We ran toward the back door, but Darlene apparently remembered that she had mapped out the house and knew to take a shortcut around the kitchen, where Emily sat on a stool at the island, mouth open.

Darlene appeared in front of the back door, light on top angrily blinking red as she slowly reversed, winding up to slingshot toward us again.

I looked to the left. "Bathroom!" I said to Jess. She had Jack in a piggyback, and she raced toward it as I hobbled after. I shut the door behind us in the small powder room. I had to wedge myself next to the toilet to find space.

"Rocky! Oh no!" I said as I heard his bark. "We have to let him in." I reached for the door just as it shook with another blow from Darlene. The door split up the center, since it was made from cheap foam core.

Rocky's barking grew louder as he got closer to the bathroom.

"Rocky, go! No!" I said. The thudding against the door stopped, and a scraping sound replaced it, like a whirring. Then, an acceleration.

The awful sound of Rocky's whimper filled the bathroom. I didn't hesitate to wrench open the door to save him. He was backed into the corner by the front door, huddled, his front two paws bleeding where Darlene had run them over. And she was reversing again, ready to strike.

I charged after her, and she slowly spun around, the small

rotating brush in the back moving like a cockroach's antenna. She paused, and then spun excitedly as she prepared to accelerate toward me.

"Keep Jack," I called to Jess in the bathroom. I steeled myself as she came toward me.

"Kill it!" Jess screamed.

I tried to calculate the distance to the bathroom door and whether we could escape out the window into the yard. Surely she couldn't break down the front or back door. Then we could run inside and grab Emily, we could call Mark from Jess's house, and he could come home and kill it, although I didn't want to think about his reaction when we told him my vacuum had turned homicidal.

During my hesitant calculations, Jess activated. She hip-checked me as she hurried past, leaping over the laundry basket at the entrance to the basement. She ran toward Darlene like an Olympic sprinter, skidded to a stop on the floor, and brought her heel down as hard as she could on it. Over and over. Until there was nothing left, except a few whirs and beeps.

Finally, Darlene emitted a *womp womp* sound, the same as when she got stuck at the top of the stairs or ran out of power.

And then her light went out.

Red-faced, Jess looked up at me and wiped her forehead with an arm before putting her hands on her hips.

"Well, that was really fucking weird," she said. "Okay, I believe you, Amy."

I heard a gasp from behind her, and Emily stepped aside, looked from the now-dead Darlene to me, and said, eyes wide, "It was her."

Fear flooded my veins as I crouched down in front of her, reaching for her hands. "Who, honey?" My voice cracked.

She pulled her hands away and shook her head, her mouth pressed into a line. I repeated the question, louder, as I looked at Jess, who slowly placed a hand over her mouth.

Emily's eyes relaxed into a dull stare. "Her."

"Who is 'her'?" My voice was louder now, nearly a shout. "Emily, I said, who is—"

Jess stepped forward and placed a hand on my shoulder. "Amy. Stop."

Emily took the opportunity to turn and run upstairs. Still crouched down, I looked up at Jess. She struggled to keep her face calm, but I saw the fear simmering under the surface.

"Go check on Melissa," she said. "I'll take the kids to my house."

CHAPTER
14

HURRIED DOWN THE sidewalk, ignoring the pain in my leg, and turned the corner of Oakton Lane, sweating and out of breath as I approached Melissa's house. As I got closer, I slowed when I heard soft, warbling music and saw a Ford F-150 with Ohio plates parked out front. Shit. I had forgotten her parents were coming, and it looked like they had already arrived.

I hesitated on the sidewalk, unsure of what to do. Melissa had specifically asked that we not socialize with her parents—for our own sake as well as hers. I knew how uncomfortable the visit would be, and the last thing I wanted to do was force some kind of literal come-to-Jesus moment between her new life and her past.

Your Roomba just tried to attack you, idiot. Go make sure she's okay.

I slowly made my way up her stamped-concrete front walk, past the black planters filled with geraniums, and lifted my hand to knock. Before my knuckles could make contact, the front door swung open.

Tony stood, smiling, arms outstretched. "Amy! What a wonderful surprise! I told Melissa she should invite some of her friends to meet her parents."

"Oh—I'm not really . . . how did you know I was here?" I said, crossing my arms over my chest, realizing I was in a white T-shirt from college that read, *Gimme Margaritas, Por Favor.*

"The Ring, of course. I get an alert any time there's motion at the front door," he said with a shake of his head. He stepped aside and motioned for me to come in.

"Oh, no thanks, Tony. I just wanted to tell Melissa something. Can she step outside for a quick moment?" I took a step backward, nearly tripping over a midcentury-modern elevated planter.

"Don't be silly." He reached forward and put a hand on my back, guiding me inside. "Everyone is outside in the yard. Come say hi, even if only for a minute."

I couldn't think of an excuse, other than the fact I was sweating, not wearing any makeup, and sporting a T-shirt that asked for tequila, so I complied. As we walked through the house to the back door, the music grew louder. It wasn't any song I recognized, and I caught a lyric that went, "When the End of Days arrives / I will be by your side."

I didn't know they made pop songs about the apocalypse.

Melissa was outside, seated on her blue-and-white outdoor sectional, clutching a glass of iced tea and frowning at a well-dressed couple across from her. Her kids were jumping on the trampoline in a corner of the yard. She did a double take when she saw me, and then her body froze.

I'm so sorry, I know this is your worst nightmare. It could be worse, I could have brought Jess.

"Look who I found," Tony said as he clapped his hands together. He turned to me. "Iced tea? Virgin, of course," he laughed.

Melissa shook her head, and I did the same. "Oh, no thank you. I just stopped by to tell Melissa something, but it can wait. Really. I had totally forgotten you have company."

Melissa's parents rose from the couch in unison. Her mother was dressed in black capri pants and a short-sleeved floral shirt. Her hair was a blond lightbulb around her head, and against her chest was a gold necklace with *Protected* written in cursive. Her father wore a blue golf shirt and khaki pants and looked like he had just made a donation to an Ivy League school to get his son admitted after he was busted for underage drinking.

"I'm Patricia," her mother said. "And this is my husband, Joe." Her drawl was more pronounced than Melissa's, and she extended a hand, her wrist jangling with three charm bracelets. Her gaze fell down to my T-shirt, and her drawn-in eyebrows knitted together.

"Amy Foster. I live around the corner," I said. I flitted my hands around like an injured butterfly. "So nice to meet you. I really should be going."

"Please, we insist. We have never met any of Melly's friends since she moved here." Patricia gave my arm a squeeze and practically threw me toward the couch.

Melly? I mouthed to Melissa, who shot me a look fiery enough to melt plastic.

"Now, Amy, tell us about yourself. How many children do you have, which church do you attend here in Winchester . . . those kinds of things," Joe said as he leaned backward and clasped a hand around his bent knee.

I looked at Melissa, who slowly closed her eyes.

"I have two children." I sat with my back straight and smiled at them. They stared at me expectantly. "Oh, I'm not very religious, I . . ." I trailed off when I saw Melissa lean back and slump her shoulders forward.

Patricia's smile didn't fade in the slightest. "Well, anyone can be saved. At any time. That's the beauty of the healing power of Jesus. He is always waiting and always loves you. Satan may tell you different, but he only speaks in lies." She tapped her *Protected* necklace and looked at Joe, who nodded approvingly.

I looked around for Tony, for any respite, for him to offer risotto or that brie en croûte, but he was fiddling with something at the grill.

"Well, Satan doesn't really—" I stopped and pursed my lips. I had two believers in front of me, and I figured I might as well take advantage before another appliance sprang to life. If I was going to be a murder victim, I would rather Melissa murder me than a possessed inanimate object. "Actually, let me ask you: so you believe the devil and demons are real?"

Patricia's cheeks grew long, and Joe leaned forward. "Very real," he said. They exchanged a glance.

"How do you know?" I said before I could stop myself.

"Because we've seen it, of course," she said. "We've seen people possessed before, many times. It happens more often than you would think."

My pulse began to ratchet up, and I had to take a quick breath so I wouldn't blurt out anything about Liz. "How often?"

Patricia put a hand on Joe's arm as if to say, *I got this.* She looked at me. "Every day. People are surrounded in darkness and listen to the devil's silver tongue. They submit to him and then open the veil between hell and our world."

"And then what happens?" I knew I should stop, walk out, go back to my house, check on my kids, not put Melissa in this position. But these people *believed*. Maybe they could help us.

Joe shook his head. "All kinds of things. They speak in tongues, things catch on fire. They create chaos and evil, just to watch the world burn."

A terrible vision of our neighborhood engulfed in flames, parents running from unseen dark forces while terrified children screamed for help, danced across my brain.

Joe continued. "Believe you me, the End of Days is closer than any of us know. Which is why it's so important to become a true believer so you can ascend to heaven during the Rapture."

The only thing I knew about the Rapture was thanks to an interview I watched about the new Creation Museum in Ohio that discussed how dinosaurs were on Noah's Ark. I had never so much as read a book of the Bible.

I looked at Melissa, who cocked her head and gave me a challenging look. *Are you finished?*

No, not yet.

"If someone has been possessed, how would they become, um, unpossessed? I'm just curious," I said, trying to keep my tone light, one of curiosity rather than true information seeking.

"Well, that's the easy part: by accepting Jesus in their heart. And the way they do that is to find a pure spiritual home. Our church, the Glorious Return of the Lord," Patricia said. She pulled a stack of pamphlets out of her purse and held them toward me. They had donation envelopes stapled to the backs.

She waved them around until I took them.

Joe cleared his throat. "Now, I can feel Jesus speaking to me, and we can see you are very interested in becoming a true believer, Annie—"

"Amy," Melissa said, correcting her father, with a smirk.

"We would love to welcome you to the church and help you save your soul," he continued.

"What would she have to do?" Melissa said with a wide smile, mood suddenly lifted. She was enjoying this payback.

"A small tithe. Only five thousand dollars to start, and then monthly after. Of course, if she recruits other true believers, that amount will decrease," Patricia said.

I stared at her and then down at the pamphlets, barely concealing a laugh. It was a multilevel marketing megachurch scheme. There was nothing spiritual or holy about these people. They just wanted money.

I looked up and shook my head. "I don't really have that kind of money, but thank you. I guess I will have to take my chances during the Rapture."

Their eyes hardened, and Patricia held her hand out for the pamphlets, which I hurriedly shoved back to her. Melissa stifled a laugh and took a long sip of her "virgin" iced tea.

See? Now do you see?

"I must be going. So nice to meet you both," I said as I turned to leave.

"I'll just see Amy out," Melissa said. She followed me, and once we got inside, she said, "Told you."

We walked through the kitchen to the front door. "I'm so sorry. I just came over to tell you—" The entire incident with the Roomba came flooding back. The screams, the sparks, the sound of metal screeching. Emily's words. But it wasn't the time to tell her that her childhood fears might be real. "Nothing. It can wait. You're safe, though?"

She leaned against the open front door and sighed. "If they don't leave soon, I'm going to be the one speaking in tongues."

I gave her a sympathetic look and a goodbye hug before I jogged down the street to my house, back to the scene of Darlene's crimes.

CHAPTER 15

THAT NIGHT, AFTER I ordered a new vacuum on Amazon, one that was not robotically controlled, I tried to explain to Mark what had happened. He looked confused and wondered if some kind of electrical surge had caused Darlene to malfunction. I murmured, "Not likely," and then grabbed my phone and walked out the front door. Enough of this shit. It was time to see Liz again and find out what was going on.

I had performed enough psychosocial evaluations at work, and it was time to use those skills. Part of me still hoped that I could uncover a sensible explanation for what was happening.

"Are you sure that's a good idea?" Mark had said as he eyed the bits of Darlene's metal in the garbage can.

"No. But what else can I do? She's my friend. Or was my friend." I rubbed my forehead, feeling how dry my skin was, and bits of it fluttered down onto my shirt. I shuddered as I thought of Liz's alligator skin the last time I'd seen her, her features melting into one another like warm candle wax.

It was just before dinnertime, the golden hour, when the heat of the day had fizzled out and the cicadas began to buzz. Birds chirped in the old oak tree in my backyard, fighting over territory with the racoons.

The aching in the burn on my leg grew stronger as I turned the corner to Liz's house, like a beacon alerting me to danger. I ignored it and kept walking, averting my gaze from Jess's house. She had left my house after the Darlene incident, realizing she should keep a watchful eye on her own house should any of her electronics decide to go haywire. No one wanted to know what would happen if her Vitamix or air fryer turned self-aware.

The rotting smell still hung in the air as I walked up Liz's concrete front steps. My heart felt like it was going to break through my chest, and I suddenly became light-headed, a wash of nausea falling over me like a weighted blanket.

I rapped twice, hard, on the door before Tim answered. He still wore his work suit, his phone stapled to his hand.

"Yeah?" he said, his eyes narrowing when he saw me.

"Is Liz home?" Normally I would have been taken aback at his brusqueness, but our current situation left no room for niceties.

He pushed open the door and moved his phone in a sweeping motion, pointing it toward the couch.

I hesitated before crossing the threshold, unsure of what I would find. I certainly didn't want to be trapped inside, with a new burn.

I followed his gaze to the living room just off the foyer, where we had kicked off our shoes at the last movie night, the last normal moment before the storm hit.

"Tim, I'm really worried about her. Ever since our last girls' night, her behavior has been concerning. I'm sure you're worried, too."

He frowned at me and looked back at his phone. "Sure." He looked up, and his jaw tightened. "I told Mark that I have it handled and that people need to be careful in our backyard with the construction."

I rubbed my forehead and steadied my voice. After a trauma or terminal diagnosis, families often wanted someone to blame, and I was sometimes their punching bag. I had to remain calm, logical, rational, and explain the facts. "I didn't trip or fall into the hole. Liz pushed me, and then left me there."

He slowly closed his eyes and then opened them again. "People need to be careful around construction sites."

Frustration and anger pricked at my skin, and I pressed my lips together to stop from snapping at him. He was still worried that we were going to sue or ask him to pay for medical bills. Not about his wife, or whatever might be happening to her.

"There's something going on with her, Tim. That's why I'm here," I said. I leaned and peeked over the edge of the couch that faced away from the front door, and saw a figure splayed out. It was Liz, and she was asleep. Or at least she appeared to be asleep.

I looked back at Tim, one eyebrow raised out of caution. We exchanged a silent glance before I tilted my head toward him and gestured toward my friend with a palm.

Do something.

Don't you care?

Don't you see what's going on?

He shrugged slightly and looked down at his phone, studying it intensely. Conversation over.

"O-kay," I said. I realized the house was far too quiet. "Where are the kids?"

His eyes were still on his phone. "At my parents' house for the night. My mom has had to help out a lot lately."

"Well, that's good." Relief flooded through me that at least someone, even if it was Liz's horrible in-laws, was taking care of their children. "Like I said, I think Liz needs help. Don't you agree?" I said carefully. I wasn't about to specify exactly what kind of help I was afraid she needed.

He looked up and met my eyes briefly. "Yes," he said before he walked away, phone in both hands, furiously typing.

Anger bubbled up in my chest, and I took a step forward to follow him, shake him by the shoulders. Wake him up. Ask him to give a shit about his wife. I didn't know if she had tried to do anything to him, but she had thrown me into a pit and possibly summoned the forces of darkness, and I still wanted to help her.

I waited to see if he would come back into the room, listening to Liz's heavy breathing, which I could hear all the way in the foyer. The creaking upstairs told me he was going back into his office, and I heard a door shut.

I was on my own.

I smoothed away some flyaways that had escaped my topknot as I took a slow step toward the couch. Careful not to make any noise as I walked across the dark wood floor, I noticed a tumbleweed of dog hair from Bucky and realized I hadn't heard or seen the dog. Usually he at least gave a cursory bark when people knocked at the door.

Swallowing hard, trying not to think that something terrible had happened to him—that maybe he was at the bottom of the pit—I approached the back of the couch.

Liz lay in a prone position, wearing only a men's nightshirt and underwear. Her hands were clasped across her stomach, as though folded in prayer. Her dark hair was splayed out around her like a fan, her red painted toes crossed. She looked like a wax figure, a doll from Madame Tussauds. Like I could reach out and touch her cheek and have my finger go all the way through her jaw and brush against her teeth. Or whatever was left of them.

I shuddered as I thought of her skin softening to butter, melting down her face, the way she appeared to me that night in her backyard.

This is Liz. Your friend. She needs you. She deserves your help.

I steadied my breath as I tiptoed across from her, watching her chest rising and falling rapidly, like she had just finished the Chicago Marathon. I waited for it to stop, thinking she was having some awful nightmare, but it didn't. I looked down at my Apple Watch and timed her breath.

Forty-two breaths per minute.

I wasn't sure what the range of normal was, but that couldn't be it.

"Liz?" I whispered. When she didn't flinch or move, I said her name again, a bit louder. Again, nothing.

Heart pounding, I took a step forward, even though every fiber of my being told me to run. To go back to Mark and round up the children. To drive as far away from Winchester as we could in one night.

I stood directly over her, my body inches from hers. She could have easily shot out an arm and grabbed me. I braced myself for her to rouse, but she just kept panting. The deep whooshing of her breath was like a white noise machine. As I inhaled, I noticed a rotten, dark smell coming from her body.

Cloyingly sweet, mixed with damp earth. That was the phrase that I had heard a podcaster use to describe how John Wayne Gacy's house had smelled. And he had more than twenty corpses in his crawl space, decaying.

I slowly lowered to a seated position on her coffee table. I noticed there was dried Play-Doh all over it and what looked like the remnants of a melted ice-cream sandwich. The Liz I knew would never have let that remain. She cleaned her house with the tenacity of a high school classmate sharing conspiracy memes on Facebook.

"Liz? It's me, Amy. Can you hear me?" I whispered. My throat felt like it was filled with dead leaves and old branches scratching the back of my throat.

Still, she didn't move. I leaned forward a little, studying her arms and legs. I hadn't noticed it before, but they were covered in light scratches, like she had run through a field of rosebushes. Most were bright red and fresh. I shivered as I remembered that she had a hedge of knockout roses near her tiki hut. I imagined her outside, running through the bushes naked, watching as the blood ran from the scratches.

I wanted to bandage them up, put antibiotic cream on them. I didn't know how Tim couldn't have noticed any of this. Or maybe he had, and it was just too much of a hassle to address. It was one thing for him to ignore the erratic behavior, but this was an actual injury. Had her children seen them? I shivered as I tried to imagine what they thought of everything.

I extended one finger, lightly running it along a particularly angry-looking mark on her forearm.

Liz's breathing stopped, and I quickly recoiled, feeling a zap of energy that ran up my finger and into my shoulder. It was like a dull electrical shock, like the time when I touched the prongs on my hair dryer too soon after I unplugged it.

I leaned back as I waited for her to open her eyes, but she didn't move. I was about to say her name again when her legs suddenly stiffened like they were being pulled by the heels. Her fingers flexed and splayed, shooting out like starfish. Her eyes were still closed, but her neck craned to the side, almost so that her cheek was touching her shoulder. Then she froze again.

As she was stuck in that position, her lips began to move. It sounded like she was whispering, almost as if she was talking in her sleep. I leaned forward, turning my head so I could hear what she said.

It sounded like gibberish from a drunk at the end of the bar who'd had too many and was trying to tell a story but unable to form actual words.

But then, it got louder. And I could make out words, but I didn't know what they were. Whatever she was saying, it wasn't in English. Or any other language I recognized.

She said the same phrase over and over again like a mantra. I figured it had to be meaningful, so I grabbed my phone and typed out what I thought was the most reasonable phonetic spelling.

Ahm nays inter fitch ay ray

Then the whispering stopped, and her body went back to normal, her head returning to upright and her hands crossing over one another, her feet relaxing. Whatever it was, it was over.

I slowly stood up, unsure of what to do. I didn't want to wake her, and Tim was obviously no help. It felt wrong, but I took a quick picture of her on the couch to show to Jess and Melissa, so I wouldn't have to try to explain it to them again, like I did with the pit accident.

I tiptoed away from the couch, and as I got to the front door, she spoke again.

"Thank you," she said in a deep, gravelly voice, eyes still closed.

The hair on my arms stood on end. It wasn't her voice. Something inside of her was thanking me, but for what?

For bringing me into our neighborhood.

I wrenched open the door and quickly shut it behind me. As I walked home, I pulled out my phone and looked at the notes I had typed.

Ahm nays inter fitch ay ray

I typed them into Google, and nothing appeared. I tried the phrase a few different ways, but still nothing. Whatever she had said, Google didn't have the answer.

Maybe it was nothing. Maybe it was just dream language. Maybe she was having a pleasant dream about Bradley Cooper and it was none of my business what they were doing.

Yet, still something made me pause. Melissa's parents, while grifters, had mentioned speaking in tongues when people were possessed. Could that be what Liz's dreamspeak was?

I found Mark in the kitchen, loading the dishwasher. I was barely able to form the words to explain what happened.

"Should I try and talk to Tim again? I can't believe he was such an asshole to you," he said as he carefully shut a kitchen cabinet. He turned around and leaned against the counter, arms folded over his chest.

I shook my head. "No, I don't think that would go anywhere. Whatever this is, it isn't natural, and there's no way he would believe me, anyway. He doesn't even want to take her to a therapist or doctor. Remember, this is the guy who said that therapy was a scam."

"True. But she obviously needs help. If things don't get better, someone needs to do something."

I had the feeling that whatever Liz had said meant something, but I didn't know what. Unfortunately, I would soon come to find out.

CHAPTER 16

I DREAMED OF JUNE that night. In the dream, I was in the backyard, watching butterflies land on the wildflowers growing next to the house. I sensed my sister's presence, a movement out of the corner of my eye as she lowered herself into a nearby patio chair. I didn't turn to look at her, too worried that if I did, she would disappear. She didn't say anything, just sat next to me. I woke up desperately wishing I had spoken to her.

There were so many things that I still hadn't been able to do since she died. I had never visited her grave, couldn't listen to any of her favorite songs or look at pictures from when we were little. I had a box of her things that my parents had given me before they moved to Florida, and it was still taped up in my basement, never opened.

But I wondered if I could face all of that if I could just somehow hear her voice again.

I HAD BEEN sitting in the parking lot of Target for close to ten minutes, trying to find the will to go inside. I took a deep breath, the heat from the afternoon building without the air-conditioning on. I'd left Jack and Emily in Jess's yard to run errands. It was our unspoken agreement, as we both knew the pain of having to drag kids through a store. I was eternally grateful, and it often felt like we were living together in some kind of common-law shared-wife situation.

I eyed the car that pulled in across from me, a black Yukon XL. There was a 90 percent chance I knew whoever was behind the wheel, as the Winchester Target was less a retail store and more of a watering hole for the local mom wildlife.

It was inevitable that I would run into at least two people I knew. The record was ten conversations, which took me two hours. There was no running in and out to grab a few things. No, Target was a social opportunity, one where you had to look at least decently presentable and be prepared to chat about everything from the latest fundraiser for the school to gossip about how the traveling soccer team's coach had gotten thrown out of the game for screaming profanities at the referee. If Winchester had an office water cooler, it was squarely inside those red and white walls.

But that's what I was counting on. I needed volunteers, recruits for the school carnival, and it would be much harder to say no in person.

That morning, I'd pulled out the binder just as Jack walked into my bedroom.

His eyes lit up as he saw the logo on the front. "Can I help plan?"

he said as he brushed his bangs out of his eyes. Before I could answer, he threw his body on the bed next to me, spilling the cup of coffee in my hand.

"Watch it, bud." I dabbed at the comforter with the leg of my pajama pants.

"I can't wait for the lollipop pull. That was so much fun. I won that elephant last time, remember? Are we going to do it again?" he said as he rested his head against my arm. His excitement mitigated my dread at having to plan it. Hopefully, I could make him proud.

I chuckled and nodded before I flipped open the binder to the "Games" section. I ran my finger down the list. They were fairly straightforward, like the lollipop pull, where the kids paid a ticket and got to choose a lollipop from a rack. If the end of their lollypop had a red dot, they selected a prize.

There was also the cakewalk; a bounce house; Bozo buckets, where kids tossed plastic balls into red buckets and received a prize if they got all the way to bucket ten; and a freeze-dance competition.

"This shouldn't be too hard," I muttered to myself.

"Mom, are you like the principal of the carnival?" Jack said as he stared at the binder.

"Kinda. I'm in charge but I will need a lot of help." My anxiety began to climb as I realized I really only had two volunteers, both of whom I'd drafted against their wills. If Liz were herself, she would have appointed herself cochair and done the lion's share of the work, without question. Other than Jess and Melissa, no one had stepped forward to help. So now I had to recruit people, in person.

Jack leaned forward and gave me a hug. "It's going to be great, Mom. I'm so excited."

I closed my eyes briefly as I pressed him to me. I had to do everything I could to live up to his sweet expectations. It was the least I could do for him.

In the Target parking lot, I watched as a blond woman with shoulder-length beachy waves climbed out of her car, wearing a pink shelf-bra tank top and black high-waisted leggings. Sarah Keener. She turned, saw me, and waved. Her face lit up with a brilliant yet insincere smile.

Exhaling slowly, I opened my door and smiled back.

"Hey there! How's it going?" I said as I added some pep to my step.

"Oh, it's going!" she said brightly. She waited for me to join her, and then we walked toward the entrance together. "It's been so long! How's your summer been?"

You don't want to know. One of my closest friends has turned feral.

"Every day is another day in paradise," I said with a forced laugh. It was my go-to line—be funny, exasperated, the overworked mom who had great one-liners. Of course, one could never actually look like an overworked mom. You could wear comfy leggings and a ball cap, but the leggings should be high-end athleisure and the hat should be from wherever you or your family had a lake house. Lake Geneva, Wisconsin, or one of the beach towns in Southwest Michigan.

"I hear you," Sarah said as we walked through the sliding glass doors. The air-conditioning hit my skin, and my sweat instantly evaporated.

Sarah chattered on about how she was so stressed because she and her family were leaving for a vacation to Hilton Head Island the next day, and she needed to buy trinkets from the $1 bin to occupy her toddler on the plane.

"Snacks. Buy snacks, and then when you think you have enough, buy more," I said. Mark and I had taken the kids on a flight last year, and they had eaten like they were going to the electric chair. But the Doritos muffled the sounds of their voices.

"I wonder if they have organic graham crackers here," Sarah mused as she pulled out a cart.

"I'm sure they do." I cocked my head to the side as though I'd just had a thought. "Actually, before you go, I wanted to ask you something. I don't know if you've heard, but I'm in charge of the school carnival this year."

I watched Sarah figure out what I was about to say, and her smile faded. It wasn't lost on me that I had been in this situation many times, just reversed.

She preempted my request. "That's wonderful. It's such a great event. I'd love to help, but this summer is just crazy for me."

I nodded. "Of course. Have fun on your vacation."

She beamed with relief and pushed her cart toward the grocery aisle with a wave.

I grabbed a cart and turned toward the electronics and books section, eyes moving around, looking for other people I knew. After we had moved here, I used to fly through, eyes down, assuming people would avoid me if I looked like I was on a mission. Au contraire, it seemed to be an invitation, like a flashing neon sign that said, "Talk to me about the upcoming school board election!" But this time, I welcomed any social interactions. I realized I was like Heather in that moment, waiting for the right opportunity to collect unwilling prey to volunteer. It didn't matter; I needed help.

I steered over to the electronics section and picked out a pair of earbuds for Mark's dad's birthday gift. We had dinner at Mark's parents that night. Next, I headed toward the toys. I figured as long as I was there, I would buy a birthday present for a party that Emily had been invited to by a classmate, for which I had been instructed by her to purchase LOL Surprise dolls. I stood in front of the display of shockingly overpriced small dolls with huge heads and tiny bodies, wondering if the LOL Surprise doll or the regular one was the better choice.

I was about to grab the one hidden in a giant egg when the store went dark. One moment, I had a hand extended toward the toy box, and the next, blackness. There were a few sounds of muffled confusion, and I heard a child shriek two aisles over.

I looked at the shelf of LOL dolls, eyes narrowed as my vision tried to adjust. All I could see was the whites of their eyes as they stared at me, a tiny toy army. And then, one of the dolls moved. The two huge round circles on the doll's face blinked.

I shrank back, a strangled cry escaping my lips. Then, it blinked again.

My feet felt heavy, unable to follow directions. My hand was still outstretched as I leaned forward slightly and looked at the doll. It stared back and then cocked its head, studying me.

The lights flooded on, and the sounds of the store increased in volume. The doll was motionless once again. With a shaking hand, I carefully turned the box around so it was facing the other way and then rushed out of the aisle, my vision still spotty.

Calm down. It was just your imagination. A trick of the lighting.

Despite every rational excuse, though, I knew what I'd seen.

I had reached the end of the aisle when I heard: "Hey, Amy! How's your summer been?"

Fifteen minutes later, I was armed with the newfound knowledge of which private gymnastics gym had the best summer classes and not much else. Julie Sommers had turned me down flat when I asked if she would run one of the games, although she did offer to take a shift handing out ice cream, so the ask wasn't a total bust.

I had kept my face pleasant when she offered, even as I realized I hadn't asked the ice-cream vendor if they would donate again.

After she left, I pulled out my phone and typed a quick email to Oberweis, the local ice-cream company, asking if they would do an in-kind gift of ice-cream bars for the event. After I sent it off, I was about to put my phone away when a new email popped up in bold type.

It was from Monarch Hospice, the organization that I had emailed my résumé to. My heart racing, I opened it.

> Thank you for submitting your résumé for the Social
> Worker position at Monarch Hospice. Your qualifications
> are very impressive, and we would be interested in
> setting up a phone interview with the Hiring Manager
> sometime next week. Please let us know some dates and
> times that work with your schedule, and we look forward
> to speaking with you.

Holy shit. They wanted to interview me. Next week.

A foot in the door, maybe. A chance, an opportunity to show what I could do. Or at least what I thought I could do.

I mentally calculated the time I would need to prep. I hoped Jess wasn't too annoyed by Emily and Jack, because I would need to lean on her and Melissa to help with the kids while I got everything together. A pang in my heart reminded me of Liz, how if she were her normal self, she would scoop up my kids and take them all day—for ice cream, to make homemade crafts, to watch a movie in her backyard. All without complaints. I had joked one time that my kids could burn her house down, and she would cover for them and take the blame.

I smiled, feeling the excitement run through my bones as I forgot about the moment in the toy aisle. This was more than a chance, more than a job opportunity. It felt almost like a calling.

Before I could get too deep into my elation, I spotted another Winchester Elementary mom and sped my cart after her.

"Joelle! How are you?"

———

TWENTY MINUTES LATER, I left Target, feeling dejected. Joelle had pretended she was on a phone call when I got her attention, no doubt intuiting that I was actively searching for help. Although it was sort of funny when her phone rang while she pretended to talk into it.

I needed help, and my next move was to tell Jess and Melissa that their husbands had to run some of the games. They wouldn't be thrilled, either, since they would want to take their own kids around to the booths, but desperate times and all that.

I pulled down Maple Leaf Drive, and the first thing I saw was a gaggle of children running down the sidewalk, screaming. As I drove closer, I recognized the screams as ones of terror, rather than summer afternoon shenanigans.

I stopped the car in front of Jess's house, where the group was headed, and got out of the car. Jess ran out of her house dressed in a sports bra and workout bike shorts, hands in the air. The children, Emily, Jack, Summer, and Melissa's twins, all crowded around her, talking at once.

"What's going on?" I said as I jogged across the grass.

"I have no clue." She held up a hand. "Calm down. Talk one at a time."

I leaned over to Jack and put a hand on his shoulder. "What happened?"

He turned to me, eyes full of fear, tears at the corners. "We went over to see if Carson wanted to play Ghosts in the Graveyard with us and saw something scary."

My gaze lifted to Jess, and we exchanged a glance. "What was it?"

He swallowed hard and looked from me to Jess before he said, "We were about to knock on the door when we saw something black inside. It was a pointy shape, like my rubber sensory ball, and then we heard a growl."

"You guys, it was probably just Bucky," Jess said. She laughed, but a crease of worry appeared in between her eyes on her forehead. She turned to Summer and rubbed her arm. "Nothing to be afraid of."

I looked at Emily, whose face had turned to stone. Her arms were straight against her body, like she was in an invisible tube. "Honey?" I tapped her on the shoulder. "Emily?"

She looked up at me, her eyes dark and flat again. She didn't say anything, her gaze unblinking.

"Emily?" I said again, to no response.

"That's it. I've had it with this shit. I'm going over there," Jess said as she threw her hands up. She started across the lawn, and the children started screaming again, begging her not to go.

Emily finally spoke. "Don't," she whispered.

Jess stopped and looked from her to me quickly, assessing. She slowly walked back. "Like I said, I'm sure it was just Bucky." She looked at Summer, who had a finger in her nose. "Yo, Sums, why don't we see if your friends want Popsicles?"

At that, the children forgot about the creature they saw at Liz's house and happily followed her inside to collect their treats. I helped her unwrap the Popsicles and hand them out, an unspoken conversation happening between us as we exchanged glances.

Whatever dark force was in Liz's house seemed to be getting stronger, and I had the horrible thought that it wouldn't be long before it outgrew her house and went looking for other places to inhabit.

CHAPTER 17

THE SAYING "LESS is more" is one that my mother-in-law never subscribed to. The anti–Marie Kondo, more was always better to Judy. When she was at my house, she was determined to organize and weed through my closets, but at her own house, it was game on. The pack rat version of "do as I say, not as I do."

"Shit!" Mark pitched forward as he stepped onto the landing of his parents' front porch, which was newly covered in fairy-garden tchotchkes.

I looked down at the now-broken stone statue of a frog wearing a crown and holding a scepter. I held up the head as Judy answered the door.

"What did you do to Pierce?" she said as she reached for the head.

"Sorry. Your son's fault," I said as I stretched my arm out and handed it to her. Stepping inside the screen door, I inhaled the familiar scent of their house: seven different kinds of potpourri all mixed together.

"You can glue it, Nana," Emily said as she and Jack rushed forward into the arms of their grandmother. "I will help you."

Judy pressed both of them to her waist, against her white-and-blue caftan, and closed her eyes briefly. "Of course, sweet girl." Her voice still held the lightest lilt of a Texas accent. She opened her eyes and looked at her son. "I'll have you know, I liked Pierce more than you."

Mark laughed. "Sorry, Mom." He stepped into the foyer and gave his mother a kiss on the cheek.

She made a harrumphing noise, no doubt wondering whether Mark had done it on purpose. In college, when Mark and I started dating our senior year, he told me early on that his mother was into what she called "discrete collections" of things, and he was not happy about it. I pictured a china cabinet filled with old tea-cups and saucers, and antique picture frames. And she did have those things. Just about five hundred additional "collections" in every inch of her house. Mark said it was like living with hoarders, except socially acceptable ones who had Hummel figurines in-stead of flattened cat carcasses. And, apparently, fairy-garden accoutrements.

Judy waved Mark into the sunken family room, where his dad, Bud, sat parked in front of the White Sox game, as per usual. Their house was built in the 1970s, and I don't think any of the decor had changed; it had just been enhanced. Then she leaned forward and hugged me.

"It's so good to see you. It's been too long," she said as she kissed my cheek. She always went in for the kiss on the lips, but after I awkwardly turned my head enough times, she had to settle for my cheek.

"Good to see you, too," I said, silently adding, *We saw you guys not that long ago.* But if Judy had it her way, we would all live together like some kind of eighties sitcom with a wacky letter carrier who stopped by for coffee every morning. I, of course, would fill the role of the incompetent mother who had to learn everything from actual adults. Which, I supposed, wasn't that far off.

I held out Bud's present with my index finger, the *Happy Retirement* bag swaying. I'd been distracted by another mom from school who asked me if I had heard that Mrs. Brown—the second-grade teacher—was retiring because she'd met a bartender on vacation in Cancún and decided to travel the world with him, and grabbed the wrong gift bag in Target. And so, even though Bud had retired ten years before, the bag was wishing him luck in his next career adventure.

Judy went to reach for it and then stopped, her hand frozen in the air. She cocked her head to the side slightly and stared at me.

"What's wrong?" I said nervously, shifting on my toes.

Her eyes grew wide, and her hand trembled slightly.

I quickly took a step back and repeated the question, but she was still frozen.

"Mark?" I said as I tried to see into the other room.

"Nana?" Emily said in a small voice as she moved toward her. She touched her grandmother's arm, and Judy came back to life.

"Oh, sorry, dear. I just had a . . . spell," she said as she shook her head. She shot me a quizzical look, her gaze moving up and down as she reached for the bag. She placed an arm around Emily and ushered her into the other room, leaving me alone in the foyer.

I felt like my feet were rooted to the bamboo-plank floor. Her expression hadn't been just blank, like a mild seizure or a moment of spacing out. It was one of fear.

AFTER MARK AND his dad had grilled burgers and hot dogs outside, we sang "Happy Birthday," and then Bud blew out his candles. He and Mark went inside to finish watching the White Sox game. Emily and Jack found glass jars in the garage and went to the front yard to catch fireflies. That left Judy and me alone outside on their patio. They had recently installed a pergola from Costco, with LED lights around the ceiling and a TV in the top corner. The strange moment earlier with Judy had passed, and she'd acted like her usual self, pulling out garnishes for the grill and fussing over arranging the hamburger buns on a platter shaped like an owl. I thought maybe I had imagined it and my paranoia really was getting worse. Still, I couldn't shake the feeling that she knew something was off.

"So what else is new with you, Amy?" Judy said as she leaned back in her chair, crisscrossing her legs under her caftan as she held a stemless glass of white wine stenciled with *Gatlinburg Gals '97*, a relic from one of her "hen weekends" with her friends.

I wasn't ready to talk about the possible job. It felt like jinxing it, so I shifted to a long diatribe about occupying the kids each day of summer break.

"How are your parents doing?" she asked as she took another sip.

I smiled. "Good. Enjoying retirement down on Sanibel Island. They ride a golf cart around every day and meet their friends for tennis or happy hour." It was a weight off my shoulders to know that my parents were happy, even if some part of them would always be missing since June died. They had spent so long after her death like ghosts, going through the motions but only half-present. So when they decided to move south, I told them I would miss them but that they should do what made them happy. It seemed that they finally were. We spoke every so often, and they FaceTimed with the kids, but I hadn't seen them in more than a year. Sometimes it felt like it hurt them more to spend time with me than not to.

Judy smiled. "That's wonderful to hear. I think of them often." She stopped there, and we both understood what she meant.

Yet the weight of not talking about June sometimes felt greater than the burden of having to share my feelings, and I shifted uncomfortably in my chair. I crossed my legs, and the bottom of my white linen pants rode up, the hint of the bandage on my leg showing. It still hurt, but I had learned to walk normally, on the side of my foot ever so slightly, so that virtually no one could tell the difference.

"What happened to your leg?" Judy said as she looked down and then up again. Her eyes widened a touch, and the same look of fear flashed across her face.

I inhaled sharply at her expression, my facade shattered. "I—I got hurt. One of my friends accidentally tripped me, and my leg got a scratch." I regained my composure and waved my hand around dismissively. "It's really nothing." I took a long sip from my wine, avoiding her eyes.

There was silence, and I finally looked up. She sat with her back perfectly straight and shook her head.

"There's something wrong. I can feel it. There's something

troubling you, and I felt it from when you walked in the door." Her voice was no more than a whisper. "Are you in danger, Amy?"

The glass in my hand felt heavy, slipping out of my grasp. I quickly set it down on the patio table. I stared at it for a moment, Judy's body distorted through the glass. Judy had always called herself an empath. Well, sometimes "empath," other times "angel messenger." Occasionally "crystal mother." I never paid much attention to any of it, because she was always a little bit of everything, like a collage of titles and experiences, all bound together with the rubber cement of her will.

Yet she had never called me out on something like this.

She knew. It didn't seem possible, but she *knew*. In the same way that Emily did.

"Who?" she said simply.

"It's Liz." My voice was so quiet it was as though I merely mouthed the words.

Her face fell, and she rubbed her forehead. Judy had a soft spot for Liz, after a long conversation at Emily's birthday party last spring. We'd rented a bounce house and an inflatable water slide, and Judy brought over face-painting supplies and patiently drew dragons and butterflies on the kids' faces. Then she and Liz huddled around the jug of peach sangria Liz had brought, getting tipsy and sharing recipes for lasagna. Liz had joked that Judy should come to our next neighborhood wine night, until I asked her if we should also invite her mother-in-law, the WASPy country club queen who called tuxedos "dinner jackets."

"I'm so sorry," Judy said. "Do you want to talk about it?"

I rubbed my forehead. My chest felt tight. "Not right now. Maybe another time."

She shifted in her chair and folded her arms together, and the pressure in my chest lifted. "I hear you're planning the school carnival this year. Jack seems beside himself with excitement."

"He is, although I've been having some trouble finding volunteers." I rolled my eyes slightly. "To think, I used to be the one who avoided these kinds of things." After I struck out with volunteers at Target, I had asked Jess to secure the bounce house and Melissa to coordinate the signage. But they were the whole team so far.

Jack was so looking forward to the carnival, and it pained me to think of disappointing him, but if I didn't get more help, I didn't see how it would live up to last year.

She leaned forward. "Well, I'm happy to help if you need an extra pair of hands."

"Oh, I don't want to put you out. I—" I stopped as I remembered Emily's birthday party. I had a willing volunteer in front of me, and I should accept the help. "Actually, would you mind doing the face painting?"

Judy brightened, and without a word, she put her hands on the arms of her chair and lifted herself, her caftan billowing behind her. She held up a finger and went inside. I sighed and took a long sip of my wine, finishing it, and then after a glance over my shoulder, I took a swig out of hers.

I reached for a glass of water on the table to chase down the wine. Except, my hand slipped right through it. Not really through it, but when I tried to grasp and lift it, the glass folded inward like it was made of Saran Wrap, barely a solid object. I retracted my hand in confusion and looked at the clear glass filled with water. It looked perfectly normal.

I slowly reached for it again, and my fingers couldn't curl

around it. They met in the middle as the flexible glass bent and cracked, spiderwebs appearing for a moment before it shattered in my hand. Sharp glass pieces, solid once again, sliced through my palm. Blood began spouting from my skin, snaking down my arm, and dripping onto my leg.

I stared at it in shock, not feeling any pain, trying to comprehend what had just happened as blood pooled onto my lap.

"I found—" Judy reappeared, a cardboard box labeled "VHS tapes" in her hands. "Are you all right, dear? You're as white as a sheet."

I looked down at my palm, which was now uninjured and free of blood. I flexed my fingers and turned my hand over. No injuries. It must have been some kind of vision or hallucination.

"Yes," I said in a shaky voice. "I'm fine."

She shot me another quizzical look and set the box down on the table. "I've had these for years. Can you use them for games? And of course I will help with the face painting."

I leaned forward and peered into the box. It was filled with small toys and prizes. I glanced down again at my hand and at the glass, both of which were as they should have been.

Despite the strange vision, gratitude flooded me at her gesture. If no one in Winchester would help me plan the carnival, I had to get creative. Even if it would be a ragtag group running the show, I had renewed hope that I could pull it off for Jack. He deserved to have something special, and I would do everything I could to make it happen.

CHAPTER 18

THREE HOURS LATER, after the kids were in bed, I waited on the corner outside of my house, my other hand grasping Rocky's leash. After we had arrived home from my in-laws' house, Jess had sent a text to Melissa and me, asking to meet to walk our dogs. After my vision with the glass, I had a sinking feeling it wasn't really about the dogs.

Rocky started to whine and pull when he saw Jess walking down the street, her Lab mix, Duffy, at her side. He was off-leash trained and was more obedient than any of our children. She wore a Bob Marley T-shirt and blue-and-white-striped pajama pants. Her feet were bare.

Melissa was a few steps behind her, wearing a cream silk pajama shorts set and Ugg house slippers. In her arms was her small white evil dog, Lucy. Lucy was a long-haired Chihuahua and only loved Melissa, even shunning Tony and the kids. She primarily lived in Melissa's bedroom, emerging only twice a day to eat downstairs and then poop on the expensive throw rugs.

"I guess we aren't going to walk," I said as I pointed to Jess's bare feet.

Melissa sauntered over, Lucy growling at us and shaking from her arms.

Jess scowled at the dog. "Your dog needs a Xanax," she said.

Melissa patted Lucy fondly, and she responded by nuzzling her head against Melissa's chest. "No more than any of us. She's just honest about it."

"What's that?" I pointed to a small cardboard box under Jess's armpit.

Jess shifted the leash and held the box out. Melissa shrank back quickly and inhaled, pulling Lucy closer to her, who responded with a squeak.

"Isn't it badass?" Jess said with a smile.

"Where did you get that?" Melissa said, taking another step back. In the darkness of the neighborhood, I could see her eyes were wide as her hands clutched her neurotic dog.

It was a Ouija board, with a picture of two hands on a triangular planchette and a board with numbers and letters.

"They sell these things everywhere. Del gave me the idea. He was kidding, but I thought it would be worth a try," Jess said. "They're used to communicate with supernatural things, and maybe we can ask it if there's something, you know, nefarious hanging around Liz."

I leaned forward and peered at the board. The picture looked innocuous enough.

"Well, it's worth a shot, I suppose," I said.

"Great!" Jess said. She sidestepped onto my front lawn and plopped down, crossing her legs as Duffy settled in next to her. She started to open the box.

"What? Now? I thought we could, like, schedule it," I said as a pit of nerves began to rise into my throat from my stomach.

"No, thanks. That is not something to mess with. I was taught that Ouija boards were a direct line to Satan himself. And that's one thing that I agree with my parents about," Melissa said. Her hand stroked Lucy's head over and over again like a worry stone, white hair flying all around her. "I won't do it."

"Buzzkill. What if it works?" Jess said. She flopped back on the lawn, arms spread out wide.

"You guys, that"—she glanced at the board and shielded Lucy with both hands—"is dangerous. Y'all know most of what my parents taught me to fear was harmless, like birth control, or Halloween costumes, or weed. But the Ouija board was the one lesson that I think we should all listen to."

Melissa reached down and picked up the Ouija box with two fingers and tossed it across the lawn. It lightly bounced and spilled open, the planchette with its legs in the air like an animal playing dead.

Jess jolted up and reached for it. She started to unfold the board. "Well, I'm not scared."

"I'm leaving," Melissa said, and turned on her heel, beginning to walk back home.

"Wait! Don't leave." I looked down at Jess and snatched the board and planchette from her, tossing them back into the box and replacing the lid. "See? It's gone. Come back. I need to tell you guys something."

Melissa stopped and frowned but slowly stepped back toward us as Jess lowered herself to the grass again, arms out.

"It seems like every time you have to tell us something, it's something awful. Not like, 'Hey, I found a new sushi place that has great spicy tuna.' Or, 'Did you hear about these new workout leggings on Amazon?'" Jess muttered from the grass, eyes closed.

Melissa raised her eyebrows expectantly and held Lucy on her hip like a baby, keeping her distance from the board.

I told them about going to Liz's house and watching her sleep and the strange movements. I told them about how her skin was covered in scratches and seemed waxy. I then showed the picture of her on my phone, and they shrank back.

"She was also mumbling something." I clicked over to the Notes app. "I tried to record it phonetically. It was 'Ahm nays inter fitch ay ray.'"

"Why didn't you just do a voice recording?" Melissa said impatiently.

I shrugged, lifting my phone in the air. "Because that would have made too much sense? It's not like I had a plan, other than to make sure she wasn't levitating and vomiting pea soup."

"*The Exorcist.* Another reason not to use that Ouija board. The demon contacted the little girl through the board and then she started doing unnatural things with a crucifix," Melissa said.

"That would be a badass stripper routine." Jess laughed, still splayed on the lawn like she couldn't muster the energy to sit up and engage in this ridiculous conversation. "The guy could come out with horns and red body paint and dance to 'Highway to Hell.'" She shot up. "That's actually a great idea. Maybe I should open my own club."

I sighed deeply. I would have thought she was joking, except Jess concocted a new business idea every other week. Two weeks ago, she'd wanted to run a nursing home for swingers but then realized there were hurdles like insurance and licensing. (Not to mention the potential medical costs of elderly swingers' breaking their hips.)

Melissa stared at her phone. Her face was illuminated by the light, shadows bouncing off her face. Even at night, her eyebrows were perfectly filled in and her lashes were long and full, thanks to bimonthly trips to the lash studio in town.

"Say again what Liz whispered," she said. I did, and she scrolled the screen with her thumb.

"I already tried googling it and it just took me to a Russian website that I think is a front for arms dealers," I said. I'd also tried Google Translate and was pretty sure my name was now on the FBI's watch list.

"Nothing wrong with Russian fronts. The place where I get my Botox is one," Melissa said absentmindedly.

"Oh, a med spa. I could own one of those," Jess said from the grass.

Melissa inhaled sharply and pulled her head away from the screen, her thumb paused.

"What is it?" I took a step toward her, and she looked up, her pupils dilated and her mouth slightly open.

She turned the phone around and showed me the screen. *Latin for Satanists.* She flipped the phone back to her face and said, "'Latin is often used for demonic incantations. Demons are thought to be solitary creatures, but there is evidence that they are actually quite social. Once a demon has ripped a hole through the mortal realm and has been able to enter, it will quickly try to widen the hole so that other demonic entities can come through. Thus, it is imperative that demonic possessions or suspected possessions be dealt with accordingly—the demon sent back to the spirit world, and the hole closed.'"

"Sure, but—" Jess started, but Melissa held up a finger.

"'Demons may attempt to widen this hole to let others through in a variety of ways, especially keening or communicating through electricity, or through incantations and meditations. The most commonly reported incantation is the Latin phrase *omnes interficere*. It translates to: *Kill them all*. It amounts to a sort of marching order for other, lower-level spirits to come assist.'"

Melissa looked up and her hand dropped to her side, her leg illuminated by the screen. None of us spoke. The night air grew thicker, like a wool blanket draped around us. My skin began to tingle, and I felt something brush against my toes. I violently shook my foot and felt something hairy scamper away. I decided it was best not to look.

Jess tucked her legs up to her chest and clasped a hand around the opposite wrist.

"Well, there we have it." My voice was shaky and thin.

There were a few more moments of silence, until Lucy, whom Melissa had set down on the sidewalk, let out a loud yelp. My blood ran icy, and my heart began to pound. Rocky started to pull on the leash and whine, while Duffy stared at Jess, waiting for a signal.

We heard a rustling in the bushes flanking my front door, and the three of us stared in terror as the evergreen began to move.

A strangled cry escaped my lips, and Melissa shook her palm at me. *Shut up.*

Something began to move across the lawn, with eyes that glowed in the dark as it crouched down low to the grass. My feet felt frozen in the spot on the concrete, even though every part of me said, *Run. Run now. Get to your children and hold them close.*

I pictured Liz crawling out from the bush on all fours, limbs bent at odd angles. Her mouth full of rotting teeth, her eyes two black holes. Her skin dripping off her bones, decaying before us. We would be too frozen to do anything before she opened her mouth and swallowed us whole. And then, she would move on to our families.

I started shaking. Then I saw a small black body, no bigger than a housecat, with white stripes on its back. A skunk.

A loud exhalation from all of us, and Jess lay back down on the grass while Melissa leaned forward and put her hands on her thighs.

I sat down on the sidewalk and brought my knees up to my chest. "I thought you said Del had gotten rid of the skunks," I said to Jess.

"He said he had. He even poured out some Rumple Minz liquor around the shed since Google told him skunks hate the smell of peppermint. Complained about it for days after since that brand of liquor is an endangered species, apparently," she muttered from the grass. Her family was very attractive to the skunk population in Winchester. Rocky had gotten sprayed three times in the past two years, all from the skunk family who had decided to take up homesteading in their backyard.

"I think we should try the Ouija," I said. "If you're afraid of it, Melissa, that means it's exactly what we need to do next. Maybe not tonight, but we don't have any other ideas."

I looked at Jess, who put her hands over her face, and then at Melissa, whose head hung down, her long, dark hair covering her expression.

"I'm sorry. I can't," she said, although her voice held the slightest bit of hesitation.

That was the best we were going to get.

I collected the board from the lawn and tucked it under my arm. "Let's take a breath and regroup next weekend, assuming nothing else happens between now and then."

"But that's the Fourth of July," Melissa said from behind her hair. "Tony has been talking about making his famous four-day ribs to bring to the barbecue."

There was a long pause, until Jess spoke.

"Really?" she said, her voice flat.

I wound Rocky's leash around my palm and started for my front door, Ouija board under my arm. "Next weekend. Ribs or not."

CHAPTER 19

I **WATCHED THE SUN** slowly come up on the horizon. It was a foggy morning, and even as the day broke, the air was hazy. I thought I heard Jack and Emily begin to stir in their rooms, so I swung my legs over the side of the bed and rubbed my face. I figured I might as well get the day started, since sleep was ever elusive. I went downstairs and was surprised to see my kids already awake and snuggled together under a blanket, watching Netflix on the iPad.

"Since when do you guys know how to operate Netflix?" I said.

Jack laughed. "Since I was four."

I pushed aside all thoughts of how I wasn't winning Mother of the Year any time soon and went into the kitchen to make coffee. While I listened to it percolate, I pulled out a mug from the cabinet. The front of it read, *Good Morning, Gorgeous*. Liz had given it to me for my birthday last year.

I looked around and tried to imagine what things were like in her house that morning. Likely, there would be no quiet moments with siblings snuggling under a blanket or a tired but mostly happy mom making coffee. I wondered if her scratches were healing, if she was still on the couch, muttering those awful words. If she was like a statue in the room that they all just ignored, not bothering to help her.

Before I could stop myself, I pulled out my phone and typed out a text to her. I had my interview for the social worker position in a few days, and I'd learned long ago that distraction is better than anticipation, so I should fill my days with things other than worrying about the meeting. But mostly, I was worried about her kids.

I typed and retyped the message, determined to keep it light.

> Hey there! Emily and Jack are missing your kiddos and wondered if they could come over for a playdate this afternoon. Wasn't sure if they would be around or not. Let me know!

I copied Tim on the text and waited for a response. Three dots appeared immediately and then disappeared. Finally, the answer came through, from Tim.

> Great. Sending them over now.

I paused, my coffee cup in the air. It was definitely not the afternoon. I craned my neck around to the oven and saw the time: 7:15 a.m. But at least the kids would be safe over here.

———

"DO YOU GUYS have Godzilla movies?" Liz's son Carson asked as he walked through our front door, trailed by Luke. He set his backpack down on the wood floor, water leaking out of the bottom of it. "My lunch is in there." He shrugged before he scampered off into the family room.

I wondered if Tim had packed the lunch, or if Carson had done it himself. I peeked inside the backpack and saw a leaking water bottle, a bag of mini muffins, and Doritos. I still wasn't sure who had assembled it.

I walked into the family room, where Luke was happily tucked in next to Emily, Goldfish crumbs encircling them.

"Hey, Luke. How's everything? How's your mom doing?"

He didn't look at me, transfixed by the bright orange snack.

I didn't want to press the issue and possibly further traumatize the kids, so I decided to wait until later to try to gather any intel in a more subtle way.

"Are you hungry?" My words fell upon deaf ears as they remained focused on the iPad screen. I looked at my phone, to make sure Liz hadn't texted. Nothing. Normally she would have sent them with a full meal and a backpack full of crafting activities that she had found on Pinterest.

I felt a longing in my chest for my friend. Before all this happened, I had never stopped to think about Liz before. She was someone whom I didn't think about, who was always in the background. She was the constant, the one we all took for granted. The one who quietly folded the blankets at the end of the night and took out the recycling. The friend who texted the day after a party to ask if I needed help cleaning up and to say that she'd had a great time. She required almost nothing, and with a pang of regret, I realized we never gave her more than that.

The least I could do now was help her kids. I peeked my head in the room, and all the kids were still sitting quietly. As I walked upstairs to my bedside desk, I heard Jack say, "Did you know my nana is doing the face painting for the carnival?"

I sighed as I sat down on the edge of my bed, staring at the event binder. I needed at least ten more people to help out, and I was running out of options. As it was, I had my friends and their husbands, my mother-in-law, and Marianne Baker, who was making goodies for the cakewalk.

An idea popped into my head. Marianne and my mother-in-law had readily volunteered to help. The older ladies in the neighborhood were always so kind and helpful; I wondered if I could ask some of them to assist. Their grown children had attended the elementary school, and they were the ones who had started the carnival tradition. They might be willing to help out, even if only out of a sense of nostalgia.

I leaned forward to pick up the binder, and as I did, I glanced under the bed, to where I had stashed the Ouija board the night before. Confusion swept over me when I didn't see it. I shoved the binder aside and lay down flat on my stomach, feeling around the carpet with my arm. Nothing, except for some stray bobby pins and plenty of dust bunnies.

I stood up, hands on my hips, looking around the room. There was no way Mark could have moved it, since he'd gone to work before I was even awake. That left only a few more options, some of which were human.

Breathing rapidly, I checked under the bed again. Then, swallowing hard, I went first into Jack's room and looked around, checking under his bed.

Next, Emily's room. It was covered in laundry that she was supposed to put away, which I had grown tired of asking her to do and had kind of given up on, closing the door when I became overwhelmed at the state of it.

I knelt down and looked under her bed, afraid of what I might find.

I squinted into the darkness under her pale pink comforter and saw a rectangular box, the picture of the planchette and hands on the side. I shot my arm out and grabbed it, pulling it toward me. Standing, I tucked it under my arm, unsure of where to stash it. I had taken a step to leave when I noticed her tall, hot-pink, plastic Barbie Dreamhouse.

Normally the Barbies were half-dressed, hair sticking up everywhere, furniture out of place. So much so that when the state of it was particularly hilarious, I would text a picture to my friends, commenting on Barbie's apparent fraternity party the night before.

The first thing I noticed was that the furniture was all meticulously placed in the rooms. That was odd. Narrowing my eyes, I knelt down, taking in the scene. On the first floor, in the living room, Ken was splayed on the ground like a chalk outline in a crime scene. One arm was bent above his head, and the other had been removed from his body and snapped in half. His head had also been torn off and placed next to him.

In the bedroom, Skipper was in her bed, with all of her limbs torn off, her hair cut and scattered around the room. Next to her, her dog was lying on his side with his eyes scratched out.

My blood ran to ice as I took in the scene.

"Oh my God," I whispered.

In the next bedroom, the Midge doll that I had saved from when I was a kid and given to Emily was in the plastic closet, sitting on the floor. She was also headless.

Finally, in Barbie's bedroom, Barbie was dressed in a pink taffeta ball gown that had come with the Christmas collection doll from last year. She stood, smiling at me, hair resting around her shoulders. And in her hand she had a tiny plastic kitchen knife. What looked like red nail polish was splattered all over the front of her dress.

I put my hand over my mouth to muffle a strangled scream. With one quick motion, I swept the dolls out of the Dreamhouse and onto the floor. Ken's head rolled under Emily's bed, lost to the dust bunnies. Skipper's hair floated all around the carpet, and the dog somehow landed on all fours, looking at me.

A cold sweat began to form down my back. *Emily couldn't have done this, could she? And if she did, why? What was going through her head?*

Panic began to bubble in my chest. My vision narrowed to a tunnel as I lifted my bad ankle and swiftly kicked the Barbie house. Pain shot through my leg as the cheap plastic immediately buckled and the second story fell down onto the first, creating a rubble of hot-pink and purple plastic flowers. The maniacal Barbie rested on top, still holding the pink knife. Her perverted smile seemed to grow wider, her teeth longer.

Good girl. You saw what I did. Did you like it?

The scratching voice clawed its way through my ear canal and up through my brain. I gasped and tore out of the room, waves of pain running through my body.

"Mommy?" I heard Emily call from downstairs.

"Hold on. Just a second," I said before I ran into my bedroom and closed the door behind me. I closed my eyes as I sank down on the floor, tears running down my face. The Ouija board was still in my hands, and I threw it across the room. It exploded onto the carpet, the planchette bouncing across the floor as the board flipped over. The cardboard box ripped at the corners and settled onto the ground.

"Mommy?" Emily was outside of my door.

"Hold on," I said again as I tried to steady my breath.

"Are you sad? You sound sad," she said. Her little voice went straight to my heart, breaking it a little more.

What was wrong with my little girl?

I scooted out of the way of the door and opened it while sitting on the floor. She was still in her pajamas, hair tangled around her shoulders. Her face slackened with fright as she saw me.

"It's okay. I'm okay. Come in here for a minute." I tried to grab for her hand, but she moved away, her eyes growing wider. I lunged forward, and she gave a little shriek as I pulled her into the bedroom.

"Sit down. You're not in trouble, but I have to talk to you."

She sat cross-legged in front of me, her hands wringing in her lap, eyes cast toward the carpet.

I took a deep breath and exhaled slowly, trying to frame what I wanted to say in the least frightening way. I relaxed my shoulders and reached for her hands, holding them in mine.

"I saw your Barbie house."

She slowly lifted her head and cocked it to the side in confusion.

"Were you playing with it yesterday?" I tried to keep my voice steady, nonthreatening.

She looked over my left shoulder and pursed her lips. Then she shook her head. "No, Mommy. I didn't play with Barbie at all yesterday. I played with my American Girl dolls."

"Really? I think you might have played with it and forgot."

She denied it again. "But Carson wants to play with them after the movie."

I nodded, knowing there wasn't any way Carson had gone upstairs and created that . . . *scene* after he got here this morning.

I decided to move on and circle back to the Barbies after I had a chance to talk to Mark about it. "So, I found something under your bed. A board game."

She smiled and laughed. "That's a funny game. Amelia told me about it."

I raised my eyebrows. "Who is Amelia?" I tried to remember if I had seen that name on her class roster list. I didn't know everyone in her preschool class and of course had lost the paper copy of the list the second week of school.

"My friend," she said with a wide smile. "She's really funny and nice and gives me lots of hugs."

I wondered what kind of preschool friend would talk about a Ouija board, but Emily went to a Montessori preschool, where many of the parents were untraditional—by Winchester standards, anyway. One of the mothers sewed her own clothes and made kombucha. So I supposed it was possible that one of the parents was also into spiritualism and had a Ouija board.

"That's great, but that's something that Miss Jess gave me, and I had put it in a special place. I don't like that you took it from me and hid it." I lowered my chin.

She tucked her messy hair behind her ears and stuck her lower lip out. "Sorry, Mommy. But Amelia asked me to do it. She said I wouldn't get in trouble."

I shook my head. "You're not in trouble, but I don't understand. Is Amelia from school? When did you see her last?"

"I saw her last night," she said with a shrug. "When it was dark out. She sat on my bed, and I told her that I was sleeping, so she said she would leave after I got the board."

My body froze, ice running down my shoulders as they stiffened into place. I sat up straighter.

"Is Amelia your imaginary friend?" My voice was hoarse, barely above a whisper.

She shook her head. "No, she's real."

"Emily, honey." I reached forward and grabbed her hands again. "No one came over last night. There wasn't anyone in your room when you were sleeping."

She pulled her hands from mine and frowned. "There was. She told me to get the board and put it under my bed, and then she left when I did it."

My voice went up an octave. "That's not possible."

Emily rolled her eyes. "It is."

The standoff continued, each of us looking at the other with suspicion. I knew when she had an idea in her head, there was no way I could convince her otherwise. She was like that even as a baby. If she saw something she wanted, there would be no substitute. It was her way or no way, on principle alone.

I knew lots of kids who had imaginary friends on whom they blamed anything naughty. Summer had melted crayons in Jess's microwave and blamed it on Susie, who she said was a half-unicorn, half-tiger who wanted to make melted crayon art. After a night of Mr. Clean Magic Erasers, Jess had just bought a new microwave.

I decided to switch tactics. "How old is Amelia?"

She beamed, assuming I had accepted Amelia's existence. "I don't know. She never told me, but she told me her favorite snack."

I smiled, despite the situation. "Sounds like you guys are good friends, then."

"Yes. She wears funny clothes and talks kind of weird, but she plays with me and it's really fun." She glanced over her shoulder at the open doorway. "Can I go watch the movie now?"

I shook my head. "Not yet. That board game is not for children, okay? And I don't like that you took it. But I am more worried about your Barbies. They are in kind of a scary scene in your house. Did Amelia do that, too?"

She abruptly stood up and ran to her room. I struggled to stand and chase after her, grasping at her pajamas but only grabbing air.

"No, wait—"

She screamed when she got to her room. I arrived a second later to see her pointing at it, red-faced.

"You ruined my house! It's broken now!" Her hands balled into fists as she looked at me, eyes flashing with rage.

"I'm sorry. I tripped on it." I fumbled for words. "But I did get scared when I saw what the Barbies were doing." I knelt down in front of her on one knee. "It scared me, Emily. It looked like Barbie was trying to hurt people."

She slowly turned toward the crumpled Dreamhouse, the hot-pink plastic piled on top of itself and the dolls' legs sticking out of the mess.

"She was."

I leaned forward. "What did you say?"

"She *was* trying to hurt people." She leaned forward and cupped a hand around my ear. "Amelia told me."

I started to tremble. "What did she tell you?" I whispered back.

Her breath was hot in my ear. "That people are going to die."

CHAPTER

I SPLASHED SOME COLD water on my face in the bathroom
after sending Emily back downstairs. My hands were shaking as
I brought them to my face and closed my eyes. Something was
happening with her. To her. This was officially not a Satanic Panic
situation; this was real.

I dried my face with a hand towel and pulled my phone out of
my pocket, checking to see if Mark had replied to the text I sent
him: Call me.

Nothing.

I clutched my phone in frustration. I knew he was in meetings
all day and likely wouldn't see the message until late that afternoon, if at all before he got home. Which meant I was on my own
to deal with this for the day.

My fingers wildly shaking, I typed out a text to Jess and Melissa, trying to explain what I'd seen. As I waited for a response, I
peeked out of the bathroom window toward Liz's house. The

chimney spouted a thin stream of smoke, as it had the other day. I swallowed hard. At least her children were here, safe. Or what I had assumed was safe.

I looked down at the Ouija board on my bedroom floor. My first instinct was to throw it in the trash. Yet, I wondered if Emily's story was true. Could it possibly be that there was something supernatural hanging around? Was that force trying to hide it for a reason?

Even though the last thing I wanted to do was touch it, I picked it up with two fingers on each hand and stashed it on a high shelf in my closet, covering it with a paint-splattered red sweatshirt.

My phone dinged with a text from Melissa.

> I'm not sure what is happening. I had awful dreams all night long, about the rabbits in your backyard, except it was the three of us who were killed. And then when I woke up, I had this—

I held my breath as I waited for the next text. What could she have?

Finally, an image came through. It was a picture of Melissa's upper arm, where she was holding up her sleeve. On her skin was a red mark, bleeding in the middle, with purple and black lines radiating outward. I sucked in a breath as I slowly lifted the leg of my pants and held the phone next to my ankle.

It was the same mark as on my leg, the same mark from the pit.

I whimpered and dropped my phone onto the bathroom floor with a loud crack, the screen shattering.

I felt tears welling up as I reached for the phone and squinted at the screen, trying to reply to the text. Jess had already done so.

Am I next? she said.

That's not all, Melissa replied. I saw Liz this morning walking Bucky. I passed her house and saw her through the window. She looks really awful. Her face was almost gray, and it looked like her hair had been falling out. You guys, this is getting really scary.

I took a deep breath and again looked over at Liz's house, at the trail of smoke wafting up into the air.

Jess texted back, asking if she was ready to do the Ouija board now. Her answer came back immediately: No. Then she added, All of this started with the She Shed, when we were outside. Maybe the way to end it is there, also. What if there really is some swamp gas or poison that's making everyone go ballistic? I think we should try and seal it off.

It wasn't the Ouija board séance that Jess and I wanted, but it was a start.

CHAPTER

"I KNOW THIS WAS my idea, but I'm not sure we should be doing this," Melissa said as she crossed the street and met me on the corner of Maple Leaf and Seneca Drives. She was dressed in long black yoga pants and a black Lululemon tank.

I pointedly looked down at her upper arm, covered in a gauze bandage and surgical tape. "I didn't hear any other ideas this morning."

We turned as we heard a gate unlocking, and Jess slowly tip-toed out of her backyard, wearing dark shorts and a Green Bay Packers T-shirt. She wore fingerless weight-lifting gloves and a back brace like the ones that wrestlers wear in the Olympics. Slung around her shoulders was a black leather messenger bag. As she got closer, I saw that she had drawn in two black lines under her eyes, on her cheekbones, like a football player.

"I'm ready," she said as she adjusted her messenger bag. Her gaze moved down to Melissa's arm. "I'd like to get this over with before I end up with a matching crispy mark."

"I agree that all of this is weird, but if you really think it's su-pernatural, why Liz? Why *only* Liz?" Melissa said as she chewed her lip. "What if we're just delusional?"

Jess leaned over and tapped her gauze bandage, at which Melissa yelped in pain. "Is that delusional?"

Melissa straightened up and put her hands at her sides, a move I had seen only once, fortunately. It was her fighting stance, set before she delivered a termination to a subordinate or when she had stepped out of her car to confront a guy who rear-ended her and then called her a dumb bitch.

It meant you had ten seconds before you really saw what she was capable of.

I put my arm in between them. "Guys, stop. We can't start fighting now." I turned to Melissa. "Yes, this is probably crazy. Maybe it's only affecting Liz because she's the most open out of all of us. Open to good . . . and bad. She was a pediatric nurse and always took care of the sickest little ones. You don't get involved in a career like that without a big heart." Then, to Jess, "Hands to yourself." I looked at the bag. "What did you bring?"

She nodded and opened it, pulling out a large hunting knife. "We might need protection."

"Are you nuts?" Melissa said. "Why do you even have that?"

"I'm from Wisconsin," she said flatly. "Deer-hunting season. I got it at Mills Fleet Farm."

At one of our wine nights, Jess had tried to explain the lore of Fleet Farm. Peppered all over Wisconsin, apparently the stores were something of a cross between a Home Depot for Wisconsin-ites (read: hunting and fishing); a Kohl's, with casual clothing; and a grocery store. You could buy a new crossbow, a pair of kicky capri pants, and a case of beer all in the same location. Adding another layer to the mythology was that there were also Farm & Fleet stores that sold similar items, yet there was no connection between the owners.

"Fleet Farm?" Melissa shook her head. "I can't do this."

"You are doing it. We all are." I stepped aside and gestured toward the red wagon I had behind me. In it was the leftover fence wood from my backyard, nails, and a hammer.

We'd agreed to meet that night at 2:00 a.m., after everyone was asleep, and try to cover the pit as quickly and quietly as possible. We knew we didn't want to be around her house at the witching hour of 3:00 a.m. and figured an hour was more than enough time to get it done. We had discussed asking Tim for permission but couldn't imagine his reacting well. He'd probably ask us to sign liability waivers before entering the property. So we figured we would ask for forgiveness later after it worked.

Jess walked over and grabbed a side of the wagon while I lifted the other, as we thought it would make too much noise if we rolled it. Melissa didn't offer to help but did silently follow us down the street to Liz's backyard.

I took a deep breath, turned to Jess and Melissa, and nodded into the darkness before we crept into Liz's backyard, back to where it had all begun.

———

"WATCH OUT FOR those," I said as I pointed to a root from the locust tree on the side of Liz's house. The air held a faint odor of smoke, although the plumes from the chimney had stopped. It didn't smell like wood burning. It was something more acrid, like burning rubber.

Or melted wax, I thought with a shudder as I remembered the way her features ran into each other on the night everything started.

"Ope," Jess said as she tripped over the root despite the warning. The wagon between us jostled, rattling the hammer against the metal.

"Shhhh," I hissed as she regained her footing. Behind her, Melissa trailed, holding on to the end of her ponytail, keeping distance between herself and the house.

The house was dark, the windows black. The night air seemed heavier, as though someone had hit a pause button and all time had stopped. I nodded silently to Jess, and we slowly crept around to the corner of the house, where we would have to walk across the yard to the pit without any cover. I glanced around the corner to make sure the path was clear. All I saw was the blue plastic Adirondack chairs around the firepit. They were overturned, splayed on the concrete, and covered in dried mud.

An owl hooted. It sounded like a warning, like it knew what was coming next. Another owl responded. A mating call. I only knew this because one night Mark and I were kept awake by two owls, calling back and forth as we silently pleaded for them to just get it on already so we could sleep.

Melissa whispered, her country accent strong, "Y'all, I don't know about—"

I jerked my head toward the backyard. "Let's just get this over with."

"Fuck yes," Jess said back.

She came around to the side, and we faced each other, holding the wagon with the wood sticking out, the top of the boards pointing at Melissa, like stakes threatening a vampire. I nodded and we took a step forward, then another.

A light breeze ran through the yard, tinkling the wind chimes Liz had made with her children last summer. My breath caught as I heard them. I always thought of the movie *Twister* when I heard wind chimes, of the aluminum cans tinkling in warning when a storm was near. June and I had watched that movie over and over one summer, making emergency storm kits for the basement and monitoring every thunderstorm on the Weather Channel.

Jess was about to step forward again when my gaze was drawn to an object near the wind chimes. I froze, which caused her to stop suddenly, making the hammer rattle again. Melissa reacted too late and ran into one of the fence posts, grunting as it thudded against her chest.

I shook my head as I squinted into the darkness, trying to make out the shape. It was over by the tiki hut on the opposite side of the yard, with the pit in front of us.

"Wait, is that—" I leaned forward even more, causing Jess to shift the weight of the wagon toward her body.

"What?" Melissa sounded like the word escaped her lips without her permission.

The more I stared at the shape, the darker it became. And then, nothing. There was a wall of black around the tiki hut, the fake bamboo and straw silent. An optical illusion.

I turned back, taking my share of the weight from the wagon again. "Nothing. I thought I saw something. Let's go."

The lawn crunched under our feet. I could feel the moisture

from the ground soaking into my running shoes. "Careful," I warned my friends as we reached the back of the lawn, peppered with raised roots and unseen divots. The worst possible thing that could happen was one of us falling into the pit.

Then I saw it in the corner. Dirt was still piled around it, construction still paused. As we got closer, I motioned for Jess to start lowering the wagon. I bent down at the waist, feeling my back strain, and I knew I would spend the next day becoming very acquainted with my heating pad. Jess bent her legs and kept her back straight, her backside moving expertly like a hinge, in a perfect squat. Melissa hovered behind us, her phone in her hand, ready to make a run for it.

In my peripheral vision, I saw a light turn on in Emily's room. My heart began to pound as I thought of the last time I was in the backyard, when Liz pushed me. Emily's light had turned on then, too.

We had to hurry.

I forced myself to look down into the pit, at the hole where everything had begun. I was surprised to find that I could see the bottom of it. From my memories of trauma and terror, it was dark, bottomless. In my nightmares, the mist rose again.

At the bottom, nestled in the mud, were white shapes. I silently pointed to them, and Jess turned her head. I leaned closer.

I blinked and looked again, but there was no mistaking what they were.

They were bones.

As my eyes adjusted to the darkness, I saw that the bottom was scattered with them. White bones dotting the mud, like dust blowing over a surface.

I don't know how I knew, but I did: they were human bones.

And then we heard it. A scraping sound that ripped into the night air. It wasn't loud, but the jagged edges of the noise peppered us like razor-sharp confetti. We froze, the wagon between us. I looked at Jess, and her eyes were wide.

Get down, she mouthed to me as she looked over my shoulders.

The hairs on the back of my neck stood at attention but I didn't dare turn around. I mirrored Jess's actions and put a knee on the ground, slowly lowering the wagon, as I saw Melissa side-shimmy behind a large tree trunk.

Jess shook her head slightly, her eyes still on me. It was dark, but I could see they were full of fear. The scraping behind me continued, growing louder and longer until it was one continuous noise. My hands trembled as they left the wagon, and I ducked my head and then turned and looked over my left shoulder.

I inhaled sharply at what I saw. It was Liz, dragging furniture across the concrete patio toward the tiki hut. She was naked, her skin pale white against the moon, and her hair was around her face like a curtain as she threw her body weight backward and slid the furniture across the concrete, one linear foot at a time. Even though I was several feet from her, I could see the scratches on her body. They were everywhere, red angry lines crisscrossing her legs and stomach.

I started breathing heavily, my chest pumping up and down. I didn't dare turn around and look at Jess, figuring if we remained still, Liz couldn't see us, like she was the T. rex in *Jurassic Park*.

The scraping stopped as Liz reached the tiki hut with the coffee table. She stood up and exhaled, her back to me. Her exhalation sounded guttural, like a Bobcat coming to a stop after a long day of construction. She put her hands on her hips and cocked her head to the side, as though she was listening to something. I froze, not moving even at the high-pitched whine of a mosquito in my ear.

I waited for her to turn around, to spot us. I waited for us to be thrown in with the bones.

Yet after a pregnant pause, she sat down on one of the tiki hut chairs, facing away from us. She put her bare feet up on the coffee table next to her and leaned back.

It was then that I finally turned to Jess, my neck protesting. I would have to put a heating pad on that the next day, too. I jerked my head toward the side of the house.

Let's go.

She nodded and made a lifting motion, her biceps flexing under the wagon. We slowly lifted it, inch by inch, my muscles crying out in pain and my legs shaking with the effort. When we were upright, we kept eye contact and made steps together, like a synchronized dance. Melissa extricated herself from her tree camouflage and began to wave us over, urging us to move faster.

Just as we were about to get to the side of the house, and relative safety, a laugh stopped us. Liz was laughing to herself. It was a low-pitched tone, more like a rumble. We turned, and from that vantage point, we could see her face. Her mouth was stretched wide, wider than was humanly possible, so the corners of her lips met her ears. We could see all of her teeth, or what was left of them.

She brought a hand up to her chin, almost in thought. Even from across the yard, I could see that she was missing fingernails. She moved her hand to the top of her head, brushing her hair back. It was then that I noticed her hair was patchy, and I could see her scalp in places.

It was like watching someone decay in real time.

We kept moving, the hammer jostling around, but at that point, we didn't care. We knew we just needed to get out. We didn't stop moving until we were back in front of Jess's house. We set the wagon down on her lawn and stood there, staring at each other. Jess's eyes filled with tears as she crossed her arms over her chest, and Melissa had her hands over her head as she bent down, face to knees.

And all I could think of was this: Emily was right. She wanted our bones in that pit next.

CHAPTER 22

I **SNUCK BACK INSIDE** my house and checked on Emily. She was asleep, her light off again. I carefully crept into my bedroom and lay down next to Mark in bed, listening to his heavy breathing as I lowered my body onto the mattress. I'd left the wagon in the garage and slowly taken the stairs, careful not to step on the creaky wood parts. I felt like a teenager sneaking back in after spending a night doing things I shouldn't have.

The clock on my phone read 3:02 a.m. The kids would be awake in a few hours, so I closed my eyes and tried to block out everything that had happened in Liz's backyard. I had just started to drift off when flashes of her appearance—bald patches, scratched-up skin, missing fingernails—caused me to open my eyes again.

Her deteriorating exterior reminded me too much of June's in her last few months. June would show up at my parents' house, or on my front doorstep, with her skin pallid and open sores on her face. Before she said a word and asked for money, I'd know that she was using again. And yet I let her in every time, gave her what money I could, fed her a decent meal. Before she disappeared again. When she would go underground, it was like she had died. I didn't know if I would see her again, and part of me was ashamed to admit that I hoped I wouldn't. So by the time I got the call that she actually had truly passed away, it felt like I had been preparing for that moment for far too long.

The official police report said that she was found under a high-way overpass. The first people to see her and call the police were on their way to work, doing normal things. They probably had a cup of coffee in hand, happy to start their day early. Until they looked down as they crossed Forty-Seventh Street.

Mark was the one who told me. I had slept through the calls and texts from my parents. It was he who had to wake me up, he who had to close the door and have his parents come get the kids while I screamed.

The days following her death were a blur of funeral arrange-ments, of responding to people who said, "There are no words," of picking out what people should eat at the luncheon, of getting the toxicology report that told us what we already knew: a large quan-tity of powerful drugs had been coursing through her body.

But it had haunted me ever since.

I tried to close my eyes again and fall asleep, tried to will my body to forget what it had experienced. I'd started to drift off when a low rumble pricked at my ears.

At first, I thought it was the distant sound of the commuter train going through downtown Winchester. We were a couple of miles away but could still hear the click-clack of the train tracks when the wind blew the right way. But then it got louder in waves before quieting again, like the wail of a tornado siren. And it wasn't the soothing sound of a train. It was more of a screeching, moaning sound. It sounded like an animal in pain. Or a person.

I was too afraid to look out of my bedroom window, too scared to see what was outside. It seemed to be coming from the side of my house, in the direction of Liz's backyard.

Keening, like we had read in the demonology book. A siren's call to other demons to join her in our realm.

I put a pillow over my head to block out the noise and pressed it to my skull.

I WOKE UP to the sound of laughter. I shot up in bed, the pillow falling to the floor. My head felt heavy, like I had a hangover, and my eyes were crusted with sleep. I looked next to me. Mark was already up and likely gone, and I didn't hear the kids downstairs yet.

I must have dreamed it, although there had been nothing to laugh about in my dreams. They were filled with bones and broken skin. With skulls and missing fingernails. With June at the bottom of the She Shed pit, arms stretched upward as I tried to grab her and couldn't.

I put my feet up on the edge of the bed frame, my burn mark protesting. It had scabbed over, but it was tight and inflexible, like the skin had begrudgingly agreed to heal but it had a few demands. I still needed to make an appointment with a plastic surgeon, but the thought of possibly having a skin graft performed turned my stomach. The rest of my body ached from carrying the wagon.

I rubbed my face and reached over to take a sip of water from the glass on my desk, when the framed photo in the corner caught my eye.

It was a picture of me, Jess, Melissa, and Liz from April. We were on Jess's front porch, sitting in patio chairs, holding up champagne glasses to toast my birthday. Del had snapped it with my phone, and I had printed it out and given each of my friends a copy in a gold frame. In the picture, we were laughing, eyes bright, with big smiles.

But the image was different now.

Our eyes were colored in, black from ink, holes in our heads. Empty. Missing. Like conduits that allowed the darkness to pour in. Like the She Shed pit.

Around the edges of the photo mat were symbols and letters. The symbols looked like they were part of a complicated math problem, with triangles intersecting and clusters of circles. In each corner of the picture was a dark spiral that looked like it had been traced many times, the ink seeping into the paper and nearly ripping it.

There was a dark scribble on my leg, with dots coming out of it like blood. On Melissa there was the same mark, but on her upper arm. I picked up the photo and peered down at it, a wave of fear slowly filling my body. Then I saw that Jess also had a mark, on her cheek. Liz was unmarked, except for the dark holes for her eyes.

I wondered whether Emily could have done this, too, or maybe I unconsciously created it in my sleep.

My hands shaking, I turned the frame over and opened it up, pulling the picture out. In between Liz and Melissa were tiny letters, easily missed, and written horizontally and slightly diagonal. The first letter touched Liz, and the last extended to Melissa.

I brought the page to my face and squinted.

It was the word "help," written in my handwriting.

I dropped the picture onto my desk, watching it flutter when I wanted it to plummet to the ground, where I could step on it or kick it.

I picked it up, ready to crumple it into a ball and throw it out, to pretend that I never saw it, but I looked at the word again.

Help.

I then noticed that there was another word underneath it. "Me."

Help me.

My ears rushed with noise, panic bubbling up through my chest. I knew it was a message from Liz, wherever she was. She was asking us, specifically, for our help.

But how on earth (or in hell, I supposed) were we supposed to do that?

I had no idea how, but we had to step up our efforts to save her, and all of us.

CHAPTER

"**DO YOU THINK** I can call the regular police line, or is 9-1-1 appropriate?" Melissa paused over her phone, index finger pointed at the screen.

I held up the photo for proof and tapped it. "'Help me.' She wants our help. The police or EMTs can't do that. She's asking us, Melissa. She needs *us*."

Melissa lowered her chin and pursed her lips, the beginning of a glare. "How are we supposed to do that? She should try contacting a priest. Or an exorcist. Or a therapist."

"We are her friends. Don't you care—"

"Guys, enough," Jess said from the backseat. She leaned forward and put her elbows on the sides of the driver and passenger seats. "Enough," she said again. "Being assholes to each other isn't going to help."

We were in my SUV, parked in my driveway. After I'd fed the

kids breakfast and tried to scrub the dried maple syrup off the edges of my kitchen island before I gave up and let Rocky have a go at it, I texted both of them the picture. Melissa said she would stop home on her lunch break, and Jess agreed to come at the same time.

I met them in my driveway and pointed to my car, as it was the only place I could guarantee we wouldn't be heard. I wasn't comfortable talking in the backyard, with the specter of Liz's house casting a shadow over us.

Melissa made a harrumph sound and adjusted the air-conditioning vent so it pointed at her face. It blew her hair back, and she closed her eyes. Her makeup was still perfect, her lipstick unsmudged. She wore a black sheath and black-and-white pumps, in contrast to my Target leggings and tank top with small holes in the front. Jess wore a bathing suit, since she was apparently about to inflate the baby pool in her front yard. Of course she hadn't put on a cover-up. It was pointless, she said, like washing your car during a rainstorm.

I swallowed hard. "I'm really worried about Emily. For whatever reason, this is all affecting her, too." I felt the beginning of tears forming in my eyes. "Please, just hear me out."

"So what do you suggest?" Melissa said, eyes still closed.

"I read in one of those library books that hauntings and possessions or . . . whatever you want to call it," I added when Melissa opened one eye and looked at me, "usually start with an event. A place. A catalyst. I'm talking about more than the She Shed. I'm talking about whatever the construction unearthed."

I pulled *Everyday Demons*—a ridiculous title that made it sound like demons were as ordinary as using a Crock-Pot—

out from between the console and the driver's seat and began to read.

"'Demons do not choose who or where to invade at random. They require a calling or a summons. That can be in the form of another demon, one who has already entered the human realm, ripping a larger hole for them to enter, or in the form of a tragedy. An event that occurs that is so horrific that it leaves a lasting impact on the location. When such an event occurs, it leaves the area vulnerable and more accessible to demonic forces, since they feed off trauma and pain.'"

I looked up and then continued.

"'Demons attach themselves to low frequencies, drawn like moths to a flame to anyone who is already feeling darkness. Once a demon has made contact with a person, it will stay with them until drastic measures are taken, usually in the form of an exorcism. But a successful exorcism requires knowledge of who the demon is and why they have come.'"

"Whoa," Jess said.

I turned around and nodded, putting my leg up on the driver's seat and tucking my knee to my chest. "Logically, we should start there. Remember the movie *Poltergeist*? Everything happened because they built on a cemetery. Maybe there's something like that here."

"Logically," Melissa repeated pointedly, "we should call the police and Child Protective Services."

"I still think we need to use the Ouija board," Jess said.

Melissa shook her head. "I already told you no, so stop asking." She sighed. "But it does make sense to look into the history of the land. Maybe it will help us find a rational explanation." She reached for the door. "I have a slow afternoon tomorrow, so I can join you two demon-hunting wonder twins. I have to go back to the office and lead a team meeting on not sending porn emails on company accounts."

"Killjoy," Jess said.

CHAPTER

24

DOWNTOWN WINCHESTER HAD kept up with the times and had a Starbucks, a craft brewery, a wine store, and a housewares store that sold things like throw pillows sporting *Winchester Born and Raised*. There were a few brunch restaurants scattered around, an upscale gastropub, and a Mexican restaurant known for their grapefruit margaritas, which people sipped at the sidewalk tables. Out of place among the other establishments, the Winchester Historical Society was located in an old church, a relic from when the town was founded. It was a looming stone structure, rising high above the rest of the downtown area, with three large turrets pointing to the sky like sharp black fingernails.

That morning, I'd emailed a docent at the society, to give her a heads-up that we would be arriving. Then a wave of anxiety filled my chest as I spotted the carnival binder on my desk and remembered I still didn't have enough volunteers. I thought again about asking some of the older women to help. Before I could talk myself out of it, I picked up the phone and called Marianne Baker. She seemed delighted to offer her help and said she would talk to the other women at their bunco game later that day. I was so relieved that I had to hold back tears when we ended the call.

As my friends and I walked up to the historical society, the shadow of the building blanketed us, and a strange sense of dread began to build among the group. We climbed up the cracked stone steps to the large archway, pushed open the heavy wooden door, and found a beautiful older woman waiting for us.

Mary Ellen Peabody, the docent I had emailed, was in her seventies but looked like an Instagram filter that had taken a picture of a much younger woman and aged her. Her hot-pink skirt suit and dangling turquoise earrings swished as she leaned forward and placed her elbows on the display glass.

"I'm so happy you all are here!" said Mary Ellen, a look of genuine delight on her face. "I know your neighborhood! Whispering Farms used to be one of the largest farms in the area, before it was eventually sold and then incorporated into Winchester." She tapped a coral fingernail on her lined cheek.

"Great. Can you give all the documents to us?" Melissa said impatiently as she placed her hand on the case. Catching flies with honey when vinegar was available had never been her style.

I shot her a warning look and then turned to Mary Ellen. "We would love to see whatever you might be willing to share."

When Mary Ellen disappeared into the bowels of the historical society, I looked at Melissa. "We have to be nice to her."

She raised an eyebrow. "Look where being nice got Liz."

Jess snort-laughed and then nudged Melissa with her hip. "Good one."

After a moment, Mary Ellen reappeared with two leather binders and an armful of documents in plastic sheeting. She gave us an appraising look before setting it all down on the glass top. She turned to me and said, "I need someone to sign out the materials before I can let you peruse them." Her eyes slid to Jess and Melissa before she pushed the sign-out sheet and a pen in my direction.

Stifling a laugh at the fact that Mary Ellen deemed my friends untrustworthy, I wrote my name with a flourish, and then Jess and Melissa gathered the materials and followed me to a long wooden table in the center of the research room. The research room was in what looked to be one of the former chapels of the church. It was markedly cooler than the rest of the building, and the stone walls extended up to the ceiling, giving the space the feeling of a cave. I didn't want to think about what kind of as-yet-undiscovered species of poisonous spiders lurked in the corners.

We spread the materials out onto the table and stood, looking down at them from a high vantage point.

"Look at this: 1965," Melissa said as she tapped one of the documents. We leaned in and squinted, looking for Whispering Farms. Winchester in 1965 looked nothing like it did today. The houses were interspersed with large swaths of farmland, and present-day subdivisions with hundreds of houses were then unbroken squares on the map.

I ran my finger along Orchard Road, the main thoroughfare to Whispering Farms.

"Look! There's us." Our houses were among the first to be built in our neighborhood—that much we knew—but it was startling to see only ten houses clustered around makeshift cul-de-sacs and the rest of the map as empty space.

"Not much has changed except for Melissa's." Jess's, Liz's, and my houses were all essentially the same in the photograph, save for a few trees removed and the front porch addition on Jess's house. Melissa's original house had been torn down and a new one built a couple of years before she moved in.

"Now you see why the builder tore it down," Melissa said. The original house was a small ranch, built like an army barrack. A perfect one-story rectangle surrounded by an enormous yard.

"Here's an older map," Jess said as she slid another toward us. "Nineteen forty-two."

Held next to the one from 1965, the map from 1942 showed none of our houses. The land was completely open and more populated with trees in dark, shadowy clusters.

"Hey, there, apple trees," Jess said. We had heard from the older residents in our subdivision that everything around us used to be part of an apple orchard, although that was the extent of their knowledge. That was where Orchard Road got its moniker.

"Shouldn't there be a farmhouse somewhere? For the family, I mean," Melissa said. "They had to have a house somewhere. It's not like the apples picked themselves."

"Weird," Jess said.

We peered at the map but couldn't locate anything resembling a house. So I scanned the other papers and slid another toward me. This one was labeled 1875. It was nearly unmarked, with large farms crisscrossing the paper and only one road by our neighborhood. A small, dark shape was the only object close to where our houses would eventually be.

The shape was located at, according to my best guestimate, the intersection of my backyard with Jess's and Liz's. If all the fencing was removed and the land looked at as a whole, the dark rectangle covered a piece of each of our property. But the more I looked at it, the more it appeared to be mostly in Liz's backyard. Right where the She Shed pit was located.

I tapped at it. "X marks the spot. Or, a weird rectangle from the 1800s."

"That has to be a house," Melissa said as she leaned forward and squinted at it. "Tony has been doing some research on the former owners of our house, and no one lived there until the 1960s. We thought it was all open land that was part of the Reagan farm, three miles away."

"Yo, Mary Ellen," Jess called across the stone room, her voice bouncing against the walls with the acoustics of a minister preaching fire, brimstone, and the stoning of witches.

Mary Ellen appeared at the threshold, frowning, her earrings swinging back and forth like pendulums. "Yes?"

I tapped the dark rectangle. "Do you happen to know what this is? A farmhouse? It's really close to where we live."

Her face brightened. "Oh, you live on that street? That's where my best friend's daughter lives. Heather Hacker. I'm sure you all know her." She smiled proudly and then leaned in, her voice lowering to a whisper. "Her mom and I went to Winchester High together, and we were prom princesses."

Jess stifled a laugh and Melissa looked away, annoyed. I feigned a smile. "How wonderful. Yes, we do know Heather."

Mary Ellen beamed and then glanced down at the map. "Oh yes, that's the old Wanneberg farmhouse. They are the ones who owned the apple orchard. Until . . ." She trailed off and a dark look passed over her eyes.

We collectively leaned forward.

"Until what?" I said.

Her eyes flitted down to the paper and then back to us. "The Wanneberg farm was involved in a tragedy. A horror, really. Very, very sad." Her eyes slowly met ours, and I realized she knew exactly how much she was milking this moment.

"Keep it coming, Mary Ellen." Jess put her elbows on the table and rested her chin in her hands.

She cocked her head to the side, like she was trying to decide how much to tell us, and I saw Melissa roll her eyes in my peripheral vision.

When she decided she had paused long enough, she continued. "The Wanneberg family owned the apple orchards all around this area." She drew a circle in the air above the map around almost the entirety of Whispering Farms. "The land was first purchased by Mr. Wanneberg's father in the early 1800s after they came over from Germany. And then it was passed down to his eldest—and only surviving—son, Joseph."

She shifted and clasped her hands in front of her. "Joseph married Mavis, who was an immigrant from Ireland. Mavis had come over with her family when she was fifteen and met her husband through, of all things, an ad in the newspaper."

I lifted my eyebrows. "Mail-order bride?"

Mary Ellen nodded. "Surprisingly, yes. Marriage was a business deal, and the ads were the old social media."

"I have had a few people ask me out on Instagram," Jess said.

"They were Russian bots, Jess. Bots with great taste in women, but still bots," Melissa said. She looked at Mary Ellen. "Please continue. I'm waiting for the horror, other than living in the middle of nowhere with a husband you barely know."

"Being in the middle of nowhere was part of it, actually. The Wannebergs had two children: a boy and girl. And Mavis was hundreds of miles from her family, who lived in Iowa, and the farmhouse was fairly isolated from anyone." She pointed down at the map, and we could see that the closest farm was miles from the Wanneberg place.

She continued. "There were reports that Mavis had been mentally unstable long before she arrived at the farm, although the prevailing thought is that it was the farm itself that made her the way she was. That being by herself, with two children, for long periods of time while tending to the farm while her husband worked in the orchards was what changed her."

"So what happened?" I whispered.

"It's said that the isolation finally got to her one night, and she snapped. She killed her entire family—her children, husband, even the family dog. She murdered them and buried them in the backyard. They weren't discovered until nearly a week later." Mary Ellen leaned forward and steepled her hands together. "She was found behind the house, dead from exposure, next to the grave where she had buried her children and husband and dog." She leaned back and crossed her arms over her chest, satisfied at our stunned silence.

I thought of Emily's "friend," Amelia. "Do you know the names of the children, by chance?"

Mary Ellen twisted her head to the side and then glanced down at the papers, running a finger down the page. "Looks like they were Josiah and Amelia."

My heart nearly stopped, and my arms began to prickle with goose bumps. An electric current ran through my body as I looked down at the map, at the seemingly innocuous dark rectangle, and tried to reconcile it with the horror of what Mary Ellen had just told us. Jess put her hands on either side of her face, her mouth hanging open, while I froze in place, my shoulders unable to move.

Melissa was the first to regain her composure. "What happened after they found Mavis and her family?"

Mary Ellen looked disappointed that our fugue state hadn't lasted longer, and I suspected that she was the school gossip in high school, a human vault of secrets that she revealed when it suited her.

"The land was auctioned off by the town after no one claimed it. I doubt anyone wanted to take ownership of a place where such a tragedy had occurred. The orchard was purchased by the Kingery family, who eventually developed it into your subdivision in the 1960s," she said.

I cleared my throat and asked the question that I almost didn't want the answer to. "What happened to the bodies?"

Mary Ellen's upper lip curled. "I suppose they were reinterred in a local cemetery, although that was never documented."

Jess shook her head, her hands still on her face. "Nope. They weren't."

Melissa's head jerked as Mary Ellen slowly looked at Jess. "Why do you say that?" Mary Ellen asked.

I put a hand up. "She's kidding. Right?" I shot Jess a murderous look, and she shrugged. "Being home with the kids for the summer has made us all a little off-kilter." I forced a laugh, and Melissa and Jess did the same.

Mary Ellen slowly looked at us, her eyes stopping at each one, and I knew our time was short before she got suspicious. I had the feeling that as soon as we left, she would be on the phone with Heather's mom, telling her about us.

We thanked her and quickly left, walking normally out of the historical society before it was safe to remove the veneer, then we huddled around the sidewalk like teenagers trying to light a contraband joint, next to a reproduction of a 1960s advertisement:

Want to make a better life for your family?

Want a safe home, away from the dirt and noise of the city?

Want a neighborhood respite, filled with children and well-kept lawns?

Then come to Winchester, Illinois, and be a founding member of Whispering Farms subdivision! With easy access on the train to downtown Chicago, and major highways just minutes away, Whispering Farms is the perfect, safe place to raise a happy family.

As I put on sunglasses to block the bright sunlight, visions of Mavis's murdered family danced behind my eyes.

"Do you think Emily is in danger?" Melissa said on the sidewalk.

I swallowed hard as I thought of Emily's Barbie Dreamhouse

and the tableau of two dead children and their dog. I knew it was Mavis's daughter trying to communicate with her, warn her that Mavis was back. "I hope not, but I'm scared. Now do you believe that this is something supernatural?"

"Demonic," Jess added quickly. "We need to use the Ouija board to talk to Mavis. Amelia already told Emily that more people are going to die."

The color drained from Melissa's face as she crossed her arms over her stomach. She started to turn away, toward the car.

I reached my hand out to stop her. "Please, Melissa. I'm going to do it anyway, because it's the only idea I have left. But I want you to be there. Remember the bracelets Liz gave us before all this started? *'Stronger with You,'*" I said.

She took in a deep breath before she lowered her sunglasses. "Everything inside me is saying no, but I'll do it. For you guys, and for Liz."

CHAPTER

25

THE PARKING LOT of Stoughton Lake Forest Preserve was nearly empty when I pulled in for the phone interview for the social worker position at Monarch Hospice. I arrived twenty minutes before the scheduled call, earbuds next to me. I knew there was no way I could take the call at home and not be interrupted, so Mark had offered to work from home for the morning.

As the minutes ticked on toward the scheduled interview, my anxiety grew exponentially worse. I reviewed my notes and tried to stay calm. Yet I still jumped when my phone buzzed.

"This is Amy," I said at the same time that my Apple Watch chose to activate and answer the call, resulting in an echo.

"Amy Foster?" Dale Keane, the hiring manager, said.

"Yes, yes," I said, reaching down and yanking my watch off. "So sorry." Not the way I wanted to start the call.

"No problem at all. Thanks for taking the time to speak with me about the social worker position here at Monarch. I would love it if you would tell me a little about yourself. I have your résumé here, but I'd appreciate it if you went through it." I heard rustling in the background, and it sounded like he muted his side of the call.

My nerves began to spark. "Well, I graduated with my MSW . . ." I detailed my experience, ending with when I left the workforce after my children were born.

"Great, great. I see here that you have experience working with hospice patients in a hospital setting. As I'm sure you're aware, it's a special skill set to work with these families. Since our focus is on palliative care—pain relief and comfort—we help families and patients prepare for the end-of-life decision-making and support them. We help family members cope with the death of a loved one, to put it simply," he said.

"Yes, I am clear on that point." I tightened my jaw and reminded myself to remain professional, even though thoughts of June began to cloud my mind.

There was no coping with her death. How could anyone explain that the little sister who'd run through the sprinkler on the front lawn with me, who'd made up silly dances to cassettes on my pink portable radio, whom I'd taught to do a back walkover in our basement, had died? She would never have a promotion, wedding, children, grandchildren. She'd barely had a moment of true happiness in her last years. She was filled with self-loathing and shame from all the chaos she caused, and that was the one comforting thought that her death had given me: that she didn't have to hate herself anymore.

He continued. "Many times, families have a difficult time accepting that it is the end. We find that patients themselves are more amenable to the concept, really. So much of the job of the social worker here is to provide that emotional support, and it can be somewhat taxing. But we need to help."

Help me.

My throat constricted as I thought of Liz's message. I'd tried to help June and failed and was on the path to fail with Liz, too. Fear and panic flooded me, making me nearly forget the phone in my hand.

"Ms. Foster?" Dale said. "Are you still there?"

"Yes, I apologize again. My phone connection seems to be a little wonky. I absolutely understand what the patients and their families require and would look forward to providing that."

But as I said the words, doubt ran through my blood.

My voice cracked as I added, "I have a strong desire to help others."

The interview ended with Dale saying he would be in touch, and I sat in my car for several minutes with my eyes closed, air-conditioning on full blast, willing myself not to break down. I had gotten so skilled at shoving away the difficult feelings of my sister's death. I had been able to compartmentalize my grief and trauma over her death in almost every situation. Deflect any questions or concerns. I hadn't been prepared for them to surface at such an inopportune moment.

Especially at a time when I seemed to be losing someone else I loved.

———

THE NEXT DAY, as I wrote down a recipe for red, white, and blue M&M's brownies, I had to concentrate on the ingredients—flour, sugar, vanilla extract—to keep my thoughts from returning to Mavis and her family.

When Whispering Farms was built back in the 1960s, it was billed as an engineered neighborhood for families. It was touted as a suburb that had it all. The best place to have kids, to form neighborhood friendships.

Little did they know that they were building on top of an evil darkness, a suppressed rage that patiently waited for someone to discover it and unleash it. Mavis would have her revenge, if she only bided her time.

As I pulled the dry ingredients out from the pantry, I thought about her and what life must have been like to drive her to do such a thing. It was unknowable, unthinkable, but part of me still understood. She was isolated from her parents, her family. In a strange country where she didn't know anyone, at a time when tolerance wasn't a virtue. Long days with her children and dark, cold nights at the house. I imagined that all she wanted was friendship. Someone to listen, someone to commiserate with.

Before the time of social media and houses so close we could peer into each other's bedrooms. Before the time when taking your dog for a walk gave you the opportunity—or misfortune, depending on who you saw—to chat with a neighbor. There were so many times when I was frustrated and angry with the monotony of my life, and seeing one of my friends was a balm for my mood. Even though Winchester often felt suffocating, like living in a scaled-down *Truman Show*, and I couldn't so much as go to the grocery store without social interaction, if our family lived alone in an isolated farmhouse without anyone around at all, I didn't know what I would do.

The madness must have crept in like the autumn chill. Little by little, until one morning the air held a bite that couldn't be ignored, a warning.

Until it was too late, and the snow had already fallen and the ground was frozen solid. And everything around was dead.

I shook my head and opened the kitchen window to let summer air blow through the house before I had to close it in the afternoon when the sun rose high. I focused on slowly stirring the batter with a rubber spatula shaped like a dinosaur that the kids had bought for me last Mother's Day.

That night was the annual Winchester Fourth of July fireworks. As was tradition, the Whispering Farms neighbors would gather in Big Rock Park in the center of town to watch the fireworks and then retire back to the neighborhood to drink wine and beer on patios and front porches while the kids ran around with sparklers and glow sticks.

I hadn't told Mark what we'd learned about Amelia and Mavis's family, as I was still trying to figure out the right way to present the information. It seemed too important to mention in a passing conversation, and I had prioritized telling him about the less than ideal job interview. And now it was time for the Fourth of July festivities and everything after.

It would be a long evening, although my friends and I had planned for a longer one than usual. The time to use the Ouija board had come, and we were going to communicate with Liz and find out what dark plans Mavis had for our neighborhood.

CHAPTER 26

I BROUGHT REINFORCEMENTS," Jess called as she walked through my front door without knocking. She stepped into the dark foyer and made her way to where I stood in the kitchen. In her hands, she held a half-empty American flag tray of clear Jell-O shots.

Melissa appeared next to me and shook her head. "No way. I saw people's faces when they tried those in Big Rock Park."

Jess laughed and moved the tray closer to us. "Live a little."

"I do want to live, and that's why I won't try it." Melissa turned and walked back into the kitchen and sat at the island, Tony's leftover caprese salad in front of her. He'd told me about how he made the burrata himself over two days. And then he'd unveiled his famous ribs, which he spent three days cooking in the sous vide before finishing them off in the smoker.

Usually, I would elbow out any neighbor to grab a slab, but I had looked at the bones and they'd turned my stomach. All I could think of was the bones at the bottom of the pit.

Melissa pulled a stack of papers out of her messenger bag and spread them on the kitchen island. "The mock-ups for the carnival signage."

I peered down at the brightly colored papers advertising the various games, concessions, and prize tables. There was also a banner to be hung under a rainbow balloon arch that read, *I Scream, You Scream, We All Scream for Ice Cream*.

"This looks great, Melissa. I so appreciate it." I turned to Jess. "Is the bounce house taken care of?"

"Oh yeah. I had a hookup, so I got it under budget," she said proudly.

I smiled. "Great. I just wanted to get that out of the way before the rest of tonight." I sighed. "A final moment of normalcy."

After the chaos of the fireworks and the neighborhood picnic—during which we'd feigned surprise that Liz and her family weren't there—we'd put the kids to bed upstairs, and Mark had gone to Jess's house to sit around their firepit and try Del's new Croatian liquor that had just arrived. He told me Tim had texted that he would meet up with the guys. I was surprised and wanted to ask more, but I simply told him my friends were coming over. I hoped that Tim would confide in the husbands, although it was doubtful. I didn't tell Mark we were using the Ouija board, as I was worried he would try to talk me out of it, and it felt like our last hope.

Jess shoved the Jell-O shot tray nearly into my stomach, eyebrows raised.

"Question: Why didn't you just use flavored gelatin?"

She shrugged. "I grabbed the wrong box and didn't think anyone would notice."

"Jess, I love you, but they noticed." She lifted her eyebrows and moved the tray closer to me. "Sure. Why the hell not," I said as I lifted one. I eyed it before popping it into my mouth. It tasted like vodka-flavored gelatin, which explained the disgusted faces I'd seen as people took them earlier in the night. I'd seen Mark spit his into his plastic cup of Coors Light. But I needed something to take the edge off, so I forced it down.

"All right," I said as I lifted the back of my hand to keep the shot inside my body. "Let's get this over with."

"Should I put on the playlist I made?" Jess said. Her portable speaker swung from her belt loop. When we stared at her, she lifted her palms. "Guess not. Your loss."

We poured glasses of red wine, picked up the Ouija board, and walked into the family room, where I had set up a blanket on the floor and candles all around the room. The candles weren't just for effect; they were necessary. As was also Fourth of July tradition, the power was out. Without fail, every year one of the neighbors blew the electrical transformer setting off fireworks. Tim actually had done it last year, and this year the award went to Andrew Hacker. I think ComEd just put us in their calendar for every July like a standing meeting.

The air in the house was stifling, heavy like a wet blanket, like the few moments before it rains.

Melissa fanned herself with her hand and then grabbed an *US Weekly* off the coffee table and used that. I saw that her hand was trembling and knew how hard this must have been for her. "Why don't you have power?"

I pointed to the window. "No one has power. It's a neighbor-hood tradition." I glanced outside and saw that the only illumination on the street was from the old gas lamps, faithfully casting a small amount of light onto the lawns.

"Don't you have a generator? We bought one after the last Fourth of July," she said as she frowned. She pulled her tank top away from her body and fanned her chest with the magazine. "Why is it so hot today? What horrible weather."

Jess plopped down on the carpet and crossed her legs, her bare feet tucking under. "No such thing as bad weather, only bad clothing."

Melissa grumbled as she sat down, too. "Easy to say for some-one who doesn't wear much of it."

I ignored their bickering and placed the Ouija board on the blanket. I thought again about how the emotional balance of our group had shifted without Liz. Melissa and Jess had always gotten digs in against each other, but without her buffer, her kindness, the remarks seemed more mean-spirited than funny. Her presence was like a propane dial on a firepit, capable of turning down the flames so they could be enjoyed without too much heat.

Finally, Melissa's brave exterior crumbled. "Can we please just get this over with so I can go home?" Her voice cracked in the middle of the sentence.

Nodding, I opened the box and pulled the board and plan-chette out, placing them in the center of our makeshift triangle. I shivered and tried to push thoughts of *The Exorcist* out of my mind, my fear that we might make things worse by opening a door with the demonic world.

We put our fingertips on the planchette. "All right," I said as I shifted closer to the board. "Let's close our eyes and try to picture Liz, to let her know we want to communicate with her." I swallowed hard as I thought of the words written on the photo.

"But what if I actually don't want to talk to her?" Melissa whispered, and neither of us answered.

I closed my eyes and thought of my friend. The memory that popped into my head was the first night we all hung out, after the incoming kindergartner park playdate. I had immediately connected with Jess first; her easy and carefree attitude reminded me of my sister when we were young. She was her own vortex, one that I could stand near and absorb energy from. One that used to wrap my own insecurities more tightly. A shield.

Jess had met Melissa outside the school and then brought me over and introduced us. Melissa just seemed relieved that we weren't going to ask her to volunteer for a committee. Her quick wit and comfort with her own priorities drew me in. Even though Jess and Melissa were opposites in nearly every way, they shared a sense of having given their fucks away a long time ago.

Liz was different. I was the one who approached her, after I saw her standing on her own, looking hopeful and nervous, as Carson ran around the school's playground. She wore black capri pants and a workout tank, the Winchester uniform, but she hadn't put on the brittle shell that normally goes with it.

"This is a lot, isn't it?" I said to her as I sidestepped to where she stood by the monkey bars.

She shot me a grateful look. "It really is. Plus I have this one to keep an eye on." I followed her gaze down to Luke, where he toddled around the playground, looking for something particularly indigestible to stick into his mouth. I smiled as Emily skipped over to Luke and patted him on the head. She knelt down and showed him a dandelion she had picked and blew it out for him. He let out a deep-throated laugh that made all of us smile.

"She's really sweet," Liz said as she crossed her arms over her chest. She tightened the ponytail behind her head. "I'm Liz, by the way. I think I've seen you walking your cute little pug around the neighborhood."

It was a normal introduction, mundane. So uneventful that I might not have remembered it at all, or might have written it off as just a surface encounter. But there was something about her—a baked-in goodness, a sense that she was truly a kind person—that made me ask her if she wanted to hang out sometime. She wasn't flashy like Melissa and Jess, who had their own energies. She was just herself. A good person. Her presence was quieter but still authentic.

After the park playdate, Melissa invited Jess and me to her house for some wine, and before I left the playground, I stopped and turned back to Liz.

"Would you like to come?" I said.

And the rest was Whispering Farms history. The four of us against the rest.

My fingers quivered on the planchette as I opened my eyes. "We would like to speak to Liz, or whoever is around her. Liz, can you hear us?" My voice came out hoarse, even though I had prac-ticed the words all day, repeating them in my head as we watched the fireworks. *Liz, can you hear us?*

The air in the room seemed to settle as we waited, the only

sound our breathing and the distant laughter of the husbands as they sat at the firepit next door. The candles cast shadows around the room, making the furniture seem grotesquely large.

"We are asking to speak to our friend Liz, who we love. Liz, if you can hear us, let us know." My voice was strong, confident, belying the terror inside. My stomach felt like a black hole.

The planchette quivered under our fingers, and I noticed Melissa's hand was shaking. Her eyes were closed tightly and her lips pressed in a thin line. I wondered what memory from her childhood this brought up. Jess's face was open, expectant, eyes bright and clear as she waited with the calm excitement of a Labrador retriever.

When nothing moved, I repeated the question, louder this time in case the spirit world was hard of hearing.

Again, nothing.

My shoulders sagged. I had been so sure the Ouija board would work, and the thought of going to bed a failure made my chest tighten.

I was startled when Jess spoke.

"Liz, where are you?" she shouted. "Hello?"

The air around us seemed to crackle and the candlelight danced against the walls. My eyes wide, I nodded to Jess. *Keep going.*

"Stop," Melissa said, wide-eyed.

Jess was undeterred. "Liz, I'm sick of this bullshit. If you can hear us, get over here and talk to us." Her words became louder as she spoke, like the volume on a radio dial slowly being turned to the right.

The planchette quivered under us and slowly began to move in a circle.

"It's happening," I whispered, mostly to myself. No one spoke as we watched it turn clockwise twice, the dancing shadows of the candles casting a flickering glow on the letters and perverse humanoid sun at the top.

I glanced down at the gel pen and loose-leaf paper next to me, ready to record any messages.

Yet the planchette stopped in the center of the board, not pointing to anything. We waited a few more beats for it to move again, but nothing. The air in the room changed again and lightened, like a helium balloon slowly floating to the ceiling.

Frustration bubbled up in my chest, and I pressed down harder on the planchette.

"Liz!" I shouted at the board, feeling a bead of sweat run down my back and absorb into my red, white, and blue tank top. "Talk to us!"

We felt the air change again, like hitting pause on the television.

"Do you feel that?" Melissa whispered, her face pale.

And then, everything exploded.

CHAPTER 27

BREAKING GLASS, A ripping sound that exploded all around us. We threw our hands over our heads as we heard a *pop pop pop*, like firecrackers going off in a circle around us. Through my arms, I could see glittering pieces of glass falling onto the carpet.

I peeked out just in time to see the red wineglass on the end table levitate for a moment and then explode, the dark liquid spraying out with the glass. Then the noise stopped, and I slowly lifted my head again. No one spoke. Jagged pieces of glass were all around us, some littering the top of the board. Deep-crimson wine ran down the walls and soaked the carpet.

I checked my body, patting it down for any cuts, as Jess and Melissa did the same. Everyone seemed unscathed, except for a large red wine stain on Jess's white tank top.

It looks like blood.

Maybe that was the point.

"Look!" Melissa shouted as she pointed behind me to the kitchen.

I swiveled my head and saw that the red wine bottle on the counter had also exploded its contents onto the backsplash. Red rivers ran down the white subway tile and onto the countertop. I was scrambling to stand, carefully brushing off tiny pieces of broken glass, when I heard a scream from upstairs. It was Emily.

I bolted, not caring if I stepped on glass in my bare feet. I felt a sharp pain in my heel, but I ignored it as I raced upstairs and Jess and Melissa went to put out the candle.

I threw my body onto Emily's door and fell into her room, the hollow-core door far too light to support my weight. Emily was thrashing in bed, grunting and screaming. She appeared to be asleep. I grabbed her shoulders and shook them, begging her to wake up. I heard my friends downstairs, arguing over whether they should get the broom or vacuum first.

Emily slowly opened her eyes, her hair tangled around her shoulders. I pulled her toward my chest.

"It's okay. It was just a bad dream. Everything is okay. You're safe," I whispered in her ear.

She pulled away from me and crossed her legs under her. Her calm expression made me pause. "It was her."

My blood turned to ice. "Who?" I whispered.

She crooked a finger at the corner of her room, and I slowly turned, afraid to look.

I exhaled when I saw. It was her American Girl doll Molly. Emily had received her as a present last Christmas from my parents. Molly was one of the original dolls and was now considered a collector's item. At the time, I questioned whether a collector-level doll was appropriate for a young child, but Emily loved her so much that I didn't dare snatch her away.

"Molly was in your dream?" I said as I pulled her close again and began to rock her.

She shook her head against my chest. "No, Mommy. Not my dream. In real life. She tried to grab me."

"Shhhh. It was all a dream," I said. I made a mental note to hide Molly once Emily went back to sleep.

"No. Miss Liz told her to do it," she said in a whisper.

Fear seized my insides as I scooped her up and carried her out of the room. I gave the doll a nudge with my foot, which I realized was leaving bloody smudges on the carpet. She remained inanimate.

Emily's body wrapped around mine, I walked downstairs to find my friends sopping up the wine with the Norwex towels I had bought at a "friends and family" party Liz had hosted.

"Tony keeps wanting to train as a distributor for these," Melissa said as I walked into the kitchen. When she saw Emily, the expensive cloth dropped from her hand.

Jess's gaze was on something outside the family room window. She was a wax figure, immobilized. "Guys" was all that she said.

Even though everything in my body told me not to, I looked.

Outside, a figure strode on the sidewalk, moving confidently through the darkness. It was Liz. She wore a billowing black dress and was gliding down the perimeter of my house like she was on a demonic mission. All around her, a mist swirled, like she was activating it with each step. As the mist moved through the grass and shrubs bordering the sidewalk, the foliage wilted.

"Liz!" Jess called through the window. Melissa and I strangled out protests.

Liz stopped and turned toward the house in a precise motion, like a student at West Point. Even in the darkness, from inside the safety of my own home, I could see that she looked different. Her hair flowed freely around her shoulders, and her face seemed tighter, more youthful. I couldn't see her hands but imagined her fingernails were back. She looked beautiful in a very disturbing way.

She looked strong.

"You didn't really think that would work, did you?" she called, her perfect white teeth glinting in the faded light from the gas lamp.

Before she turned and continued walking, she laughed.

A pressure began to build in my chest as I watched her saunter down the street. *I'm not letting her do this, especially not to Emily.*

I set my daughter down. "Watch her," I said to my friends as I started toward the front door.

"Amy, no!" Melissa shouted, the vowels emerging long and pronounced, as Jess sputtered out a protest.

I didn't slow down. All I saw was the burn marks, the dead rabbits, the Barbie tableau. The beloved Molly doll turned into a nightmare.

My anger masked any fear I might have felt as I wrenched open the door and jogged down the sidewalk, barefoot and still bleeding, toward Liz. I saw her figure rounding the corner, the mist still swirling around her.

"Liz! Liz! Stop." My voice came out louder than expected, a razor-sharp edge to my words. I wasn't asking her to stop, I was fucking commanding her to.

She stopped quickly, arms at her sides, but didn't turn around. I had to catch my feet on the sidewalk to stop my momentum. The soles of my feet screamed in protest. I lurched forward, arms outstretched. She stepped back, and I fell on the sidewalk in front of her, palms scraping the pavement. Realizing she was just above me, close enough to strike, I pushed myself up. My palms were dirty and covered in scratches.

My shoulders started shaking in fear as I looked at her. Her eyes were all black, hollow. Her face held no expression.

Soulless.

I pressed my injured palms to my stomach. "Liz." My voice was barely above a whisper. "Liz?"

Her expression didn't change.

"It's me, Amy. Your friend? We just want to help you, Liz. We know you're in there somewhere." I didn't dare take a step toward her, but I saw a flash of recognition in her eyes. Somewhere, somehow, Liz had heard me. "Tell us how to help you, please."

Still, nothing. And I wasn't brave enough to go closer, to put a hand on her, even though that might get through to her.

"Mavis." The name escaped my lips before I could stop it.

Her eyes seemed to widen, become almost reptilian. And then she smiled, looking me up and down. One of her hands moved from her side, sliding upward on her back as her elbow bent. She was pulling something out from the low back of her dress.

I couldn't breathe, couldn't move, so I waited to see what she would do next. In the distance, I heard a crackle and a yell from the direction of Melissa's house.

My name, being shouted from Melissa's house, by Jess and Melissa. Her smart doorbell app, controlled from her phone, flashed and blinked as the words came out of the speaker. Her phone must have notified her when it sensed motion in front of the house. It was supposed to be used to tell people to come back later, to send away the siding companies who tried to get you to commit insurance fraud by making a hail-damage claim, or the mosquito companies who tried to lock people into a two-year contract.

But this time, it said: *"Amy, run! Run now!"*

At the same time, I saw what Liz was reaching for. Out of the back of her dress, she had pulled a knife. She calmly held it down by her side. A threat. A warning. And then she pressed the tip of it to her decaying hand, and a thin trickle of black blood ran down her finger.

I turned and sprinted home, rounding the corner. Too terrified to look back to see if she was following me, I pumped my arms hard, ignoring the lingering ache from the burn mark, ignoring the stinging of my palms, my aching feet.

I stumbled up my lawn and to my front door, and only then did I dare glance back. I turned to look as Jess and Melissa opened the front door, waving me inside. When I reached my foyer, I scanned the sidewalk.

Liz—Mavis—was gone. But the mist remained.

CHAPTER

28

"**WHAT A NIGHTMARE.**" Mark stood on our front lawn, one hand on his hip, and the other resting on a shovel. He shaded his eyes and surveyed the front yard. It was covered in dark brown patches of dead grass. The annuals planted by the Garden Club of Whispering Farms (of which Heather was the president, naturally) on the corner of Maple Leaf and Seneca Drives had wilted into a mushy pile, and the crab apple tree in the parkway in front of our house had turned black and lost all of its leaves overnight; it looked skeletal.

Bones, I thought as I shivered despite the morning humidity.

After I'd made sure Emily wasn't seriously hurt, Melissa and Jess had helped me clean up the house and left shortly after. Well, they each took a long swig directly out of a bottle of white wine in my fridge for reinforcement before they walked out the door. The red wine was, of course, gone. We all said very little to each other, quietly trying to process what had happened.

"Del thinks it's some kind of beetle infestation. Or maybe it's related to the flies," Mark said. He slumped forward on the shovel, a sheen of sweat on his brow. He was pale and looked like he needed a nap. He had come home last night after I texted that there had been an accident, and the second he walked in the door from Del's house, I sent him to bed without explaining anything. While we were battling with Liz, the men were all drinking copious amounts of beer around the firepit.

I had woken up to a distant buzzing sound, which at first I'd thought was the Spadlowskis' leaf blower again, but when I went downstairs, I shrieked for what felt like the thousandth time in twenty-four hours. Overnight, a fly infestation had overtaken my house. What looked like hundreds of slow-moving, fat black houseflies lazily lofted around our first floor, landing on the chandeliers and circling the can lights in the family room. I tried to kill as many as I could before I woke Mark up to run to the hardware store for flypaper and traps. Then we all went outside and hoped to come back in after a couple of hours to a house filled with fly corpses.

The kids had a bucket of chalk and were making hopscotch patterns on the driveway. Multicolored chalk dust ran up their arms and down their legs. Miraculously, Emily seemed unfazed by what had happened, although she had dark circles under her eyes, a physical reminder of what she had seen the night before.

I'd peeked in to wake her up after I discovered the flies. She was still sleeping in my bed, as I wasn't letting her out of my sight after what had happened.

"Good morning, sweet girl. How do you feel?" I said, sitting on the edge of the bed.

She brushed the hair from her eyes. "A lot better. Can we get ice cream today?"

As much as I wanted to jump up, grab her shoulders, and interrogate her, I was grateful that she didn't seem traumatized. I'd envisioned years of therapy and a morning trip to urgent care. A possible visit from Child Protective Services, and having to explain the unexplainable.

Mark let the shovel fall to the ground and then put his hands on his knees. "I'm so hungover."

"I can tell." I raised my eyebrows.

He half raised his body up. "Oh, before I forget, the guys planned a dinner thing for two days from now."

Next door, I saw Del in his yard, examining the dead patches of grass on their lawn. The brown patches traced the path that Liz had walked, demonic bread crumbs. She had marked her territory like a dog peeing on a fire hydrant. Del looked just as rough as Mark.

"You guys are getting together again? I don't think any of you will have liver function left," I said.

He shook his head, and then stopped and pressed a finger to his temple. "Ow. No, it's a respectable dinner. I think Tony called it a progressive dinner or something like that. It's where you go from house to house and everyone has a different course. Like a bar crawl but with food." He saw my face and added, "I thought it sounded like fun."

"Who all is participating?"

When he told me, I shook my head. "No. That sounds awful."

He slumped his shoulders. "It will be fun," he repeated.

"Why did you guys think inviting Heather and Andrew was a

good idea? She's a snake. And you once described Andrew as 'the kind of guy who yells "*Cannonball!*" every time he jumps into a pool,'" I said.

Mark shrugged. "Andrew was there last night when we thought of it. It wasn't like we could say they weren't invited."

"Mark, listen. I didn't tell you last night what happened while you were out, because you weren't in any shape to understand. But I know what caused all of this." I gestured to the dead patches on the lawn.

His face grew long and his eyes wide as I explained what happened with the Ouija board and then Liz after.

When I finished, he said, "We should call the police."

"And tell them what? It's not like we have any actual proof, other than my friends and me as eyewitnesses, and I'm almost certain Melissa wouldn't want to do that."

"Then what do you want to do? I think—" He cut off; Del was strolling over to our yard.

Del had a sheen of sweat on his round face as he trudged across the dead grass. "Rough morning for you, too?" He looked at me, eyes bloodshot. "I heard you ladies had an interesting night."

I cocked my head to the side, unsure of what Jess had told him.

He continued. "She told me about it all. How you all used the Ouija board, got scared, and broke some wineglasses, and then Emily had a nightmare."

I looked at Mark, who raised his eyebrows. I could see the relief behind his eyes that there was another, mundane explanation for what had happened. Even if it was a lie. But if that was what Jess wanted Del to think, or what *he* wanted to think, I wasn't going to refute it.

"Something like that," I muttered, and he turned to Mark to resurrect a joke from the night before.

I took it as my opportunity to go inside. I couldn't feign interest in their evening of laughter while the girls and I were in darkness. Closing the front door behind me, I sank to the ground, back against the wood. I didn't understand how things had gotten worse after the Ouija board. We must have widened the opening between our neighborhood and Mavis, allowing more of her darkness to come through. I covered my face with my hands. We may have cursed our friend and our families forever. Melissa had been right.

I stood up slowly and went into the kitchen, where Jack and Emily had left a stack of printer paper and markers out. I began to gather them up into a pile, smiling at the picture Jack had drawn of the school carnival. It was of the bounce house, with small stick figures inside, some in midair. I was reaching my hand over to sweep the drawings into a tidy pile when my hand froze.

Emily's drawing was of two figures. One was her, with two braids and a pink dress. The other, behind her, was a dark shape with long hair. It had a stick arm and hand reaching out, nearly touching her. Threatening her, although stick-figure Emily didn't seem afraid.

I stared at it, and another thought came to me. What if the child in the picture wasn't Emily but Amelia? And she was showing Emily what her mother had done?

A burning sensation began to build in my stomach, and I felt like I was going to throw up. I grabbed the paper and wrenched open the front door, intending to show it to Mark. I stopped when

I saw there was now a group of husbands gathered on our lawn, rehashing their evening.

I walked past Del, Tony, Mark, and Andrew, paper folded carefully to hide the drawing, and headed down the sidewalk to show my friends. I didn't have to walk very far to find them, as Jess was in Melissa's front yard, hands on her hips, looking as distraught as I was.

I jogged over to them and saw that they were each holding a slip of paper. My heart thudded as I wordlessly held up Emily's drawing. Jess lifted her hand: Summer had drawn the same one. Melissa's hand shook as she unfolded her paper with the same drawing, one from each of her twins.

"Our kids" was all I managed to say.

Melissa was visibly trembling, and I stepped forward and put an arm around her shoulders, which she shrugged away. I looked to Jess, who slowly sat down on the lawn, dead brown spots all around her like markings for a grave.

I looked down at the paper again, before I crumpled it up and then ripped it into pieces, the confetti sprinkling the lawn. I took a deep breath and then sat down on the lawn next to Jess.

I had a choice at that moment. I could give in and accept that I had lost someone else close to me. Maybe that was my lot in life—to keep trying to save my loved ones but always losing. June, Liz—who would be next?

I couldn't accept it. I looked up at my friends, an idea forming. "This can't be the only time something strange happened at Liz's house, right?" Neither of them made eye contact, but I continued. "Who lived in the house before Liz? Maybe if we talk to them, we can find out if they experienced anything out of the ordinary, and if so, how they stopped or prevented it."

Melissa slowly sat down, the three of us forming a triangle on the dead lawn. "I really can't do this anymore. Everything we do seems to make things worse. I had to delete the Ring camera footage so Tony wouldn't completely flip out, and no way am I going to show him these drawings." She shoved the papers back in her pocket.

Jess sprang up, letting Summer's paper fall to the ground. Without a word, she pivoted and jogged across the street. We watched as she stopped at Nancy Johnson's house, rapping on the door loudly. Nancy and her husband had lived in their house for decades, their family one of the founders of the neighborhood. After a moment, Nancy answered the door, and we heard the sounds of a murmured conversation.

"I found out who lived in Liz's place before," Jess said as she ran back. She looked at me and put her hands on her hips. "It was Marianne Baker."

CHAPTER

29

MARIANNE BAKER WALKED through the doors of Starbucks wearing a blue-and-white-striped maxidress that wafted around her ankles. Her hair was blown straight out around her chin and she wore layers of bracelets nearly up to her elbows. Even from across the bustling coffee shop, I could hear their charms clink together.

I lifted my coffee cup in greeting, and she turned and smiled. She sat down at the table across from me, her dress blowing around her legs. She clasped her hands in front of her.

I had called her under the guise of meeting for coffee to discuss the cakewalk for the carnival, and she'd readily agreed. I almost felt guilty about my real motives after how excited she was to get together. But I was desperate.

"Thanks for meeting me today," I said. I tucked my hair behind my ears to hide my shaking hands. I took a quick breath, trying to steady my voice. "And thank you so much for helping with the cakewalk goodies."

She leaned forward and rested a hand on mine. "I'm happy to help. I miss the days when my kids were little, but I do remember how grueling they were."

I nodded, and we discussed who she had recruited and the various treats she was baking for the prizes. I fixed my face into a grateful, relaxed expression.

"And it really was such a lovely neighborhood to raise a family. The wives all became friends, and we raised our children together," she said. "We would pull a card table out into the cul-de-sac and play cards while the children played in the yards."

I nodded. "That's sort of what is still happening. Not the cards, but all of our kids are growing up together. And the moms are friends." I felt my throat constrict as I silently added, *Or we all used to be*. The weight of what we were on the verge of losing threatened to overwhelm me, until I shoved it back down.

She nodded. "Oh yes. If one of us would need to run out, or do laundry, or just pop to the grocery, the rest of us would just keep an eye on her kids." She sat back, a faraway look on her face. "What a wonderful way to grow up."

"So why did you leave Whispering Farms?" I said as I took a sip of my coffee, trying to look nonchalant.

She turned away, and the distant look returned. "It was time." A flicker of something I couldn't identify passed across her eyes. "Our kids were grown, and it made sense. The house didn't feel right anymore."

I couldn't dance around the subject. "My friend who lives in your old house isn't feeling right, either. Liz Kowalski. I'm just wondering if you two are sharing an experience in common."

Her blue-lined eyes widened, and she shook her head. "We weren't sure what it was. It was just a feeling. A darkness, possibly. My husband thought it was all in my mind." She gave a hollow laugh. "But I was terrified. I had nightmares every night, of a woman whose skin was falling off. I had visions of her attacking my children, and even my dog, Murphy. I consulted everyone. A counselor. A priest. Even a spiritualist." She gave me an appraising look.

"What did the spiritualist say?" I leaned forward.

She smirked, her pink lips pressed together. "She said she felt something dark in my backyard. She did one of her potions or spells out there and then told me to plant more grass in the corner of the yard." She shook her head. "It was a waste of money. My husband said she was a scammer. So I assumed it was baby blues and didn't tell anyone. I kept it to myself, and did the best I could."

It was a familiar story. Postpartum depression was often discounted, society expecting moms to be in baby-bliss mode after having a baby, despite the lack of sleep, hormones, pain from delivery, and feelings of isolation. We weren't supposed to show anything but joy, and we were certainly never supposed to complain. I knew this because I'd felt that way after having Jack, like my life had changed, and not for the better.

I swallowed hard. "Liz dug up the grass in what I'm assuming is the same corner. And that's when it all started. I think there is something there—a true darkness."

The corners of her mouth drew down. She looked at her hands and said, "Then tell your friend to move."

"I can't. It's too late for that." My voice was a shaky whisper.

She put a hand over mine and gripped it. "Then move, yourself. And tell anyone you care about to do the same."

I shook my head and pulled my hands away. "We want to fight it. We want to save Liz, and the neighborhood."

She frowned before she put her palms on the table and stood. "You better make sure it's worth fighting for, then." She turned and left.

As I walked back to my car, my phone dinged with a text. It was from Liz, sent to the group of us. It read: See you tomorrow at the dinner.

The progressive dinner. But Mark hadn't told me Liz and Tim were invited. I quickly typed out a separate message to Melissa and Jess, but before I could hit Send, their messages popped up.

After several confused and panicked exchanges, we discovered that they hadn't, in fact, been invited. We had no idea how she'd found out.

Considering the last time I saw Liz, she'd been holding a knife, I couldn't imagine what she had planned. Our sanctuaries were about to become her playgrounds.

CHAPTER 30

"HOPE YOU ALL like blood." Tony held out a bright orange cocktail as Mark and I walked through the door of Melissa's house. He chuckled to himself. "Blood orange cocktails, that is. The drink has freshly squeezed blood orange juice, small-batch bourbon, simple syrup, and lemon and lime juices. Garnished with a Wisconsin-made maraschino cherry, of course. I found them at a specialty farmer's market." He looked expectantly at me as I took the drink from the engraved sterling silver tray.

I nervously glanced out the front window, afraid Liz was going to appear. Even though everyone had denied inviting them, she knew. And I had no idea what she had planned next for us.

Tony stared at me, so I took a slight sip of the drink. It was cloyingly sweet and reminded me of Liz's rotgut boxed wine. "Mmmmm," I said as I forced a smile. Mark waved his off and headed to the kitchen for a beer. I followed him and found everyone in Melissa's beautiful kitchen. Melissa had renovated it after she moved in, removing the dark wood cabinets and replacing them with white Shaker fronts, replacing the granite with marble, and upgrading all the appliances, including a red Viking range.

On the large marble island with a dove-gray bottom, there were trays and trays of different cocktails. One was smoking and appeared to have dry ice inside. Jess and Melissa turned in greeting, lifting rainbow-hued cocktails in my direction. Del had an ornate bottle of bourbon next to him. Heather and Andrew were animatedly talking to him, something about how trying to find a summer home in Michigan this year was particularly challenging. Right now, I was somewhat grateful for their presence, since it would block any talk of Liz.

I placed my cocktail on the countertop and saw Tony frown out of the corner of my eye. Leaning against the island, I looked at Jess and Del and down to the bourbon bottle next to him.

"Didn't want to try a blood orange cocktail?" I asked him.

He lifted a rocks glass and shook his head. "What can I say? I'm a purist."

"What appetizers are you serving?" I said. My stomach hurt at the thought of repeating what Marianne had told me: to make sure our neighborhood was worth fighting for. I felt like we were sitting ducks just waiting for Liz to attack us again.

Jess's eyes brightened. "I made cocktail meatballs and a spinach-and-artichoke dip. Del planned to do everything, but I had a housewife moment and offered."

Melissa sidled up to us. "Don't tell Tony how bad these are." She daintily lifted an electric-green martini to her lips and pretended to take a sip as she smiled at her husband over the rim of the glass.

"Oh, Amy, I've been meaning to ask how the carnival planning is coming along," Heather said. She smiled. "I really wish I could have helped out more, but I've been so busy planning our next home renovation. We are putting in a four-seasons room in the back of the house"

I matched her faux smile. "It's been great." I gestured to Jess and Melissa. "I'm so lucky that my friends have pitched in and that the older ladies from the neighborhood have offered to help, since finding volunteers was a bit challenging."

I didn't tell her that I had had a breakdown that morning to Mark over all of it. The carnival was the next week, and although I had checked off all the boxes and arranged for the games, food vendors, and prizes, the weight of what had happened with Liz, and Emily, made it hard to breathe.

"Maybe you should just cancel it. With all the stuff that's happened this summer, I don't know if it's such a good idea," Mark had said as he hugged me in our bedroom, after he saw my tears.

"Mark, it's days away. I can't cancel it now," I said.

"You can. Just do it," he said.

I paused and briefly allowed myself to think about what a relief it would be to let it all go, throw in the towel. It all felt like too much, and I didn't know if I had the emotional fortitude to hand out small stuffed animal prizes and pretend nothing was happening.

I was about to agree with him when I heard a shriek outside the bedroom. I turned my head from Mark's chest and saw Jack standing in the hallway.

"What? You're canceling the carnival?" he said. His fists were balled up on either side of his body.

I extricated myself from Mark's embrace and wiped my cheeks. "No, of course not."

Jack eyed me suspiciously, and I walked over and put an arm around his small shoulders. "Everything will be great, I promise. I was just being silly."

He wiggled away and gave me such an innocent smile that it nearly broke my heart. "Okay, good. You're the best."

"Did you guys hear about what happened to our tub?" Tony said now as he made the rounds of the kitchen.

Melissa's head snapped in his direction.

Heather put a hand to her chest as she took a sip of her purple drink. "No, what? Not your custom clawfoot."

He set the tray down on the island, happy for the room's attention. "When we woke up this morning, it had all kinds of stains on it. Dark brown stains, like hard-water marks, but they were in horizontal lines, five of them." He lifted his hand and made a claw, slowly dragging it through the air.

I involuntarily shivered as I thought of a beast slowly digging its claws through the porcelain, smiling as its nails scratched the surface. Melissa was obsessed with that tub, a treat she'd bought herself with last year's bonus. Liz knew if there was something to destroy in her house that would hurt her—get the most bang for her demonic buck—it would be that tub.

Heather gasped. "That's terrible." She leaned forward and said conspiratorially, "I have a wonderful restorer if you'd like a recommendation. Make sure to mention my name when you contact him."

Jess laughed and then stopped when Heather's head snapped

to her. There was a moment of uncomfortable silence before Melissa said, "Let's move to Jess's."

———

"I CAN'T BELIEVE this." Jess stood in her kitchen with her hands on her hips as she surveyed the garbage scattered all around the kitchen. Duffy had gotten into the trash, and there were remnants of coffee grounds, used napkins, and spent kale stalks on her white tile floor.

I bent down to help her scoop it up and heard Del say, "Uh-oh. Jess?" I popped my head up, and Del was holding an empty silver tray that had been sitting on the stovetop.

"Shit," Jess said. "Duffy!"

"Were those the appetizers?" I said as I picked up a dirty paper towel with two fingers and stuck it in the trash bag. I looked up at Del. "Why don't you take everyone outside?"

He nodded and ushered everyone to the back patio.

"Damn it," Jess said. She rubbed her forehead. "Of course, I'm the one who screws everything up tonight. I can't get my shit together for things like this." She closed her eyes.

I leaned over and touched her arm. "Hey, it's just spilled milk. Do you have anything else in the fridge? We can quickly make something, and no one has to know."

I craned my neck around and peeked outside, where they all sat at the patio table. Even from inside, I could see the annoyance on Melissa's face as she sat next to Heather, nodding and trying to look pleasant during what I was sure was another soliloquy on the wonders of saltwater pools or something equally obnoxious.

Jess sniffled, and I leaned forward and hugged her, crouching down to where she sat on the kitchen floor, surrounded in garbage.

"Hey, it's fine, really, hon. Don't be so hard on yourself. Things happen," I said.

She covered her face with her hands and took a deep breath, wiping under her eyes and brushing her hair back. Her cheeks were red and splotchy.

"Why can everyone else prepare a fucking progressive dinner, and I can't even make appetizers without something happening? I feel like I'm always failing at things like this. I just want to prove that I can do things that Sharon can do." She looked at me, eyes bloodshot.

"Because we have a lot going on right now. And you're great at so many things, who cares if one of them isn't appetizers?"

Jess wasn't usually a crier. I had seen her cry *maybe* two times before, and once was when her sump pump overflowed into her basement during a torrential rain and ruined some of her only keepsakes from childhood. This clearly wasn't about the appetizers. She was full of unexpected contradictions, one of the things I always loved best about her.

"I just wish one of the things I was good at was normal mom stuff," she said with a sigh. She leaned back against her kitchen cabinet and closed her eyes.

I nodded. "I know. All of the work always seems to fall on us, even if it's unintentional. Finding babysitters, remembering that we need extra milk, sending in the field trip form. It's all small stuff but it takes up extra brain space." I put a hand on her shoulder, and she opened her eyes. "I see you, and I understand."

She smiled. "Thanks. I don't know what I would do without you, buddy."

I twisted my mouth to the side in a smile. "Same, buddy." I heard Melissa laugh outside—a placating laugh—and knew her patience was about to run out. "Let's get this figured out. I will clean the kitchen while you look for something else to make. Do you have anything in the freezer?" I said.

She cocked her head to the side for a minute, thinking. "I'm pretty sure there's garlic bread in the garage freezer." She shrugged.

I nodded. "Perfect. We can quickly make it and cut it up into bite-sized pieces. Marinara?" She confirmed, so I added, "Side of dipping sauce."

"I'll get the bread from the garage." She slowly stood up and stretched her arms overhead in a yoga backbend before she stepped over a pile of burst tomatoes on the ground.

I started frantically throwing the trash on the floor into the bin as Jess left the kitchen. I heard the door to the garage open and close and stole another look outside. Melissa caught my eye and made a discreet sweeping motion across her neck. *Kill me.* I held up a finger and then rotated my hand around, giving her the signal to stall. Usually, she would have been inside a long time ago, seeing what was going on and trying to help. But tonight, her help was occupying and entertaining Heather.

Then two things happened at once: I picked up a carton of used eggshells, some of the leftover whites dripping down my front, and I heard a buzzing sound coming from the garage. Then a cry for help.

"What the—" I stood up and jogged over to the garage door, the buzzing growing louder. "Jess?" I reached for the door and tried to open it, but it was locked. In the garage, I heard Jess yelping, "Help!"

"What's going on? Open the door!" I said. I heard a metallic crash from the other side as a buzzing came and went, like something flying past the door on the other side. I pounded on the door again. "Jess! Open the door!"

I smacked my hand against the door and desperately tried to jiggle the handle to open it.

"Amy!" she said from the other side.

I kicked the door and it didn't budge, but I felt a shot of pain from my toes. It was a heavy-duty fireproof door made of metal covered in white faux wood.

I heard her call my name again, sounding more terrified. I screamed for Del as I ran over to the sliding glass door and yanked it open. The crowd looked up in unison and scrambled to their feet. Del brushed past me, nearly knocking me over as he ran to the garage door.

"Jess, open the door!" He pounded a fist on it and tried the handle to no avail. "Jess!"

Everyone was crowded around the door, talking and yelling at once. Melissa grabbed my arm, hard.

"What's going on?" she said as her fingers gripped my biceps.

I shook my head. "I have no idea. She's trapped in there, though."

"Del, the garage door. Open it from the outside with the code," Mark said, and pointed to the front door.

Del sprinted out the front door and raced across the yard to the driveway.

"Hang on, Jess, Del's getting you out," I called with my cheek pressed to the garage door.

She screamed in response. Then the buzzing stopped, and we heard the clanking of the garage door opening from the other side. I ran out the front door, Melissa and everyone else at my heels. I stopped suddenly when I got to the driveway and saw what had happened in the garage. Heather muttered a curse under her breath.

Jess sat on the floor of the garage, sobbing and holding her cheek. Del was crouched down next to her, arms wrapped around her. Next to her was a smoking weed whacker.

"What happened?" I asked Del.

His face was white, and he wordlessly shook his head. I bent down on one knee and tried to see what had happened to Jess. She wouldn't remove her hand from her face and continued to cry loud sobs that left her gasping for breath.

Melissa stepped into the garage. "Jess. Are you hurt?"

Jess's sobs grew quieter, and she looked up, eyes red and swollen. Her face was a mask of fear, her eyes wide and mouth drawn. "The weed whacker turned on by itself and cut my face."

We looked in unison at the quiet landscaping tool, a thin plume of smoke emanating from the motor. It wasn't plugged in, and I could see the sharp thread sticking out from the reel.

"How bad is it?" Melissa said.

Jess slowly removed her palm from her cheek, and we took a collective, sharp inhale. There was a bright red slash across her face, running from her hairline to nearly her nose. It didn't appear to be bleeding that badly, but the skin around it was puffy and swollen.

The photograph.

My insides felt like they were tightening, and my body started to tremble as I realized the photo foretold this: Jess with a mark on her face.

Now we all had one. Like diabolical matching friendship bracelets.

Mark went inside to get Jess an ice pack and a wet cloth while I remained rooted in place, feet nailed to the garage floor. Everything around me grew softer, like I was coming into focus, the background falling away. I couldn't take my eyes from Jess as Del held her and she whimpered in pain.

This was what Liz meant by seeing us tonight. We were so stupid to believe she was going to show up in person, like normal. Landscaping tools couldn't just turn on by themselves. She had marked each one of us, just as she had in the picture.

I didn't know how we were going to stop her, let alone pull her back from the pit of hell. The darkness was overtaking our neighborhood, and we were powerless against it. We didn't have much time left before we would all belong to Mavis.

CHAPTER

HEN MOVE, YOURSELF. And tell anyone you care about to do the same.

Marianne Baker's warning floated through my mind before I had even opened my eyes the morning after Jess's injury. Her words were like the hissing of a snake, lightning before catastrophic thunder.

We had helped Jess bandage her face after Heather and Andrew went home, the rest of the evening canceled. She refused to go to urgent care, insisting after she stopped crying that she was fine and had just gotten spooked.

"Must have been an electrical surge," Del said as he carefully picked up the weed whacker from the garage floor.

"It's not plugged in, Del," Melissa replied, her voice rising.

Mark and Del had exchanged a pointed glance, each of them beginning to put the puzzle pieces together from what we had told them.

I opened my eyes and reached for my phone. It was 5:00 a.m., and Mark was still asleep next to me. At the top of the screen were two text notifications.

The first was from Melissa, sent just over an hour ago: Jess, how are you doing?

She replied a few minutes later: My face will be fine, but I'm not. I can't do this anymore. I'm sorry. I'm going to talk to Del today, but I think we need to move somewhere else before things get worse.

My heart sank as I read her words. Not that I could blame her, but I couldn't imagine her leaving and living anywhere else. I hadn't even told her or Melissa about Marianne's warning. I was about to reply when Melissa responded: Understandable. I've been having the same thoughts.

A heavy feeling settled over my shoulders as I typed and deleted a variety of responses. Their thoughts were valid, reasonable. Expected. I should have been thinking the same thing. And yet I couldn't imagine a world with all of us scattered to the four winds. I still harbored some tiny hope that we could find a way to stop all of it and get our friend back, no matter how far-fetched it seemed.

I put my phone down without responding. I couldn't think of a reply that wouldn't discount their feelings but would inspire hope. I thought maybe something would come to me later and I would find the perfect words to rally the troops. But for that moment, all I could do was remain silent.

I SCREAM, YOU SCREAM, WE ALL SCREAM FOR ICE CREAM

I looked at the sign in Melissa's hands, my eyes lingering on the word "scream."

"What do you think?" Melissa said as she tapped the front with her index finger. She looked terrible, her hair in a greasy bun, her clothes rumpled. I had never seen her look so disheveled. I was sure I looked the same.

"Looks great. Thanks for taking care of it," I said. I turned and pointed toward the entrance to the school parking lot. "You can start setting up over there." She turned and shuffled away.

Our morning had started early, with Mark and I packing up the car and heading over to the school before 8:00 a.m. while Judy sat with the kids. She had arrived with an enormous box full of face-painting supplies and a sign with sketches of different designs the kids could choose.

I was busy setting up the ticket table, while workers secured the balloon arch. I could hear Melissa's voice wafting over as she ordered them around while Tony and their kids delivered the various signage to the proper booths.

Jess had texted me the night before, asking if it would be okay if she skipped the carnival due to the mark on her cheek. She didn't think she could face everyone and all their questions but said Del was going to bring Summer and could help direct the bounce house company for setup. To my left, a steady stream of white noise emanated from the bounce house as four questionable workers inflated it.

It was carnival time.

———

AN HOUR LATER, the sounds of children screeching and cheering had reached a dull roar as families milled around, moving from game to game. A long line of children snaked out of the bounce house as they waited their turn. Judy was hard at work at the face-painting booth, and Marianne's friends were stationed at the games, wide smiles on their faces. Several children had stuffed animals and prizes under their arms, and parents walked around with baked goods they had won at the cakewalk.

Marianne Baker had arrived with an SUV full of pies, cakes, and cookies. I tensed as I walked over to help her unload, my shoulders stiffening in anticipation. As I lifted a chocolate chip cheesecake out of the back of her car, the moment I'd waited for arrived.

"Did you think more about our conversation the other day?" she said. She turned to me, a tray of powdered brownies resting against her stomach. Her face was creased with worry, and river-rock earrings swung and brushed against her cheeks.

I averted my eyes and busied myself with putting the cheese-cake on the rolling cart next to the car.

"I did," I said in a tone that indicated I didn't want to talk more about it. The carnival wasn't the time.

Marianne didn't say anything more as we finished loading the cakewalk prizes. I flashed her a smile as she closed the trunk of her car.

"Thanks so much for all of this," I said as brightly as I could muster.

I heard Jack's cheer from across the parking lot and saw that he had again won the lollipop pull. I smiled from my spot at the ticket counter, handing out two pink tickets to the O'Connell family. Jack scampered over to the bounce house line, his stuffed dragon prize dangling from his hand. Emily was with Melissa and her children at the ring toss game, and behind them waited Tim's mother, Ann, and Liz's children.

Heather and her friends stood in a semicircle at the edge of the bounce house line, frowning and rolling their eyes at the seeming success. Sharon stood next to Heather, intently staring across the parking lot. I followed her gaze to Del and Summer and prayed she wasn't going to try to cozy up to her ex since Jess wasn't around.

Mark was seated next to me, and he leaned over. "I'm so proud of you. I know it wasn't easy to be in charge of all of this, especially with everything that went down this summer."

I gave him a grateful smile. "Thanks. I didn't think I could pull it off, but here we are."

He leaned in for a kiss, but before our lips could meet, a strong wind blew across the parking lot, sweeping the tickets off the table.

I had just bent down to pick them up when another gust, this one stronger, made the tickets scatter across the asphalt. I'd stood up to collect them when I heard screams.

My head snapped around the parking lot—booths were swaying, and the signage was nearly horizontal to the ground, the thin metal stands bending in the wind. The balloon arch swayed dangerously back and forth.

"I thought it was supposed to be sunny today," I said to Mark as my heart began to thud in my chest.

He looked bewildered as he began to rise from his chair. I stepped away from the booth as another gust of wind came through. This one, though, was sustained, like an enormous fan had been turned on. Hair blew backward as the booths began to fall.

Then, two things happened. The balloon arch began to pop, loud bangs echoing like gunshots as children started to scream. Worse, though, the bounce house started to lift off the ground.

"Oh my God," I shouted as I watched the four workers struggle with the lines and sandbags that were supposed to keep it grounded. "Mark!" I said before I broke out into a sprint toward it. As I ran, I frantically searched for Jack. He had been in line just moments ago, but I didn't see him. Melissa and Tony huddled around Emily and their children, protecting them from the debris whipping through the air.

I was nearly hit by a flying lollipop as I ran toward the bounce house. Instead of dying down, the sustained gust grew stronger. The bounce house lifted off the ground and fell to its side, the screams of the children inside and the parents clouding my vision. My hair blew back in the wind, and my skin felt like it was being rubbed by sandpaper, but I kept running.

Mark sprinted ahead of me, reaching the bounce house, and began to wrestle it to the ground. A worker began to reverse the inflating mechanism. The yellow and red sides began to wrinkle as it slowly sank to the ground.

The wind finally eased up, and Mark and the bounce house workers grabbed for the flaps on the outside and began to pull children out as other parents tried to lift up the sides to let the children out before it collapsed on them.

I reached the bounce house as terrified, red-faced, and crying children were being lifted out of the collapsing structure. But I still didn't see Jack.

"Mark! Jack! He's still inside."

Mark dove inside, his feet still sticking out. Everything went silent as I waited for him to rescue our son. His body began to back out, and I prayed that he had him.

When he was finally out, in his arms was a hysterical and bloody Jack.

Blood poured from Jack's nose, and his hands were covered in red as he screamed, the color of his face matching his hands. Mark clutched Jack to his chest, blood smearing across his white shirt.

"We need a towel!" I shrieked as I reached them. A cacophony of chaotic parents began to frantically look for one. "Shhh. Shhhh," I said as I put my arms around Jack.

He couldn't speak, just screamed. Del ran up next to us and ripped off his blue T-shirt and handed it to me. I balled it up and gently put it on Jack's face, causing him to scream more.

I looked to Mark, who put his hand over mine on Jack's face.

"It's okay. It's just a bloody nose. You must have gotten hit with something when the house blew over. You're going to be fine," Mark mumbled, the words running together like a mantra.

Jack stopped screaming and started breathing quickly, nearly hyperventilating.

"You're going to be all right, buddy," I said, my voice breaking. "Just hold this on your face and the bleeding will stop."

My hand on the shirt, I looked over my shoulder for Emily. She was still with Melissa and Tony. They were both crouched on the ground, hugging her and their kids, examining them for injuries.

The carnival looked like a war zone. Brightly colored prizes littered the black asphalt, while baked goods were splayed on the ground like organs pouring out of a disemboweled torso. The balloon arch sagged to the ground, half the balloons deflated or popped.

Families were crying and hugging each other, scooping up their children and carrying them off.

The signage was all over the ground, and my eyes fixed on the large banner we had hung across the balloon arch.

It was covered in leaves and dirt, and the only words still visible were: *We All Scream.*

CHAPTER

32

Everyone okay?

I sent the text to my friends the night of the disastrous carnival. After Jack's bloody nose had stopped, Mark took him and Emily home while I stayed behind with a few of the other parents to clean up what was left of the event. Melissa's family left without saying goodbye. I didn't blame her. Del stayed behind to help while Summer left with Sharon. I could only imagine what Jess had heard.

Thankfully, Jack seemed calm and happy by the time we put him to bed after I got home. Emily barely spoke, her eyes haunted and afraid. I tried to remain logical about what had happened, reminding myself that Liz might not have been responsible. But still, some part of me felt as though she had to have been involved. There weren't any other reports of wind damage in the area; it seemed isolated to the carnival.

I waited for a response, to make sure my friends were safe, emotionally and physically. But no one texted back.

Silence was worse than anything, so I sent a follow-up text two hours later as I was making dinner.

I hope you guys are okay.

I rebooted my phone twice as I ate ice cream alone in the kitchen while Mark fell asleep on the couch, exhausted from the day's events, and again as I loaded the dishwasher. And yet no response came.

Later, I lay in bed watching Bravo, trying to immerse myself in the latest Real Housewives drama—something about one of the women insulting the shoes of another—but had to turn it off. If only our problems were that mundane.

I woke up the next day and checked my phone, feeling like a clingy girlfriend who knows she's about to be broken up with but can't accept it.

My friends had responded.

I read through the group text. I stared at it until the words blended together like melted ice cream, hoping if I just kept reading it, I would find hope. A small hole that I could wiggle into and make larger. To make them reconsider.

The first text from Melissa had been sent early that morning: Tony and I talked and we have decided to put our house on the market next week. It's just not safe to stay here anymore, especially after what happened at the carnival.

Five minutes later, Jess had responded: Sorry Amy, but I'm

wondering if we should do the same. The carnival wasn't your fault, but I'm scared. Holy shit this is terrible.

Then they quickly moved into a discussion of who they were each using as a Realtor. The last one in the thread was from Melissa: We may have a buyer already who wants a quick close.

So my worst fear was happening. Liz had finally driven them out of the neighborhood. I had assumed if anyone ever moved away, it would be because of a job change or wanting a bigger house. No one could have looked into a crystal ball and predicted they'd leave due to demonic activity.

My first instinct was to respond immediately. I wanted to ask them how they could just up and leave, turn their backs on our neighborhood and our friend and me. Instead, I asked them where they were planning to move. I assumed across town or somewhere close.

Melissa: For now, I might see if Tony would want to decamp to Santa Rosa Beach, Florida. I can work remote for some time while we figure things out. I think getting as far away from Winchester as we can is the right decision.

My chest constricted. Not only was she going to leave the neighborhood, she was crossing state lines. All the good times, the bonds we had, were part of a dying season, the wisps and whispers of autumn on a brisk September morning. The warnings that seem to say, "I hope you had a good summer, because winter is coming."

They weren't doing it to hurt me. They were trying to protect their families. I understood that, but part of me wondered if there was something wrong with me that my first instinct wasn't to grab my young and run from the predator. Why didn't I think to flee immediately? Was my instinct to fight wrong? After all, we had no idea how to fight what was happening or who would get hurt next.

I closed my eyes and inhaled deeply before I responded. Are you sure? I know how hard it will be for you guys to go so far away.

Melissa's response: It's harder to stay here.

I sent another text: Can we all talk? And waited for their answer. I wanted to sit down, face-to-face, and talk through all of it. Enough with the bullshit texting. We were closer than that, we were better than that.

I waited all day, periodically checking my phone even though my Apple Watch would have buzzed at a text. But none ever came. They were moving away, and our friendship would begin its slow decline. Sure, we would stay in touch with texts and phone calls. After a while, those would morph into just birthdays and first days of school. It would then move to social media, until finally it ended with the yearly, obligatory Facebook birthday wishes, delivered only because of the site notifications.

And I would be left here, alone, with Liz. To watch as she continued her destruction. Maybe she would stop if we all moved away. If she really wanted to destroy our neighborhood, maybe the sacrifice of breaking up our friend group would be enough. She might come back and be the Liz I used to know. The friend that I loved, the kindhearted mother hen.

I shivered as another possibility entered my mind: Or maybe we would be at the bottom of that pit next, no matter what. Maybe she would find us no matter where we were.

CHAPTER

33

"TO A NIGHT out," Mark said as he lifted the glass of prosecco in front of him from the table. We were out to dinner at the Winchester Golf & Tennis Club at his insistence. His parents had come over to watch the kids, even though I'd tried to protest. In the aftermath of the carnival, all I wanted to do was stay inside and wallow in my dark thoughts.

On top of everything else, I had received an email that morning from Monarch Hospice, politely informing me that I hadn't gotten the social worker position. I read it and quickly deleted it, exorcising it from my inbox. It felt like one more devastation that summer, one more spindle removed from the wheel that represented my dreams. No job, no friends, what next?

I gave him a small smile and lifted my glass to his, clinking it, before I took a sip with my eyes closed. I appreciated his gesture, and I did need to get out, away from our house and all the chaos, but it was hard to forget about everything. After all, we were only a mile from our neighborhood.

I looked out over the golf course, at the sun slowly setting on the green horizon. It was a warm night, but there was a thickness in the air that promised a summer storm. The golf course was lit with solar lights along the path that wound back to the tree line. The patio was red brick and dotted with tables, decorated with LED lights overhead.

It was beautiful, and should have been the setting for a perfect evening.

I leaned forward and put my elbows on the table, determined to spend a nice date night with Mark. It had been so long since we'd had a quiet moment together, away from the kids, away from our friends, away from the darkness.

"Did I tell you what Jack said the other day?" I asked with a smile.

He leaned forward, relaxed, and shook his head.

"Well, I caught him staring at his forearms, looking strange, and I asked what was wrong, if he was hurt or needed ice. He said, 'No, Mom. I was just looking at the chargers in my arms.'"

Mark said, "Chargers?"

I nodded and held out one of my arms, tracing a finger along a blue vein. "He thinks his veins are chargers, like something that would connect to an outlet."

He threw his head back and laughed. "Always about the electronics, right? If he had an electrical system in his body, would it mean we could power him down at night?"

I took another sip of my wine and gave him a wry smile. "If only."

He crossed his arms over his chest and leaned back. "Have you talked to Jess or Melissa lately?"

A pang of anxiety ran through my stomach. "We haven't really spoken since the carnival."

He put a hand on my knee. "They're dealing with a lot. They'll come around."

I gave him a grateful smile. "I hope so." I didn't tell him that my hope had dwindled down to the faintest, smallest whisper.

After a delicious meal of risotto with scallops, beef Wellington, and a lot more wine, we were ready to leave. After we paid the bill and stood up, a group of women at the corner table caught my eye. There were four of them: a tall blonde, a short brunette, a redhead, and one with glossy mahogany lowlights. I had to look twice, as at first glance, the four of them resembled me and my friends.

"Ready to go?" Mark said as he put his wallet in his back pocket.

I shook my head slightly, and the women came into focus. It had been a mirage, an image created by my subconscious. These women were at least a decade older than us and, other than hair color and stature, didn't look anything like us.

"Let's do it," I said, and Mark held his arm out for me to lead the way.

Our exit path took us past the table of women.

"How much wine have you had, Belinda?" the blonde asked with a laugh.

"Not nearly enough," the redhead said as she held up her hand to signal to the waiter. "Another bottle, and keep it coming!" The four of them broke out in loud peals of laughter.

I smiled at them, the sadness that was always in the back of my mind brought to the forefront. Once upon a time, that was us. Drinking wine, laughing, sharing stories about our families and children. I would never have that again.

When we were in the car, a question to Mark came bubbling up. "Honey, you don't really think that everything that's happened this summer has been a coincidence, do you?"

His eyes remained fixed on the road, and I could tell by the way he tensed his shoulders that he had been waiting for this question. "I don't see how it could be anything else but a coincidence."

We sat in silence as I tried to determine how I wanted to continue—if I wanted to continue. But I figured I had nothing to lose.

"You don't see how all of this is connected? Liz pushing me into that pit, the grass dying, the landscaping tools attacking Jess . . . you don't think it's all part of something?" I kept my voice even, logical, to match his demeanor.

He exhaled slowly. "I can understand why you might think so, but no, I don't think it's all related. I think Liz is having a midlife crisis, we have terrible clay soil and a fungal infection sweeping the neighborhood, and the weed whacker was an electrical surge from the ComEd transformer that was blown out on the Fourth of July. I think it's just a series of strange happenings but not a larger picture. It's just been a summer of bad luck."

I wanted to tell him he sounded like the women who don't realize they're pregnant until they're pushing out a baby after a bout of "stomach pain." At the very least, every single horror movie where they blow off all the signs that they're being haunted or stalked by a serial killer, until the only one left is the Final Girl.

But instead, I said simply, "I know it's more than that."

He nodded and looked like he was going to say something, but we were home. He pulled into our driveway and gave me a kiss on the cheek before we went inside. I was suddenly grateful for my momentary restraint. We ended the evening on a high note, something that was nearly extinct these days. I didn't want to look like the conspiracy theory meme with the guy standing in front of a wall of paper, looking crazy, pointing out the connections while wildly smoking a cigarette.

After we relieved Mark's parents, I sat by myself in the kitchen for a long time, thinking about all that had happened. The very real fear of Liz's slipping away, Emily's continued strange behavior, and my own feelings of helplessness felt like a weighted blanket around my shoulders, pressing my body down, down until I wanted to curl up on the wood floor.

I put my head on the kitchen island, resting my forehead on the cool granite. I knew I had a choice. I could surrender and stop fighting. We could move away from Whispering Farms and never look back, chalking up the summer to a chapter in our lives that we would never discuss.

Or I could fight. Like I had fought for June, even though it had ended so horribly.

June.

I had surrendered when she died, pushing her to the cobwebbed dark part of my brain. But maybe it was time to finally bring out the dusty memory box.

I stood up from the island and walked down to the basement, to the storage room with cardboard boxes on wire shelving. I stood on my tiptoes and carefully reached for a white box. Inside were the things my parents had given me from June. I had never even looked at them.

I peeled back the flaps and peered inside. There were a few of her T-shirts, some unused candles, trophies from her high school track-and-field days, and a black leather notebook. I carefully opened it and flipped through the pages.

There were doodles of spirals and triangles around mundane things like grocery lists and reminders to pay bills. I ran a finger along her handwriting, distinct, round loops that always made me joke that she had the penmanship of a child.

I flipped to the final page, and in the center, in her very small and childlike writing, was a sentence that broke my heart.

I need Amy to forgive me.

I didn't know when she had written it, but I assumed it was during her endless cycle of getting clean and relapsing. When she would come back and try to make amends, and each time, my heart grew stonier, until it was a fortress. By the end, I was grateful because the fortress protected me from falling apart when she died and gave me a foundation to keep standing on.

Yet with those words, my fortress crumbled to dust.

I put the notebook in my lap and my hands over my face. Every tear I had held back, every sob I had suppressed, flooded out in my cold basement storage room. I could hear her whisper, asking for what she needed. *Forgive me.*

When my breath steadied, I took the box upstairs into the light. I put it next to my bed, and the notebook with my sister's words on the desk. I looked at it for a long time before I fell asleep, wishing more than anything that I could hear her voice just one more time.

CHAPTER
34

RAIN PELTED AGAINST the windowpane in the kitchen, an angry chorus of water that made it difficult to see down the block. The trees whipped back and forth, releasing leaves onto the street, as branches scraped against the roof. We had meant to have those trimmed at the beginning of the summer, before storm season hit, but then everything happened with Liz.

I had the Weather Channel on in the background as I slowly unloaded the dishwasher. Jim Cantore frowned as he pointed to a dark red circle that encompassed the entire Chicago area. There was something called a derecho headed our way. A "record-breaking storm system," he called it. Normally, it would have been exciting, equal parts fun and scary. But after what I had experienced over the past few weeks, scary was anything but fun.

The television said we were still just under a severe thunderstorm warning, not a tornado alert. In the Midwest, no one bats an eye until there is an actual tornado warning complete with sirens. Even then, you check the storm's path to see if your part of town is included. And then go to the basement only after going outside to look at the sky, take some pictures, and then take shelter when an actual funnel cloud is spotted on your street.

The storm wasn't anywhere near panic levels, so the kids were in the playroom engaging in a fierce battle of Hungry Hungry Hippos while I finished up the dishes. I thought of how little things seemed to have changed from when Mavis was alive. So much of the domestic labor fell on the women, an unspoken expectation.

I closed the kitchen cabinet, went into the family room, and sat down on the couch. I watched the rain fall as I thought of my sister's words in her notebook, and of the pleas for help from Liz on the picture.

My sister was gone, but Liz was still here. I felt that she was still in there somewhere, unable to control the darkness inside of her. The demon inside of her.

Mavis Wanneberg.

I didn't dare say her name out loud, but I turned it over in my head. I had googled her name, in the hopes of finding some bread crumb that would help us. But there wasn't so much as a picture of her anywhere. It was as though she hadn't existed.

I would have thought that a woman who murdered her entire family would at least have a write-up somewhere, or a blurb on a true-crime website. Shit, they made entire podcasts about much less. But it was as though Mavis wasn't even worthy of that. She was truly invisible.

I tried to imagine her descent into madness. Did she realize she was losing her grip on reality? The research we read on Mavis didn't give a date for the murders, but rather: the winter.

Winters in Winchester can be long, drawn-out affairs that leave even modern-day residents begging for sunlight. Gray snow blankets the ground for months, lasting much longer than what the calendar might suggest. Houses are always drafty and cold, and that's with modern HVAC systems.

I couldn't imagine being alone in a farmhouse with my family in the dead of winter. The days short on sunlight, the nights long with ice and wind. And Mavis was an immigrant, far from her family, who likely didn't know anyone. The closest house was miles away, not exactly conducive to making any friends.

I had an image of her sitting at her rough-hewn kitchen table, alone. Shivering in the cold after her children and husband went to sleep. Staring at the extinguished fire, just waiting for morning to come, when it would all begin again. The domestic labor and child minding were relentless, tasks that would never be completed.

I had spent mornings like that, when we first moved. Emily was so little, and I didn't know anyone yet in Whispering Farms. Each day felt like a continuation of the next, one long, dark day without any light. Except the light had come; spring did arrive, it always did. The light started to peek in when Emily began to sleep more, Mark began to help out more, and then my spirits lifted when I met Jess, and Melissa, and Liz. My life quickly went from very small, very suffocating, to full. Fulfilling, even.

Mavis had had none of that. Her life had remained dark and small until she couldn't handle it anymore.

I closed my eyes. I could almost feel her rage, her anger at the way her life had turned out. And behind it, a deep sadness at being isolated. We as mothers weren't supposed to be isolated in such ways. Going back thousands of years—millennia—women raised children together, in social pods. It takes a village and all that. We were supposed to be able to help each other, to play card games in the street, like Marianne Baker. Motherhood and child-rearing were never meant to be isolated experiences.

My shoulders drooped, and I put my feet up on the coffee table, glancing at the whitewashed fireplace. Liz, Melissa, and Jess had helped me paint it last summer, all of us taping it off and laughing as we brushed the red brick with the paint-and-water mixture. It turned out so well we helped Liz do the same to hers a few weeks later. We were each other's village for things like that, always ready to lend an extra pair of hands.

But not everyone had that.

An idea was lodged somewhere in the back of my mind, patiently waiting its turn, until it moved to center stage. It had been marinating and growing stronger until I was ready to understand.

Before June died, some part of me always knew it would end badly. There would be a cycle of rehabs, relapses, and tears. We went through all of it, despite knowing that it would not result in the happy ending we all so wanted. We would not be featured on the covers of brochures, a smiling family who had slayed the monster.

We always knew it would end with tearful goodbyes in a packed church, with nodding silently while people offered platitudes.

We had known. And we still kept going.

Just the same way, there was something deep inside me that whispered about Liz. About the *why*. About the village of my friends.

I ran upstairs and rifled through the papers in my desk drawer, the notes I had taken from the demonology books and historical society. I skimmed through them, letting the spent pages flutter to the carpet until I found the one I was looking for.

> *Mavis Wanneberg. Killed her family because she was*
> *isolated.*

The difference was: Liz wasn't isolated. She had all of us. She had a community of women around her to support her and raise our children together.

And maybe that very thing was the motivation for Mavis's revenge.

She was unearthed, and her rage still remained. Her feelings of hopelessness had survived a century of burial. She wanted to destroy us and our neighborhood because she was angry that she had been left alone, resentful that we didn't have to suffer the same fate. If that was what motivated her, then we had to attack it from that angle.

Maybe the concept of friendship wasn't that different from possession. It took a different form, of course, but we all borrowed the best parts from each other, sharing in the traits and strengths that we admired. We each brought something to the friendship, and we fed on that energy to make ourselves better. A shared possession, without diabolical intent.

If this was true, then the antidote was clear: Friendship. Camaraderie. There were no secret spells or potions that would defeat the evil force consuming my friend. No, it was something much simpler: us. We needed to confront what was happening together, in a show of solidarity, and show Mavis that our bond was stronger than anything she tried to throw at us. Literally, in the case of the weed whacker with Jess.

We were the key. We had *always* been the key.

Except, I had never felt further from Jess and Melissa. The distance between us may have only been emotional, but it felt as though they had both already moved away. Mavis had succeeded in that sense. She had taken Liz from us and torn the rest of us apart. For now, she had succeeded. We were becoming as miserable and isolated as she was.

But I couldn't—wouldn't—let her win.

CHAPTER
35

GROWING UP, I was something of a serial best friend. I had close friends, the kind who would finish my sentences and have long sleepovers, sharing our deepest secrets. The first was Sarah Brosnan, who lived across the street from me. We became best friends by default in fourth grade, spending the summers together inventing dance routines in our front yards, blasting music on my pink portable radio. Then, in seventh grade, the wedge of boys and kissing appeared, and Sarah became popular and I did not. By the time we went to high school, we barely waved to each other in the hallways.

In high school, the pattern repeated itself, this time with a girl from my English class. We became fast friends, inseparable, before we got into a fight over who was allowed to wear the dress that we both loved to the spring dance, and while we eventually made up, it was never the same.

In college, the pattern continued.

And then came adulthood and postcollege life. While I had work buddies and a social circle, the closeness of those friendships never repeated itself. I had nearly accepted it, that adult friendships were meant to have a hefty dose of space.

But all of that ended when I moved to Whispering Farms and met Liz, Jess, and Melissa. They were truly my first friendships where I felt like I could be myself, where I felt there was a place for who I truly was, an Amy-shaped slot in our group. And, looking back, it was from that safe place where I truly started to blossom, to feel like a grown-up.

I had to give it one more try, a final plea to ask them to reconsider helping Liz. I picked up my phone and typed out a text, my heart in my throat.

———

WE SAT FOR a moment in the uncomfortable silence of my backyard, the white noise of the cicadas all around us. A faint odor of burning wood filled the air, from where the Baileys had burned their redbud, a tree unfortunate enough to have been in Liz's path the night of the Ouija board.

"I know it sounds ridiculous, but we have to do an exorcism," I said, trying to keep my voice steady. "All of us. It will only work if it's all three of us."

Melissa slapped a hand on the table and began to stand. "Amy, I agreed to come over here and hear you out. But this has gone too far." She stood and crossed her arms over her chest, shaking her head. "My entire life was spent in fear. My parents told me if I wore shorts, I would upset God. They said child molesters were lurking around every corner. They said if I didn't wear my best dress every Sunday to services, I would literally go to hell." She looked at us, eyebrows raised high. "But you know what? The scariest things are the ones that are real. Child molesters weren't lurking around the corner, they were living down the street. One of the high-ranking members of their church was arrested a few years ago."

"Whoa," Jess whispered. A large bandage was on her face, taped across her cheek.

Melissa nodded. "My point is that I was raised to be afraid of a boogeyman but nothing real. But Liz and whatever all of this is? I'm afraid of that. When I left Ohio, I told myself I wouldn't let my upbringing ruin my life, so I promised myself that I wouldn't be afraid anymore, especially of things I couldn't see. Well, I can see this, and for that reason, I'm out."

She turned to leave, and I scrambled to stand, knocking my chair to the side. It clattered as the metal hit our concrete patio. "Wait, please." I held a hand in the air.

Stop. Please. Listen.

I had a momentary flashback to when my parents and I tried to convince June to go to rehab the last time. We had gathered for an intervention, and she took one look at the room and tried to run out. We knew if she left, it would all be over. She died three days later.

I couldn't let Melissa leave.

Melissa stopped and crossed her arms over her chest, eyebrows raised. Jess remained seated, her mouth pressed together in a tight line that I knew was holding back everything she wanted to say. A physical indication of how badly she wanted to tell me that I was wrong. That I was being selfish to want them to stay. That this was more about my own fears than fears for Liz. Part of me was afraid she was right.

"Mavis murdered her family because she was alone, isolated. She didn't have anyone. She didn't have us. You guys." I looked from Jess to Melissa, but their faces were impenetrable. "You guys—including Liz—saved me. Just knowing you guys were nearby, knowing that you guys understood, has saved my life. Your support, whether overt or quiet, has made me a better person, friend, wife, mother."

Jess's face softened, but Melissa's remained stony. One down.

I continued. "I don't talk about it much, but I need to. I was destroyed when June died. I couldn't forgive her, or myself. It devastated my parents and made me doubt that there was good in the world. It made me feel helpless, alone, and afraid. But when we moved here, something changed. Your friendship made me realize that there were good things in the future. That life could be weird, funny, spontaneous." I twisted my hands in my lap. "You guys brought me back to life."

Jess looked down, and I realized she had begun to cry. Melissa's face relaxed, but she wasn't convinced.

"Our friendship, the four of us, means more to me than you guys could ever imagine. I know that other people see us and wish they had what we have. No one has what we do."

Melissa's eyes remained fixed on mine, and I saw a flash of emotion behind them.

"I used to think that people like Heather and her friends embodied Whispering Farms. But I know now that's not true. It's us. It's not just where we live, it's who we are, as terrible as that thought sounds. It's me. It's you guys. It's Liz. It's our home. And we can save it, but only if we do it together."

I looked at my friends, my heart racing, out of breath.

"I was told to make sure that whatever we do with Liz is worth it. And I know it's unimaginable to think about what we've had to endure, and what we might have to do, but I know it's worth it. It's an awful sacrifice, but a worthy one. Please," I added.

Jess gave a small sob and put her hands over her face. I sat down next to her and put my arm around her shoulders. Then I looked up at Melissa. For what felt like hours, she just stared back at me as she mulled over my words, like water rushing over a stone.

"Please," I said again. "Just consider it for now."

Jess looked up at Melissa, with my arm still around her shoulders, and said, "C'mon, Melissa. We can do this."

Melissa took a step backward and slowly lowered herself onto the love seat. She clasped her hands in her lap. "You're asking me to go against everything that I fought to forget. You know you're asking me to do that, right?"

"I know. I'm sorry," I said.

She stared at her hands, interlocking her fingers. She sighed and dropped them before she looked up. Her face was hard, and my heart beat even faster as I was sure she was going to say no.

"Fine. Let's get that bitch out of our friend."

CHAPTER 36

THE THREE OF us were mostly silent as we drove to downtown Chicago the next day. The weight of what we had to do hung thick in the air, swirling around us like the mist Liz created on the sidewalks.

After ninety long minutes, we arrived at the Equinox Bookstore. The front of it looked unassuming, like a place that hosted local authors talking about the native bird population. A small store with two windows and the name stenciled on the front with white paint sandwiched between two other stores, it felt like a location where a soccer mom might run in to grab the latest book her book club was reading, one that she would never actually read, just pounding wine at the meeting instead. Essentially, every book club in Winchester.

Except the Equinox Bookstore was anything but a suburban respite. For starters, it was in North Center, west of the yuppies who lived in Lincoln Park and north of the drunken postcollege grads who cosplayed as weekend warriors while doing shots at the Cubby Bear every Friday night. It was also between a sex toy shop and a dispensary.

"Ohhhh," Jess said as I parked the car across the street.

"No," Melissa and I said in unison. She was next to me in the passenger seat and neither of us so much as turned around to see what Jess looked at in appreciation. We knew it was the Candy Vault, apparently famous for their variety of dildos, according to the placard out front.

I glanced at Melissa and saw her eyes were trained on the dispensary. "No for you, too. We are here for business."

I tried to peer into the windows of the bookstore, but it was too dark. Equinox was an occult bookseller that Melissa had found online. We needed reinforcements, knowledge, and expert advice on how to approach an exorcism. Melissa had flatly refused any notion of asking her parents if they knew any actual demon hunters but offered to find a place that might know something.

As we approached the front door, a strong wave of anticipation nearly made my knees buckle. We could have been just steps from finding out information that would make everything stop, and the thought was overwhelming. What was more overwhelming, though, was the idea that we wouldn't.

I pushed open the door with my friends following closely behind. It was dimly lit inside, and it took several moments for my eyes to adjust. While my vision was coming into focus, the smell of incense overwhelmed me. It reminded me of my first-year dorm, when my next-door neighbors smoked copious amounts of weed and burned incense all night to cover the smell. I don't know why they bothered; our RA distilled her own liquor in her room, so she didn't care what anyone did.

The inside of the Equinox Bookstore was painted a dark blue. The bookshelves were white and full of brightly colored books, an array of pink and green spines like you'd usually find on beach reads. In one corner sat a glass case with talismans, charms, and sparkly jewelry.

"Where's the demon section?" Melissa said impatiently as she eyed a collection of crystals under a glass box.

"I don't know. Look around. I—" I said before I was cut off.

"Hey there, ladies," said a voice that at first appeared to have no body. But then a figure stepped out of the shadows. "Welcome to Equinox."

"Oh! Hello," I said.

The woman in front of me was a surprise. I thought someone who worked in a place like this would look more, well, like a witch. Or Wiccan. Instead, she looked like someone I would invite over for dinner, wearing olive-green joggers and a white T-shirt.

"So, how can I help you? I didn't mean to, but I was ear-hustling and heard you're looking for books on demons?" she said. She put her hands on her hips and rocked them forward and back, like she was a used-car salesman ready to negotiate.

"Yup, demons. Exorcisms of demons, specifically," Jess said. I turned to look at her, and she lifted her palms. "What? We are."

I waited for the woman to laugh at us or at least ask why, but she just nodded and turned, motioning for us to follow her. I guess we weren't the first group to come in with such a request.

We walked past wind chimes, candles, spell books, and sage

sticks, to a small bookcase at the back of the store. A purple blanket was draped over the top of the shelves, like it was the entrance to the back room in a porn store.

She carefully lifted the blanket, pausing halfway through to smile at us. "Don't want to scare the children who come in here."

"You allow children in here?" Melissa said.

She nodded. "Sure. Their parents usually bring them in after stopping by next door."

I wondered whether she was referring to the sex shop or the weed dispensary but didn't really want to find out.

She crouched down to one of the shelves. "Exorcisms are right here." She waved a finger at a row of books. "But this one is the gold standard." She pulled out a thin, green-jacketed book. The cover was bare, save for black lettering: *Exorcisms in the Modern Era*, by Kristin Charity.

I reached for it, to flip it open, but Jess plucked it out of her hand first. She opened it and her eyes grew wide, and she quickly shut it.

"We'll take it," she said.

The saleswoman led us to the checkout area and rang up the book. As I handed over my credit card, she narrowed her eyes on me.

"So, who has it?" She slowly looked at each of us. Seeing our confused faces, she looked down at the book and then up again.

"Oh, none of us. It's our friend Liz. *We* aren't possessed," I said a little too quickly.

Melissa leaned against the countertop. "Do we look demonic?"

The saleswoman pointed to Jess's bandaged face. "Did this Liz do that to you?"

We didn't say anything, our silence as confirmation.

She whistled and shook her head. "Strong one. I've seen a few people come in here, telling stories like that. Usually it's just someone looking for an excuse as to why their wife or girlfriend is acting differently. Like, 'She can't possibly be in her right mind to break up with someone like me, so she must be controlled by Satan.'"

Melissa made a confirmation noise. "Oh, I get that."

The saleswoman gave her a questioning look, and Jess chimed in, "Grew up in a religious laser-light-show cult."

"Ah." She nodded, and then her brows knitted together. "But if this is real, and you decide to perform the ritual, make sure you have protection. Something physical, like a cross if that's your thing, or crystals. Anything imbued with positive, protective energy. Something that your friend—wherever she is in there—will recognize."

The book safely tucked under my arm as we left the store, I asked my friends, "So what's our safety item for protection?"

"A gun?" Melissa said as she opened the car door.

"Very funny," I said. "Maybe we can get some crystals?"

"The bracelets," Jess said as she hopped into the backseat. "Remember those small woven bracelets that Liz gave us?"

"Absolutely. The bracelets," I said as I started the car.

Stronger with You. Whether or not that would be the case, we would do this together, our fates joined.

CHAPTER 37

I POURED MYSELF THE largest glass of wine possible, like a recent college graduate at a bottomless-mimosa brunch, and carried it into the family room, where Mark was watching a movie starring Mark Wahlberg. Mark Wahlberg's character seemed to be combating terrorism with his signature sneer and abject confusion.

I sat down, and he glanced at my wineglass, looked back at the screen, and glanced at it again.

"Long day?" he said as he muted the television. His dark blue eyes stared at me intensely, one of the reasons I fell in love with him when we first met. He always wanted to give me his full attention when we talked. I knew from my friends that this was unusual. Their husbands always thought they could multitask, talking to their wives while they watched television or messed around on their phones. When, in fact, it seemed like the basic ability to do two things at once was relegated to the female species.

"On the way to the bookstore, we hit traffic from the White Sox game. The Eisenhower was a mess." The Eisenhower Expressway was perpetually under construction. It was, without a doubt, the most poorly constructed and designed thoroughfare in the Chicago area, and it was the only access from the western suburbs to downtown. Dwight D. should have been turning over in his grave because his name had been given to such an atrocity.

As we had driven through the section that butted up to a cemetery, Jess said from the backseat, "Del told me they said they moved the bodies when they built this highway, but I bet they didn't."

I shivered, thinking that we were sitting in traffic over people's family members. Skeletons, even, at this point. Once, they had been breathing, living people who had a favorite food, a book they hated, a treasured song. Now they were part of the roadway we drove over as we cursed traffic and listened to AM radio.

"Why couldn't Mavis have possessed whoever approved the plans to do that instead of Liz?" Melissa had muttered, mostly to herself.

As I took a long sip of wine, Mark laughed. "Well, now I understand why you had to make it a double, then."

I looked at him and a pang of longing ran through my bones. So much had happened, and my friends and I had gone through so very much, and he didn't know about most of it. Sure, we had kept secrets from each other in our marriage, but they were mostly about who ate the last of the ice cream or who had forgotten to shut the garage door overnight. Never something like this. I didn't want this to be the beginning of more terrible secrets.

I set my wineglass down on the table and then quickly picked it up and took another large gulp of liquid courage. And then I turned to him. "I have to tell you something."

He raised his eyebrows and leaned forward, putting his forearms on his knees, hands clasped together. "Okay."

"It's about Liz." His eyes briefly closed for a moment and then he looked at me, silent, waiting.

And I told him that my friends and I were going to perform an exorcism.

His face remained the same, impassive and neutral, as I went through it all. Not so much as a flinch or a lean back against the couch.

It felt both cathartic and terrifying to tell him, like a confession. It was as though I floated above my body, listening, realizing how ridiculous and awful the words sounded. But I had to tell him, like a marital therapy session. Looking back, it might have been easier to confess if I had been cheating or had a gambling problem and spent our life savings at Rivers Casino betting on Japanese horse racing.

When I finished, I took another deep drink and waited for his response.

He slowly looked down at the floor and pressed his fingertips together, over and over.

"Mark?" I said quietly.

He glanced up, his face creased with worry, and he looked like he had aged ten years in those few minutes.

"Amy, you realize how this sounds, right? You can't be serious." His tone wasn't angry or accusatory but calm. Even. Like he was yet again explaining how to work the new wireless security system we had installed last year, which I still couldn't figure out how to operate.

I was equally calm in my response, although my chest burned with anger and frustration. "Yes, I know how it sounds. Believe me—I know. Just saying it makes me feel worse about it all. But there is something very wrong with Liz, and we know it's not self-created. She's in real danger. We all are. We have to try, in the hopes of getting it all to stop." I leaned forward, my voice shaking. "Please, Mark. I need you to support me."

He rubbed his forehead. "I believe that you believe in this. But I just can't rationally accept the idea that an exorcism is going to fix everything."

I sat back on the couch and took a long breath in and then let it out. I stared at the coffee table in front of me, my eyes trained on the leg that Rocky had chewed. "Okay, well if you can't accept it, if your mind doesn't let you go there, then at least understand that this is something I—no, we: Jess, Melissa, and I—have to do. We have to at least try before something worse happens next." I looked up at him.

He shook his head slightly and hunched his shoulders forward. There was a long moment while I waited for him to say something. Say anything. Tell me I needed professional help, tell me he was going to lock me away.

"If it's what you need to do," he said quietly, his eyes never lifting toward mine.

It was the best I was going to get from him. He couldn't wrap his mind around what had happened, or what needed to happen next. But at least he wasn't going to try to stop me. And we had been honest with each other.

"It is," I said.

"When is this all happening?" he said.

I swallowed hard. "I'm going to text Tim and find a time. And if it goes according to plan, we should all be safe after it's done."

"And what if it doesn't? If you truly believe there's a demon inside of her—and I'm not saying I do—what happens if it attacks you guys or hurts Liz even more?" His voice was flat.

I shook my head, even though a jolt of fear ran down my arms. "I can't even think about that possibility. It has to work. We've gathered all the evidence and research we can. We have a book with an incantation and the process for the ritual. It will be successful because we won't let it be anything else."

"What are you going to tell Tim?" he asked.

"Just that we are coming over to spend time with her, so he needs to get the kids out of the house." *And out of harm's way*, I silently added.

Mark stood up and walked over to me, perching on the coffee table across from me. He leaned forward and grabbed my hands. His eyes were wide, full of concern.

"Please be careful, no matter what happens," he said.

"We will. I promise," I said.

He leaned forward and hugged me, tight. He kissed the top of my head before he swiveled around and sat down on the couch next to me. I rested my head on his shoulder.

Even though I felt a weight had been lifted off my body by confessing, a tinge of frustration still remained. Of course he wasn't going to buy into the story. But his unwillingness to see reality cemented my determination.

Moms were the ones who had to fix problems. From small

things like a skinned knee to bigger ones like supernatural forces trying to take over our families. It was up to us to save the neighborhood. And I knew that was how it had always been and how it would always be.

It was time to fight, and moms were the ones on the front lines.

Mavis, we're coming for you.

CHAPTER 38

C ome over at 9pm tomorrow.

I looked down at the text from Tim, and my hands began to shake. I placed my phone on the kitchen island, but not before I typed out a message to my friends.

It's on. 9pm.

I'd texted Tim earlier that morning under the guise of organizing an "intervention" with Liz. I told him that I knew she was going through something, a "midlife crisis," and wanted to talk to her. I said I thought it was best if she didn't know we were coming so we could surprise her.

If I stopped long enough to think about what we were about to do, what we hoped to accomplish, my insides grew cold and every fiber of my being told me to run away. I knew, in my gut, that it would only work if we were all there, but that didn't stop me from feeling a deep sense of doom and responsibility for whatever might happen.

After searching high and low, I finally found the bracelet that Liz had given me. It was tucked in a drawer of my desk, behind a stack of bills. It was dusty when I pulled it out. I rubbed my index finger along the letters. *Stronger with You.* I slipped it on my wrist, pulling the drawstring tight.

Jack and Emily were painting in the playroom. I had a window of quiet time, as I was worried one of them would knock the water over or fight over the paintbrushes. I pulled the demonology book out from under my bed where I had stashed it.

I sat at my desk with the book, taking notes on a legal pad. The only pen I could find was purple, so the pages of notes looked more like a high school girl's letter to her crush than a road map for exorcising a demon.

Kristin Charity's *Exorcisms in the Modern Era* truly did seem to be the gold standard. The first part highlighted a few recent stories of exorcisms, mostly from houses where spirits terrorized the families, but it ended with a full description of the ritual. Kristin had interviewed Ed and Lorraine Warren, a couple famous in the demonology world for being able to contact and banish dark forces. My eyes stopped on a passage halfway down page 204.

> In doing a ritual to send a demon back to their realm,
> the exorcist must be very careful to protect themselves.
> Demons have the ability to jump from one person to
> the next, finding a new suitable host when necessary.
> If they are threatened or cornered, they will seek out
> a more comfortable place to inhabit, usually a person

who has doubts or is vulnerable to being infected. That
is why utmost care must be taken to cleanse yourself
of negativity before the ceremony begins.

I shivered, a creeping sensation moving up my back to the top
of my head. I pictured a dark, twisted cloud filled with tortured
screams floating up out of Liz and into one of us.

After the possessed person is secured physically, with
care taken since demonic forces often increase physi-
cal strength, an incantation is read. It's to temporarily
paralyze the demon, and to speak directly to the per-
son inside. The inhabited must be empowered to fight,
as they usually have given up hope of regaining their
consciousness. Once they begin to fight, then the real
battle begins. It's a battle for their soul, of the light and
the dark.

Underneath, in a shaded box, was the incantation. My breath
quickened as I stared at the unfamiliar Latin. They were ancient
words, wrapped in tradition and superstition. Shrouded in evil.
And I would have to stay up all night to figure out the proper pro-
nunciation of the passage.

After the ritual is done, if it is successful, the demon
will be released. It will start to look for a new host to
finish its work. That's why the next step is critical: the
dark spirit must be banished with fire. The most com-
mon way is to corral it into a fireplace or a pyre, but

*oftentimes, one has to work with what is available to
them.*

I paused and looked up. Liz didn't have a proper fireplace, just a fake electric one in her family room. Which meant we would have to light the demon on fire while it hung in the air. We would need to do it outside, so we didn't accidentally burn her house down.

I read through the passage again and took notes, preparing to send it to Melissa and Jess. After I had written twenty pages, and drawn diagrams and maps of our plan, I set the purple pen down, my hand aching. I then took pictures of the research and texted it to my friends. After a few moments, they responded.

This is . . . a lot. I'm getting nervous, Melissa replied.

We got this was Jess's response.

Yes, we do, plus you have to banish your fear or Mavis'll hop right into you, I typed back, and then put my phone down.

I gathered the papers together in a stack and put it safely back under my bed. The last thing I wanted was the kids using the papers for more watercolor art, although that would have been apropos with the way everything else had gone.

The silence of my house felt crushing, like the walls were holding their breath, watching with a terrified gaze. I felt the terror, too, but there was no choice but to ignore it. We had to confront Liz, and we had come too far down this awful road to question our commitment to the journey.

I opened my laptop and began to painstakingly research how to pronounce each of the words of the incantation, laser-focused. My life—all of our lives—depended on it.

———

AFTER MARK CAME home that night from work, I left. It was time to do something that I had avoided for five years. I had only a few hours before it was time to go to Liz's house, but I needed to do this first.

I parked my car in the asphalt lot of St. Mary of the Angels cemetery. It was almost dusk, giving the grass and concrete head-stones a light glow. I swallowed hard as I opened the door and walked across the expansive lawn, taking note of the names around me. So many names, so much loss. Some of the dates told me there were young children buried there, parents somewhere out there who had faced unimaginable grief.

I walked past husbands and wives, families buried together. Some of the markers had pictures of loved ones, with expansive displays of flowers and small gifts. And some of them were over-grown and covered in dirt, not having had a visitor for years.

I swallowed hard as I made my way through the cemetery, until I reached my sister's grave. I slowly sank to my knees and ran my finger over the grooves of her name.

June McCall.

Tears blurred my vision as I whispered to her everything that I never got to say. I told her about Emily and Jack, and how I wished they knew her.

And then, finally, I said what I had come to tell her.

"June, I forgive you. I saw what you wrote in your notebook. I forgive you—I've always forgiven you. I need you to forgive me, too," I whispered. "And I need to forgive myself."

I ran my finger along her name again and brushed the debris off her stone, before I turned and left. A sense of catharsis came over me as I drove home, fully prepared to face Liz and her demons, now that I had faced my own.

It was time to see what I was truly made of.

CHAPTER

39

THE MOON WAS nearly full, casting a strange glow on the neighborhood streets as I walked to the corner to meet Jess and Melissa to try to save our friend. They were both already at the street sign on the corner of Maple Leaf and Seneca Drives, standing silently. The air was humid, and time felt like it was on pause. A mosquito buzzed in my ear as I approached them, and I felt a pinch on the back of my neck as it bit me. I slapped at it and pulled my hand away, a smear of blood on my palm.

I was still shaken from my conversation with Emily before I left. She had asked me where I was going when she saw me heading toward the front door with a bag. I told her I was going to Miss Liz's house with my friends to hang out.

Her eyes widened, and she shook her head, stepping back slightly. "No, Mommy. Don't do that."

My pulse quickened. "It will be fine. We just haven't seen her very much lately."

She took another step back, her head swiveling back and forth. "No. It's not safe."

I knelt down on one knee, placing the black bag of supplies next to my leg. "Why not?" I didn't know if I wanted the answer.

"I had a bad dream that bad things happened to you at her house," she said. She bit her lip and twisted her hands in front of her body.

My voice was a whisper. "What kind of things?"

"Monsters came and took you away. They pulled you into the basement, and you never came back out. And Miss Liz was laughing," she said.

I held out my arms, and she took a step toward me. I pulled her against my chest. "That was just a dream. Everything will be fine. It was just a nightmare," I whispered into her hair, closing my eyes.

"Don't go," she said into my shoulder. "Amelia said scary things would happen. That she doesn't want you to go, and that she doesn't want us to get hurt."

Determination built in my chest as I leveled my eyes at hers. "Look at me. Nothing will happen to you or to me. Or anyone. We are going to make all the bad things stop. And then we will all be safe. I promise."

She didn't respond, just hugged me tight. I closed my eyes and hugged her back.

"I promise," I whispered into her hair.

As I approached Jess and Melissa on the street corner, I saw their eyes were wide and lips pressed together. Melissa wore black workout pants with a pink tank top, and Jess was in all white: white running shorts and a white T-shirt with *Manitowoc Turkey*

Trot 2012 on the front. At their feet were two bags of supplies. In Jess's hand, she held an aluminum water bottle.

"Do we have everything?" I whispered. Down the block, I heard Heather's designer dog barking.

Jess lifted the water bottle, which I recognized as a free promotional item we got from Mark's work last year. I must have left it at her house at some point. Instead of water, it was filled with gasoline.

"I got some strange looks at the gas station when I filled this up and then put it in the back of the Prius," she said. She lifted her hand and sniffed it. "I'm never getting rid of that smell, I can already tell."

I nodded, and she put the gasoline bottle in my bag. "Solid work." I turned to Melissa. "Do you have it?"

She bent down and opened her bag, pulling out the exercise bands she used for doing online barre classes in her basement. She also produced a rope and bungee ties that she'd used to secure the turtle-top storage container to the roof of her car when her family drove to Florida last summer. I noticed a gold crucifix around her neck, a new addition.

In my bag, I had two grill lighters. The incantation spell was in my back pocket. I held up my wrist and waved it around, the *Stronger with You* bracelet tight. My friends did the same.

"Wait, I have one more thing," Jess said. She pulled out three shirts from her bag. They were brightly colored and covered in parrots.

"Jimmy Buffett shirts?" I said. "Are you serious?"

She nodded as she tossed each of us a shirt. "Extra level of protection. Maybe if Liz sees them, she will be reminded of who she really is. Plus, she would never do anything to hurt Jimmy." She yanked her T-shirt off and pulled hers over her head. It read, *Fins to the Left, Fins to the Right.*

"This feels like an 'It's all for you, Damien,' moment," I said grimly as I began to put on the shirt.

Melissa grumbled, but she donned one. I had to laugh as I looked around at us, a nervous, squeaking laugh. We looked like we were ready to tailgate out of the back of a pickup truck, not pull a demon out of our friend.

Melissa raised her eyebrows at me and shook her head. "This is so wrong." Her twang was back.

"What about any of this feels right?" I said as I smoothed the pink-and-blue shirt down over my hips.

"You guys will thank me—and Jimmy—when these shirts save our collective asses," Jess said.

"All right. Should we proceed?" I said.

They nodded, pink-and-blue blurs in the dark.

We were ready.

A silent moment passed between us, everything unsaid but understood. We knew what we were about to do was the epitome of dangerous, and I just hoped our friendship was enough of a shield to protect us.

"Let's go," I said.

JESS BOUNDED UP the stairs to Liz's door, and I had a flashback to the night when everything started, when the only thing we were worried about was our hangovers the next morning. She lifted her fist to rap on the door, but it opened before she made contact.

Tim stood in the doorway, wearing a black suit with a blue-and-red tie. "You guys are late," was all he said. He did a double take when he saw our T-shirts and then shook his head, eyes closed.

Jess slowly turned around, mouth twisted in anger, and looked at us. Melissa shook it off first.

"Hi, Tim. Good to see you." Her tone was placating. I assumed it was the same composure she used at work when dealing with difficult clients, or possibly with the intern she'd had last year who spent all day on TikTok and repeatedly said, "That slaps," during conference calls. "Don't worry, we can sign any liability waivers you require."

He responded with a smirk.

Jess tried to crane her neck around him to peer inside the house. "Where are the kids?"

"My mother came and picked them up an hour ago." He stepped aside for us, impatiently waving his hand around.

"Where's the dog?" I remembered that I hadn't seen Bucky the last time I was at the house, either.

Tim rolled his eyes. "At my sister's. He started snapping at Liz and acting strangely." He again waved at us to come inside.

My body tensed as I took a step forward. I ignored it and walked over the *Home Sweet Home* welcome mat.

The house was still, dark. I had an awful sensation that we were being watched. That every piece of furniture—and the walls themselves—had eyes and their threatening, amused gaze was on us.

Did you really think this would work?

"Where is she?" I said in a low tone as I stepped over the overnight bag by the front door. I carefully put my black bag on the opposite wall.

"Upstairs, I think. Maybe the kitchen," he said, his gaze on his phone screen. He briefly looked up, eyebrows raised, and nodded his head toward the kitchen. "Go ahead."

We turned and took a step toward the hallway to the kitchen, hearing the front door open. Tim stopped and turned before he closed the door behind him.

"If she doesn't snap out of this, I told her I'm taking the kids and leaving for good. She's a mess, and it's getting pretty fucked up. Good luck. I'm staying in a hotel for the night. I can't be around her anymore," he said. He shook his head and slammed the front door shut.

I wanted to chase him down and punch him in the face for being so clueless. How could he not see that this wasn't something she had chosen? That his wife's soul was in danger and crying out for help? No, he wouldn't ever realize something like that. Only we could.

We exchanged a look in the hallway, collectively taking a deep breath. My eyes focused on the gallery wall next to me, professional pictures of Liz's family at a nearby forest preserve. She had obsessed for weeks over their outfits. She was so proud of those pictures, so proud to show off her family.

We weren't just doing this for us, but for Liz and her kids, her dream of her family.

I swallowed hard before I called, "Liz? Liz, where are you?"

Melissa waved a hand around to catch my eye and pointed to the backyard.

Yes. Right. "Liz, it's us. Melissa, Jess, and Amy. We just want to talk. We miss you. Can you meet us outside? We have something we want to . . . show you." My words echoed through the silent house.

Show you? Jess mouthed, and I shrugged frantically.

I was about to call her name again when I heard slow footsteps on the wood floors upstairs. With each reverberation, my panic increased until I could barely breathe.

Thud.

Thud.

Thud.

Her footsteps were methodical, even. She was taking her time, calmly walking toward us. We were the prey, and she was the apex predator. She didn't need to run; we weren't going anywhere. At least, anywhere that she couldn't find us.

She knew just as well as we did why we were there, and it was her chance to finally finish what had already started.

"Please, can you meet us outside?" My words came out shaky, thin. Weak.

How on earth are we going to do this when I can't even speak?

A noise like the earth opening up. A low rumble, like thunder just before a thunderstorm begins. There was a word wrapped in that reverberation: *No.*

I looked at my friends. Ridiculously, we hadn't planned for that. We had assumed we could at least get her outside into the backyard. If we couldn't even do that, I had no idea how we were going to do the rest.

The three of us remained frozen in place as she walked down the stairs. I felt like a deer on a country road late at night, seeing headlights but unable to move out of the way. Unable to save myself.

Jess gave a strangled cry as Liz walked into the kitchen. She looked energized. Revitalized. Her hair flowed around her shoulders, snow white and reaching almost down to her waist. She wore a white sheath that reached the ground, almost completely sheer.

Her face was pulled tight, like she'd had a 90210-worthy facelift. Her mouth was bloodred, her lips pursed together in a smirk. As she took us in, she smiled widely. Her incisors were sharper, her nails filed into points. She looked like a dark priestess. An entity ready to open up the veil in between our world and the dark supernatural, and let loose all the demonic forces.

She had been waiting for this moment to invite the legion from hell to Whispering Farms. Everything before now had been preamble, a tease.

She didn't say anything as she stood, perfectly still, in the doorway. Waiting for us to do whatever it was that we had planned, so she could finish us off.

She had bided her time, and now the prey had come to the predator.

CHAPTER

THE FOUR OF us seemed to be frozen in the kitchen, a horror movie on pause. No one spoke or moved, and the only sensation besides the blinding panic in my head, telling me to run, was the sweat that trickled down my back, soaking my shirt.

Jess was the one to press Play. "Look, we wore these shirts for you," she said. She dramatically pointed to her chest, a quivering smile on her face. "We know how much you love being a Parrothead. Maybe we could all go to a concert together. Remember how you wanted us to go last summer and we said no? We really want to now. I want to hear the song—"

I quickly elbowed her, as we were not there to blabber about Jimmy Buffett. I looked at Liz. She began to hum quietly, a deep, throaty hum that sounded like disconnected stereo speakers. It circled my brain and began to lull me into a trance. I forgot what we were there for, allowed the noise to overtake me. Wherever it wanted me to go, I was ready.

Liz outstretched her arms toward me, a warm sensation moving through my body. It was as though she were a magnet, and I was the metal. My entire being wanted to take a step toward her. I didn't care about what she had become, I just wanted to let the humming overtake me. The sound promised rest and respite, an end to suffering, if I just allowed it. Peace, happiness, contentment.

I had never wanted anything more.

I had lifted my foot to step toward her when a noise shattered the hums. It was Rocky barking in our backyard.

The facade was lifted as all four of us turned toward the barking. I shook my head, feeling foggy, as I looked at my friends.

"Get her!" shouted Melissa as she took a step toward Liz. Jess was the closest and lunged at her, grabbing her arm. Liz tried to jerk back, but Jess was too strong. She grabbed Liz in a bear hug, and I sprang into action. I threw open Melissa's bag of supplies and grabbed a bungee cord. Melissa wrapped her arms around Liz to help Jess, and I stepped forward and began to wind the cord around our friend. I then reached for the barre class band and hooked it around her torso.

Liz began to hum and growl, deep animalistic sounds that felt like they would explode my organs. I faltered as the hum began to overtake me again.

"Ignore it! Focus!" Melissa shouted as she narrowly avoided a forward headbutt from Liz.

Liz paused, then swiftly snapped her head backward and hit Jess on the lip. It split open and blood began to seep from Jess's mouth, staining her teeth.

"Jesus, Liz, always the face with you," Jess said as she wrapped her arms tighter. She turned her head to the side and spat.

Sweating, I secured another bungee around Liz, and she stopped trying to wrestle away from us.

"She's not getting out of this," Jess said as she kept her arms around Liz and then spat again.

Liz stopped squirming and began to laugh a throaty laugh that came straight from her gut. Straight from hell. Her face twisted into Silly Putty, her mouth stretching from ear to ear, showing off two rows of teeth. The skin on her nose began to peel upward, like her entire face was a thin mask.

My stomach began to churn, and I felt vomit rise in my throat. I needed to cover her face. I spotted Tim's W flag on the countertop—apparently the Cubs were on a losing streak. I put it over Liz's head to hide her grotesque features, and Jess shoved her into a kitchen chair.

We stopped and stared at the figure sitting on the chair, face covered, immobile. She looked so helpless, like a hostage.

"Amy," Melissa snapped. "C'mon now."

Yes. It was time.

I pulled the incantation out of my back pocket. I didn't dare look up from the paper or else I would lose my nerve. I started to speak, my words growing stronger and more confident with every syllable.

"*Exsurgat Deus et Satanas expellatur. Expellantur hinc qui oderunt. Omnes qui servunt Satanae et viribus eius, abite hinc. Legio diabolica, invasores daemonici, expellemini. Sicut cera igne liquescit, liquescet impia vestra praesentia.*"

> *Let God arise and Satan be banished. Let those that hate be driven from this place. All those who serve*

> *Satan and his powers, be gone from here. All your*
> *wicked legion and demonic invaders, be driven away.*
> *As wax melts in a fire, so will your wicked presence.*

The air began to crackle with electricity, the kitchen lights around us dimming and brightening. I faltered for a moment and looked at Jess and Melissa. They urged me to continue.

Liz remained a statue under the cover.

"*Hinc abite, vobis imperamus. Abite. Vos eicimus.*"

> *Leave this place, we command you. Be gone. We cast*
> *you out.*

As I finished the last line, I looked up as my friends cried out. Liz was calmly standing. The bungee cords fell to the floor, nearly floating with an effortless flick of her arms. She slowly reached up and pulled the flag from her face, and I noticed her fingers were nail-less points, like skin claws.

She faced us, her eyes dark holes, all pupils. She chuckled, a terrible sound. And then I felt the most intense pain I'd ever felt. It was in my stomach, a burning sensation that felt like a lit match. My friends began to cry out in pain, too.

Melissa lifted her shirt, and we watched as words appeared on her smooth skin.

Your

In horror I looked to Jess, who frantically clawed at her shirt.

Children

I screamed as I lifted mine, staring down at the black words popping upward, like someone was inside my body, pushing the letters out.

Are

I felt light-headed, and the air began to smell like burning hair. Liz stood calmly and smiled. We had failed.

"Next," she said, finishing the sentence.

Your children are next. Our children. She would kill us here and now. And then come for our kids. They would be taken over by demonic forces or used for food as she brought other dark entities to our neighborhood. They would feed on all of us until there was nothing left. Until we were all bones like the ones in the pit. And then we would be forgotten, like Mavis and her family.

"Liz, no. Please." My voice was thin, and my vision clouded with pain. My knees buckled, and I wanted to slump to the floor, pass out. "I know you're still in there. You don't want this. You would never hurt our kids." I took a deep breath as a wave of burning pain ripped through my midsection. Jess was leaning against the kitchen wall, her face gray, and Melissa was doubled over, hyperventilating.

"You would never hurt them. I know that. And we would never hurt yours." I steadied my breath. "Your children are our children. We are a family."

"Family," Jess panted from the wall.

Melissa whimpered, her face hidden by a curtain of hair.

There was a murmur of pain as Jess put a palm on the wall and stood. The angry red gash on her face was illuminated by the hanging light over the kitchen island. The front of her shirt was dotted with blood.

"Family," she repeated. "Mavis, we know it's you. We know

what you did. And we know what you want. You want to ruin our lives and destroy all of us, because you never had what we do. So I'm going to make you a deal: Take me instead. Not Liz."

Melissa yelped as I put my hand out, reaching for Jess. "Jess, no!"

She didn't look at us, staring at Liz, her arms still at her sides. "Take me instead." She spread her fingers wide before putting them on her hips. "I'm stronger than Liz. I do CrossFit. I can do more damage than Liz. You don't want her. Take me."

The air around us crackled again, like sounds coming through a walkie-talkie. Mavis was considering it.

Melissa slowly stood, her face red, her hair plastered to her skull with sweat and tears. "Take me, Mavis. Liz is a better person than me—than all of us. I'm ruthless."

My heart seized in my chest as a wave of emotion spread throughout my body. I opened my mouth and whispered, "Take me. I never appreciated anything here. I deserve it." I closed my eyes. "I'm sorry, Liz, for never realizing how much you did for us. How much we all did for each other. So take me. Let Liz go."

The kitchen was silent, and I opened my eyes. Liz's face began to melt, her eyes moving down to her cheeks and the top of her head opening, like her skin was being unzipped from her bones. A dark cloud moved above her head as the dummy suit of our friend fell to the travertine floor.

The cloud buzzed like it was filled with a million flies ready to lay eggs in a rotting corpse. The shape contracted and then expanded, considering each of us. I shrank back against the wall, tripping over our bags of supplies.

Fire.

I ran to the foyer and grabbed my bag, nearly blind with fear.

I ripped it open, the fabric scratching my hands. I reached in, frantically groping around as Jess and Melissa began screaming and yelling for me to get the gasoline and lighter. Except all I felt was soft material. I looked down into the bag. It was a collection of men's T-shirts and underwear.

A terrible wave of recognition passed through me as I realized that Tim had taken my bag by accident and left me with his over-night clothes.

"He took it!" I shrieked from the floor. "Tim took my bag!"

"No!" I heard Jess call from the other side of the island.

"Find something else!" Melissa screamed. "Or we're all going to die!"

My head snapped around as I looked, my eyes going to the knife block on the countertop. The dark cloud was still hovering, cornering Jess and Melissa, who had stepped back against the wall of cabinets next to the back door. A knife wouldn't do anything. The cloud wasn't solid.

Fire. I needed fire.

Liz always had candles on the countertop. From the floor, I spied five white candles clustered together next to the oven. I crouched, grabbing the matches from the counter. They were long, fancy ones in a gold envelope that I remembered she had bought at HomeGoods.

Now I needed an accelerant.

"Amy, please!" Jess said, her voice cracking.

I needed gasoline, except that was in the bag in the back of Tim's car.

There was propane outside, but I didn't have time to detach the tank and bring it inside.

What else burns?

I had a quick flashback to the night when everything started, when Liz served us that terrible wine. The sweet rosé from a box. Gasoline wine, I had called it. Enough to burn our insides. And maybe a demon.

I wrenched open the fridge door and mercifully, the wine was still there. Apparently, Mavis was more of a red wine fan. I yanked the half-full box out and ripped open the top.

The dark cloud surrounded Melissa, pausing to rip the gold crucifix from her neck. She closed her eyes, her lips moving in silent prayer. Jess saw what I was doing and waved her arms.

"Now, Amy!"

I tossed the pink, sticky liquid in the air, toward the shape. It paused in the air, suspended in surprise. My hands felt like they were covered in sugar water as I struck a match.

"Melissa, get down!" I shouted before I tossed the match in the direction of the shape.

Except it didn't burn. Even though the wine tasted like gasoline, it wasn't an incendiary. Panicked, I looked around the kitchen. My eyes zeroed in on a bottle of cupcake-flavored vodka. That had to burn. I grabbed it and tossed the sticky liquid toward the shape, lighting another match.

Melissa ducked as the dark cloud exploded with fire. There was a primal scream from the center of it as it began to rotate inward, like a funnel cloud. Wind whipped across our faces.

"Mavis, leave us alone. Leave our neighborhood." My words seemed to be swept up in the wind, absorbed by the rotating energy. I began to chant the exorcism incantation again, my words growing stronger.

The energy began to pick up steam, and we collectively bent down, covering our faces and heads with our hands. There was a bang and a screech, like a car crash of metal on metal, and then, silence.

The air crackled four times before it went still. I slowly lifted my head from my arms and stood. Melissa's and Jess's faces were streaked with dark sludge as they examined their bodies, patting them down for injuries.

"Are you guys . . . you?" I said.

They nodded, and we looked at Liz on the ground. She was in the fetal position, her legs tucked into her chest. Her eyes were open, unblinking. But she looked like herself again.

I took a step toward Liz, crouching down and extending an arm toward her. With a shaking finger, I touched her back. It felt like it was on fire. She recoiled when she felt my hand on her.

Melissa and Jess came closer, and I looked up at them, shrugging my shoulders slightly as I moved my hand away.

"Water," Melissa said, and moved toward the sink, waving her hand in front of her face at the smell lingering in the kitchen's air. She filled a glass and held it out to me.

"Liz? Liz, it's us. You're safe now. Can you hear me? It's Amy," I said in a low tone.

She blinked once but didn't turn her head.

I extended my hand and put it on her cheek. I whispered her name again.

She slowly turned her head to me and looked up at me with red, bloodshot eyes. For the first time since it all began, her eyes looked like hers. She blinked a few more times and then moved her arms. Her hands shook as she put them on the floor and tried to push herself into a sitting position. She cried out in pain and then fell back to the floor.

"Shhhh, don't move. You've been through a lot. Just blink twice if it's you," I said.

Her gaze shifted toward me and she stared, and for a moment, my heartbeat quickened. Then, slowly, she blinked twice.

The three of us sighed deeply, shoulders collapsing down.

"We have to go outside," Jess said as she took a step toward the back door. We looked at her questioningly. "The pit. It's still open. We need to seal it off."

My head reared back. How could we have forgotten that detail?

"Amy, stay with Liz. Jess and I got this," Melissa said.

"Hell yes we do. Let's grab some shovels from the garage." Jess jogged out of the kitchen door to the backyard, Melissa behind her.

Liz made a croaking sound, and I leaned down to hear what she tried to say. Her breath still had the faint odor of darkness that we'd first smelled when the pit was opened up.

"What . . ." was all she managed to eke out.

"We'll explain everything. Don't worry. You're safe now," I said. I didn't know how we were going to tell her what had happened or how much. I didn't know if we should tell her the whole truth, if it would help or hinder. She would never forgive herself if we told her everything, and the last thing I wanted to do was cause her more pain.

I looked outside and saw Jess and Melissa filling the pit with dirt and comparing who had the better shovel. It was the most normal thing I had heard in weeks.

I was about to turn back to Liz when a small figure outside made me stop. It was a gray shape, hopping around the yard, underneath the rosebushes. A rabbit. I gasped; it was a sign from June. I watched as the rabbit hopped away, disappearing under the roses.

I rubbed Liz's back, trying to get her to sit up and take a sip of water. I had to muscle her body into an upright position and lift the glass to her trembling lips. Most of the water spilled out of her mouth, like she had forgotten how to eat and drink.

She swallowed and put her head on my shoulder. I tilted mine toward her and rested my chin on the crown of her head. I couldn't imagine what she had seen or thought over the past few weeks, if she had been in there the whole time, like a prisoner of her own body, unable to call for help. I wondered if she would ever be able to tell us about it, or if she would block it out. But that would come in time; for now, all that mattered was that we all were safe. That our love and friendship had been enough to battle the darkest of forces.

Liz was back. Mavis was banished. We had done it. We had exorcised a demon from our friend and our neighborhood. Just suburban moms, who are routinely dismissed and pushed aside, whose position in society seems to be in the background, taking care of everything. And yet, we had figured out how to save everyone.

Suburban moms had saved the world.

EPILOGUE

DOUBLE, **DOUBLE TOIL** *and trouble;*
Fire burn and cauldron bubble.

I heard the words from my front yard come wafting through the open kitchen window. I craned my neck around the corner and peered out. A group of children in Halloween costumes ran across the grass. They were dressed like witches, their long black dresses and pointed hats blowing in the unseasonably warm autumn air. In their hands, they held pillowcases and black and orange bags full of candy, swinging across their legs.

I started toward the front door, where I had a black bowl of Reese's Peanut Butter Cups waiting for the trick-or-treaters. I opened the door and smiled and passed out the candy as they opened their bags. I looked down the street, where Mark had Emily and Jack in a larger group of kids from the neighborhood, going door to door. Del pulled a wagon of beer behind him. They were stopped at the Spadlowskis' house, where they always had candy for the kids and libations for the adults.

I had offered to stay inside and pass out candy, since last year we had set the bowl out on the front step and all left. Within five minutes, the bowl had been emptied by a few greedy trick-or-treaters, something that made Mark inordinately annoyed. I was quick to point out to him that he told me as a kid they had done the exact same thing when they saw a bowl unattended. But still, I offered to stay home and ration out the precious candy.

It had been three months since we'd banished Mavis to whatever level of hell she came from. The four of us had mostly healed—well, the burn marks on our bodies had. Jess's face had the lightest hint of a scar that was easily covered with makeup. Her dermatologist had told her it should continue to lighten and eventually fade completely. If only our memories would do the same. I still had nightmares about the exorcism, even though we had triumphed. Emily, thankfully, told me Amelia didn't visit her anymore. I had hugged her tight and told her that Mommy had stopped all of the bad things.

She looked up at me, smiled, and said, "I know." She was aware of so much more than she would ever tell me.

After Liz had come to, she'd asked what happened. She remembered nothing from the possession, which seemed like the best possible option. Her last memory was the day they broke ground on the She Shed. We gently explained to her what had happened, and she thankfully didn't ask too many questions. It made me wonder if she did remember a few things but had chosen to block them out.

She had emerged as herself, with one thrilling change: She asked Tim for a separation after she took a survey of everything that had been neglected over the summer. Herself included. He didn't put up much of a fight and moved out to a condo in a nearby town with remarkable haste. She had just started back to work at the pediatric hospital, too.

"Candy corn Jell-O shot?"

I heard Jess's voice come through the back door.

I walked to the kitchen, where she set down the tray of orange, white, and yellow shots she held in one hand, her portable speaker in the other. "No, thanks. Those look radioactive."

She shrugged and lifted one, swallowing it in one gulp. She grimaced. "Awful. Never again." She pecked at her phone and her Halloween playlist came through the speaker, starting with "Freaks Come Out at Night."

"Boy, is that true," I laughed.

"Trick or treat," came a call as the front door opened. Liz and Melissa walked into the kitchen together, laughing.

"Did you see Tony's costume?" Melissa said, perching on a stool at the island.

"It's hysterical," Liz said with a smile. Her face had regained its fullness, and her hair was growing back in where there had been bald patches. Her nails still weren't back to normal, so she had glued fake nails to her fingers.

Melissa turned to me. "He's dressed as Lucille Ball, so I guess that makes me Ricky Ricardo."

"I thought you guys were coming over later," I said as I pulled a bottle of wine out of the fridge.

Melissa shrugged. "Trick-or-treating ends in an hour anyway, and I got bored with sitting in my house alone. Besides . . ." She looked to Liz.

Liz pulled an expensive-looking bottle of champagne out of her bag. She held it in the air. "We wanted to toast you, Amy. To your new gig."

I smiled and put my hands on my chest. Last week, I'd made the decision to open my own private counseling practice, specializing in women and children. If the events of the summer had taught me anything, it was the importance of community support. I was still sketching out details, but Mark and I were both excited for my next professional adventure. I'd had to go through hell to see where my opportunity was, but now it was in sight.

I pulled four fancy crystal glasses out of the cabinet, ones we'd gotten for our wedding but never used. They were warranted, on this night of all nights.

Liz popped the cork on the champagne and carefully filled the glasses. "I'm so happy for you, Amy. You deserve this, and I'm just thrilled to be a part of it."

I smiled at her, and we each took a glass.

"How about a toast?" Liz said as she considered her glass.

Jess, Melissa, and I shot each other nervous looks, thinking of the last time we toasted together. But Liz didn't notice.

"To Amy, and to all of you guys." Liz's gaze fell upon each friend. "Thank you for being there for me, and my family, when everything happened this summer. I don't know what I would do without you all. You really are lifesavers," she said with a smile.

You have no idea, friend, I thought as we clinked our glasses together. I took a small sip, the carbonation fizzing in my mouth and slightly burning my throat.

The doorbell rang, and I set my glass down. "One sec. Must be the last of the stragglers trick-or-treating." I grabbed the bowl of candy.

Not trick-or-treaters; in fact, it was Heather Hacker at the door. She stood, holding a stack of papers in her hand, dressed all in black with cat ears on her head. On her face, she'd painted black whiskers.

"Hi there, neighbor." She smiled brightly, her red lips moving upward in a smile.

"I'm assuming you're not here for candy?" I said with a laugh.

She smirked. "Not quite. I'm on keto now." She turned to the side to show off her figure, and I nodded appreciatively, mostly out of duty.

"I'm here to hand-deliver invitations to a small soiree I'm throwing." Her tone told me I was supposed to feel lucky to be included. She held out one of the papers in her hand.

It was a pale pink embossed invitation with her monogram on the front.

"It's a reveal of our new four-seasons room. You have to see it to believe it," she said.

I looked up, and my hand holding the paper froze. My body grew cold and my shoulders were at attention. Because when I saw her face, it . . . . changed. Her features ran together like melted chocolate, her cheeks running down her face to reveal her cheek-bones underneath as her eyes glowed. First red, then black. Her teeth fell out, one after another, bouncing on my concrete front stoop, as her lips stretched across her face to her ears.

"'Tis now the very witching time of night, when churchyards yawn and hell itself breathes out . . . ," she said in a low growl.

I remained in place, not able to move or speak to call my friends to the front door.

It's happening again.

Then, as quickly as it'd melted away, Heather's face returned to normal.

"Shakespeare?" she said with a laugh. "I can tell you've never heard the quote."

"I—what—" I sputtered out as the invitation in my hand shook.

"I'll put you down as a yes," she said. She turned to leave, stepping off the stoop and walking down the front path to the driveway. Before she reached the end, she turned and winked, giving me a demonic smile that showcased her incisors.

I couldn't move; my body was rooted into place.

"Amy?" I heard Jess call from the kitchen. "Get back in here before the champagne gets warm."

I could only stare at Heather's figure as she left my yard.

I watched her walk down the driveway and prepare to deliver the next invitation, and wondered what her plans for our neighborhood were.

Whatever they were, the four of us would be ready. It was the She Shed that started it all, but we would finish it.

ACKNOWLEDGMENTS

The inspiration for this book came to me the morning after a ladies' night with my friends. We had lamented that we didn't have a space of our own, away from the chaos of our daily lives. And so I began to brainstorm writing a book about friendships and finding a soft place to land in the ridiculousness that is often suburbia. As a longtime horror fan, an idea began to generate that would meld the two concepts. Thus, the haunted She Shed was born. From there, I began to see everything around me as worthy of a few scares, even my beloved Roomba.

But I didn't do this alone, and there are many people who helped me bring this book into the world.

Thank you to my agent, Holly Root, who responded with more than a few exclamation points when I emailed the pitch (appropriately titled "Weird idea") for this book. Your enthusiasm and excitement for this book carried me through all the tough writing moments.

To my editor, Kate Dresser—I knew from our first conversation that you understood what I was trying to do with this book, and I'm beyond thrilled that we are working together. I'll never forget when you told me during that first chat to just go wild with the story. So I did, and then you pushed me even harder, and the book became better than I had ever imagined. And to the whole team at Putnam, thank you for such a fun and rewarding experience with getting this book out into the world.

Thank you to all of my writer friends, especially Jillian Cantor, who understand the extreme highs and lows of this strange author life.

To the whole K-L crew—thank you for always supporting my endeavors, and for the daily memes and Nic Cage gifs. I'm especially grateful that I was allowed to watch horror movies growing up. Thanks, Mom and Dad! And to the Leurck crew, thank you for all of the love throughout the years.

And to all of my wonderful friends—especially the Mom Crew of Anne, Kim, and Meredith—thank you for providing the inspiration and hilarious moments, some of which will now live on in book form. Your excitement to read this book is unmatched, and I loved bringing a piece of all of you to the page. You all have taught me that we can do anything. The forces of darkness beware, for we have wine and snacks.

To my family—Kevin, Ryan, Paige, and Jake—thank you for putting up with all the hours I was locked in the bedroom, typing away and dreaming up suburban hilarity. Now please, go clean your rooms before our house is condemned.

Finally, to the readers—thank you for coming on this journey with me, and for celebrating the power of friendship.

DISCUSSION QUESTIONS

1. Despite the She Shed's jocular beginnings, the four friends share a deep need for such an enclave. What does the She Shed represent to them?

2. Amy, Liz, Jess, and Melissa are all quite different. But their reluctant acceptance of their suburban roles and their hatred for what they call the Mom Mafia unite them. Do you think their bonds of friendship would have been just as strong if the Mom Mafia didn't exist?

3. Amy realizes something is off with Liz when Liz fails to clean up her house after their movie night. What would be the first sign of demonic possession in your best friend?

4. The demon offers its first tangible threat by slaughtering the bunnies on Amy's lawn, which is only discovered during the

neighborhood block party. Why do you think this was the demon's first statement of threat?

5. When Liz becomes possessed, she isn't afraid to wreak havoc on the town. Do you think other people in the neighborhood noticed the drastic change in Liz to the same degree that her friends did? Would others have sensed the presence of something eerily abnormal? Discuss.

6. Author Maureen Kilmer touches on some darker themes: addiction, depression, isolation. Outside of the story's obvious horror elements, in what forms do we see darkness or evil surrounding a character? Is darkness limited to a certain kind of character? If so, why?

7. The suburban life is relentlessly social, awfully competitive, and continually hectic. The husbands of Whispering Farms Subdivision should share (mostly) the same burdens as their wives, yet the women seem to bear the weight of exhaustion more readily. Discuss the husbands' methods of coping with their respective living situations as compared to their wives.

8. Amy has her hands full with her two kids for whom she must engage with the PTA and pretentious block parties. But what she wants to do is make a difference. Name a few reasons why Amy might dread organizational projects for the school.

9. The pressures of motherhood don't always allow for many bonding moments between mother and child. On top of

searching for a job, Amy must orchestrate top-tier playdates and take her kids out for ice cream and pizza, all the while cleaning up after their messes. But when Mavis emerges, Emily's ability to see Amelia brings Amy's more intimate moments with Emily into focus. Discuss how the pressures of motherhood can both bring one closer to individuals and create distance in one's relationships.

10. Amy quickly learns how to deal with a volatile Liz: how to decipher the real Liz from the possessed Liz. Amy can render these two versions as clearly distinct. Would you find it difficult to see your friend in the same way if they had attacked you, despite knowing they were possessed?

11. Once Amy realizes it's up to her, Melissa, and Jess to save Liz, she tries to rally her friends to exorcise the demon. Instead, she's left with empty text messages from Jess and Melissa, who decide it would be best to leave town—and Liz. Do you understand the impulse to leave town? In what instances do loyalty (and exorcisms) trump fear and safety?

12. During one of their movie nights, Amy mentions that she "was a serious horror movie fan as a teenager" (p. 8). Meanwhile, Melissa grew up fearing the mildest of threats: birth control, Halloween, weed. Discuss how their respective backgrounds inform their reactions to the Ouija board. What strengths do each of the women bring to the table both in terms of demon-fighting and excelling at the suburban way?

ABOUT THE AUTHOR

MAUREEN KILMER graduated from Miami University in Oxford, Ohio, and lives in the Chicago suburbs with her husband and three children. She does not have a She Shed and thankfully has not had to battle the forces of darkness (unless going to Costco on a Saturday counts). *Suburban Hell* is her horror debut.